FULL MOON OVER MADELINE ISLAND

*Right when you
thought it was safe
Life bursts through the door!*

JAY GILBERTSON

May you
both enjoy
This!

C'mon —
The Ladies
are
Waiting

Jay Gilbertson

This is a work of fiction. Names, characters, places and incidents either are products of the author's imagination or are used fictitiously. Any resemblance to actual events or locales or persons, living or dead, is entirely coincidental.

ISBN: 1478349395
ISBN-13: 9781478349396

Printed in the United States of America

Also by Jay Gilbertson

Moon Over Madeline Island
Back to Madeline Island

Dedicated to you, my readers
Who believe in Eve & Ruby
(and me)

Now let's get cracking!

Nothing is impossible,
the word itself says
'I'm possible!'

—Audrey Hepburn

CHAPTER ONE

Standing in my bathroom, I'm humming along with a favorite old bluesy tune; *Easy Street* while tying up my stubborn red curls with a flowered silk scarf. My best friend, Ruby Prevost, and I recently pulled off my daughter Helen's wedding here at our cottage on Madeline Island. Not a single heart-attack or drunken brawl and not one thing got broken. Two wedding guests did manage to fall into the lake, but that's to be expected when you have a wedding right next to one, mix that with too much to sip and there you go.

Rocky, my fluffy gray cat, sits on the toilet watching me with major attitude in his flicking tail. Most likely he's wondering why I've not fed him yet and how my priorities could be so totally messed up. He should know better, we've been together a *long time*.

Not everyone enjoyed the wedding. I think Helen's adoptive mother, Saundra, felt a pang of sorrow at the sight of watching her daughter marry. But hey, life moves on and you either gotta roll with it or step aside! At least that's the line I told her and by the look on her face I only made her feel worse.

Come August—me—Eve Moss—am going to turn forty-eight! Fifty is waving from the sidelines. Seriously; I'm not ready. I adjust a stubborn black bra strap doing its *extra support for big girls* best shot, brush on some cheek color, dab of pink lip gloss and then I stand back and try and see what it is that's changed about me over this last year. The cracked and silvered mirror reflects the same me. Yet there *is* something different. I'd be a fool to think otherwise. Being overweight keeps the wrinkles at bay, but my eyes; they reflect back something else I can't put my hand on. Wisdom? Am I catching on to this life-thing? Funny what a wedding will do to you—makes you wonder if this is the right path, if this is where the hell you should be. I think it is. For some reason, I feel as though this summer is going to change me in ways I never would have imagined.

I scoop up Rocky and then plop him down on my bed while pulling on a pink top and torn jeans Ruby hates. I was reading *My Side of the Mountain*, for the first time before falling asleep last night, so I carefully replace my bookmark hoping Sam Gribbly can make it through the winter in that tree of his.

"Are you going to stay in there forever, darling?" Ruby asks with a pout from the threshold of my bedroom. "I *hardly* think that's the proper lip color for this dreadful deep cleaning task we're about to undertake. I've breakfast nearly prepared and coffee on the fire—come."

I glance toward her. Dressed in a flashy green, sleeveless top and matching bottom, she's ready to board a yacht, not push around our old Hoover. Barley a size one, she's a powerhouse of energy and those glistening blue eyes have more intelligence behind them than she'd ever let on.

Lifting Rocky back into my arms, we head after the quickly disappearing Ruby as she leads the way down the creaky wooden stairs. Though a good thirty years older, this British dish is my best girlfriend. For nearly a year we've lived together in this rambling old cottage on an island off northern Wisconsin, two miles from shore, completely surrounded by Lake Superior.

Morning sun has begun its journey from round mirror to round mirror that I hung in what I consider interesting groups around the two-story living room of this grand old log cabin. At the bottom of the stairs, Rocky leaps out of my arms; dashing down the hallway toward the library. After admiring the view of the lake out the open French doors, I follow Ruby into the kitchen, to the seductive aroma of freshly brewed coffee.

As Ruby hands me a steaming mug; the phone rings. "Eve and Ruby's messy madness—Eve speaking," I say and take a much needed sip. Ah, my motor starts up with a clang.

"Girrrl," a woman's deep voice drawls into my ear making me grin. "You all's gonna need some help over there—huh?"

"No kidding sister!" I mouth *Sam* to Ruby and she shakes her head. "You almost killed us last night. I don't know how you knew where to pull onto Stockton Island—it was pitch black. You're one lucky lady you didn't kill us all."

Sam. I imagine her in a bright, flowing top and matching headband that shows off her gorgeous dark skin. She has mysterious (and sometimes annoying) psychic abilities that still blow me away. Her cornrowed hair and mega-huge hoop earrings always seem able to warm up our world. 'Course, since I undid and then straightened her hair for the wedding, I wonder if she'll leave it that way.

"Now you all know I don't believe in luck," Sam chuckles. "Lilly's got a whopper of a hangover"—I hear her in the background moaning—"We're putting together some lunch for later and you can depend on us to help de-weddin' that place. Besides—we've got apron orders to fill!"

Lilly Thompson is tall and rail-thin and can whip together fabric into something stunning without using a measuring tape. Like Sam, who the hell could guess either one's age? Lilly has patience and kindness woven together like a tune. Sam and Lilly live on the mainland and take the ferry over together Monday through Friday; usually in Lilly's white 1988 Lincoln Town Car. I call it her boat.

"We sure appreciate all your help. The boys should be here any minute for breakfast. Let's make today a semi-working Monday with the added benefit of knowing that somewhere on a beach in

Hawaii—the newlyweds are enjoying a fancy drink and sunshine galore."

"A—men. See you soon—long's the ferry's runnin' on time."

I un-tie a drawer-knob from the yellow curly phone cord, hang it up and head over to the sink. Reaching over, I fling aside the shutters, lift up the window and breathe in the morning air. Cotton-ball clouds float high in the soft morning sky, black birds caw and cackle in the forest and the creek running by the barn is alive with the sounds of toads looking for love. April on Madeline Island can be a noisy business.

"I *do* hope Helen has the sense to slather on some of the sunscreen I sent along." Ruby says, hauling over the paint-spattered stepping stool. She floats up it, selects a battered copper pan from the rack suspended over the waist-high stump table and hands it to me as she steps back down.

"She's such fair skin—that one—just like me."

"I helped her carry that tote you gave her," I say as I take down mismatched dinner plates, which is all we use; makes for an interesting table. "It weighed a ton with all the tubes and bottles you had stuffed inside— they're only going to be over there for a week!"

"I was simply trying to help, darling. Besides—it wasn't *all* sunscreen in there. I included some—*marital items* as well."

I hold up my hand and roll my blood-shot eyes. "Don't tell me, I *so* don't wanna know—you are too much."

"Good heavens. Americans are so sexually repressed. Why in England—married couples have been having the most delightful—"

—Howard and Johnny, the couple from next door, burst into the kitchen. Thank God.

"Hey ladies," Johnny announces, out of breath. He adjusts his baggy shorts and moves his sunglasses up into his thick, brown-going-gray hair. "Thanks for your message inviting us over for a *Ruby's house special shrimp omelet*—I brought my personal dish-washer." He points to Howard who closes the porch door behind them.

Johnny is a good head shorter than Howard, his chiseled face and forlorn eyes are irresistible.

Howard runs a hand through his silver mane; a pained expression crosses his furrowed brow. "I'm not sure what was more detrimental to my health, the insane driving abilities of Sam or the fact that wine doesn't seem to mix well with—"

"—That phone," I say, and Johnny hands it to me. "Can I help it if I'm so popular? Good morning—this is Eve," I singsong into the mouthpiece.

"I'm going to kill her!" Helen's faraway voice crackles into my ear. "Ruby sent along all sorts of—of battery operated *gadgets*—and one was **alive**! There I was—stuck in the security line at the Minneapolis Airport with this beeping sex-fish-thing in front of—"

"—Helen. Slow down," I slit my eyes at Ruby. "I hardly think you should be discussing sex gadgets standing in the airport." I turn away from the group in the kitchen and lower my voice, trying to figure this out. "Are you and Ryan having troubles in the bedroom? I mean, this is supposed to be your honeymoon."

"This has nothing to *do* with Ryan."

I turn back around and stand next to the stove admiring the yellow and chrome of its fifties design and wonder if maybe I'm too old-fashioned and am missing something here. I'll humor her a little, to calm her down.

"You mean you're going on your honeymoon with someone *else*?" I laugh into the phone a little too hard and Ruby nearly drops an omelet she's just flipped. "I mean, we went to a lot of trouble to get you married—to *Ryan*!"

"I am with him—Ryan I mean. Listen, give the phone to Ruby—would you? Then maybe *she* can explain her sick little joke." Helen's voice has taken on an edge I'd rather stay clear of.

"Hang on—have a wonderful time and don't forget to at least *think* about sending one email. We haven't quite got the hang of texting. Yet." I happily hand the phone to Ruby, take up the steaming omelets, hand silverware to Johnny and motion the boys to follow me. "Not sure exactly what's going on, I think Ruby needs a moment to clarify her tote-filled-intentions. Let's have breakfast on the porch with all that great sunshine. It may be chilly around the edges, but spring is officially here. Grab the toast, will you Howard?"

"*Honestly,*" Ruby says pulling up a chair on the veranda and dramatically opening her napkin and sitting down. "If I'd so much as had an inkling as to what was in that box Helen's college friends asked me to pass along...*why*...I'd have never included it with *my* tasteful marital offerings of exotic oils, delightfully scented candles and a CD of seductive orchestrations performed over a background of ocean waves." She smacks the table and we all grab our coffee mugs.

Johnny says coyly, "Um, could you pass the—"

"—I would be bloody *mortified,*" Ruby dramatically declares as she shoves the butter over to Johnny. "Imagine—there's Ryan, standing proudly next to his bride as her designer handbag zooms into the X-ray machine. Suddenly, a perplexed look crosses the security guard, who in turn summons a comrade. The line of passengers behind them begins to build."

"I can hardly eat I'm so dying to hear this," I dead pan and get *the look*. "Hurry up already!"

"If one would allow me to continue," Ruby says with the least bit of a grin forming at the edge of her lips as she tucks one side of her bob behind her ear with such drama I have to shake my head. "The concerned security guard halts the line completely and begins pulling out the bags contents in earnest. Quite suddenly, one of the things he'd placed on the conveyer belt begins to move. Flipping and flopping like a live fish! It flips off, landing with; I'm sure, a rather dramatic *plop* smack dab on top of Ryan's deck shoes. The crowd of passengers waiting in line cheer!"

We laugh.

"It's good to know that Helen has friends that don't let her take herself so seriously," I say shoveling in a cheesy-shrimp bite, wondering how Helen will get revenge. "She does need to lighten up a bit, but a battery-operated flip-flopper—that was going too far."

"Wow, what a story," Howard remarks and Johnny reaches over to him and wipes jam from the corner of his mouth. "I think those kids went a little overboard."

"You're spot on, love."

Sam, Lilly, Ruby and I are all down by the boathouse; the scene of Helen's recent wedding. Having them marry on the end of the dock with Lake Superior in the back ground was something I'll remember for a long time. I was honored, as well as floored, that she had asked Ruby and me to host it in the first place. Helen and I only recently found one another and since I'd given her up when I was a teenager, well, we had a lot to catch up on.

I'm fighting with this damn tent and losing. "I suppose we could simply roll it up," I suggest to Sam and Lilly. "This would be awesome for the Apple Festival this October—not that I'm even *suggesting* we have a booth again."

Sam shakes her head and Lilly waves me off. They know we'll all be there hawking our aprons.

"Let's go find those men to help us with the frame here," Sam says and we put the clumsy, heavy tent-frame over by the tables.

Lilly purses her lips and says, "I wanted the tent over the bar and hors d'oeuvres to be strong while at the same time to work with Helen's lake-cottage theme." She pats her towering hairdo with pride. For some reason Lilly can't let go of the beehive.

"That tent sure did look damn *fierce*," Sam adds putting her hands on her wide hips for emphasis. She unhooks one of her hoops that got stuck in her teal headband. "My niece is using that word more than I can tell you and now look, it's stuck in my head too—but honey, you do have fierce 'bout you, you *do*. Now let's get this tent took down and rolled up and put away. We've got other business to tend to."

"Yes sir—I mean ma'am," Lilly lisps and we dig in. Lilly's dentures don't seem to fit her too well giving her a clicky lisp that makes you listen more closely.

"Such a dreadful shame it all has to come down." Ruby comes over to help fold the chairs we had arranged in rows on either side of the path facing the dock. "I believe that was the loveliest wedding I've ever thrown, not to mention the *brilliance* you all added to it—certainly."

"And how many does *that* make?" I ask, knowing full well the answer.

"Well—I suppose this *was* the first, darling. Imagine what the next one will be like, should Helen, you know…divorce and then care to re-marry." She tucks several hairs up into her black scarf tied on *do-rag* style. "That Ryan is such a handsome love, I *do* hope we're not too much for him."

"Good grief Ruby," I toss a roll of canvas into her arms. "Those two are going to be together a long time. Besides, how often do you have the privilege of becoming part of a family with such complicated ancestry you'd—"

"—Have the best reason in the world," Lilly jumps in, "for a lifetime of *therapy*!"

"Lord in heaven," Sam adds, "I don't know *anyone* who don't need therapy."

"*I* certainly haven't ever had the need," Ruby admonishes us as she tosses the roll into the back of my ancient yellow and red VW van. "But I still think we should give that Berry Splinner a ring. I think between the lot of us, we've enough material for—well an entire *season*—I should imagine."

"I think you mean Jerry Springer and I doubt very much,"— Lilly pauses, while stacking several folding chairs that were about to topple—"That we're all that different than most women out there in the world. Not really, not when you, as Sam would say, lift the proverbial hood and poke around in there. Or did you say that, Eve?"

She lifts her shoulders and then rolls them back and forth. A professional yoga instructor as well as belly dancer, she knows her shoulder rolls. I envy her defined arms and wish like hell I could wear a sleeveless blouse like hers and not be afraid my arm jiggles wouldn't scare people. God, if *I* look that good in my sixties.

"Who knows?" I reply. "I'll run the chairs back to Al's Place later. Bonnie said there's no rush. And then all we have left to do is haul the rest of the tent and these tables up to the barn."

"You're such a slave driver, *really* darling."

"Girrrl—don't I know it," Sam says and I laugh.

Ruby and I ran vacuums up and down hallways, through the vast living room ending in the kitchen, where someone must have dumped handfuls of chips over by the yellow fridge. Sam and Lilly swept the veranda, which runs the entire length of the north and east side of the cottage. Then they opened all the French doors from the living room, allowing a cool lake breeze to billow the long green curtains that flank each one.

Now the gang is back upstairs in the boathouse putting together today's apron orders while Ruby puts out wedding leftover's for us to lunch on. Given that the boathouse sits below the cottage over in the northeastern corner, perched over the lake, it stays a good ten degrees cooler. That makes for a happy apron-making crew. Every week day we each usually bring a dish to pass; since there was so much left from the wedding, we're simply emptying out our fridge.

Ruby pulls a long silver tray out from a cupboard. "This crab is simply *divine* and my heavens, I can't get over the size of these cocktail shrimp—it's a wonder Helen's mum didn't want a single thing to take home."

"That woman,"—Sam pops a shrimp into her mouth on her way to the bathroom in back—"She most likely has her seafood flown in daily, live no less, and hand-picks the lucky one that gets to sit on her fine china."

"She means well," I add. "I honestly think she does. She's used to money—lots and lots of money, according to Helen."

"Who's got used money?" Johnny asks as he and Howard come into the kitchen.

"We all have used money, honey," Howard says as he waltzes over to stand next to Lilly at her sewing table, ruffling Johnny's hair on the way. "Lilly, what do you know about duck costumes?"

Everyone turns to listen in. I put my electric sheers down and wonder if this has anything to do with me. Sam sends me a knowing grin on her way back to her machine.

Lilly pushes her rolling chair back from her sewing machine and folds her arms across her chest. "Well, I've done King Kong and that certainly could be considered *similar*—in a way, I should think...all that fur...versus feathers. Hmmm, the ostrich trio, *that's* more bird-like." She ponders, lifting her bifocals into her hairdo. "Oh yes—I helped a local church group do *Noah's Ark* and my ducks were something to be proud of. I even got an award for best costume. Nearly forgot about that. What do you have in mind?"

Howard folds his strapping arms over his chest and turns to me. "Can you transform Eve into a duck? A duck that will encourage people to donate *used* money to Toad Hollow?"

Lilly clears her throat, plunks her glasses back down upon her well-defined nose and says, "Well of *course* I can." We all sigh, somehow relieved. "But I wonder if we should consider Ruby seeing as Eve has..."

"—These," I say and shove my ample bosoms out for all to see. All eyes turn toward my chest.

"Eve will make a *fetching* duck," Ruby retorts with attitude. "Besides, who'd care to toss cash toward an uppity Brit with absolutely no tah tahs whatsoever? Of course—I suppose I could *sing* for cash, Toad Hollow is such a bloody worthy cause."

"Okay okay," I relent. "I'll do it. *Anything* to keep that woman from singing." Ruby grins.

I'm out on the verandah, by the back door at the cottage, sorting through our recycling. Up here on Madeline Island, there's no pickup for everyday trash, let alone recycling, so I'm the one. To be honest, I get a kick out of the entire process as it really does make sense. I mean, how many water bottles does a gal *need* anyway? We use the same ones over and over, the well water here is terrific and thank the Water-God that it's not full of iron or my panties would not be pretty.

"There you are, darling," Ruby clambers down the half-round stoop and sits onto one of the many wicker love seats. "I just rang off with Alice Anne. She says that with the way things are shaping up at Toad Hollow, why in no time at all, we'll be open for business. Oh dear, is that in poor taste?"

"Well I suppose not, I mean it *is* a type of business. A place for teenage pregnant women has to run like one anyway. More of a service I should think. Here, can you make out the number on the bottom of this bottle? My eyes are going all to hell." I hand it over.

"It's a number one, and good *heavens*," She studies the label, "That was such a lovely dressing...Salad Girl's Curry & Fig." She hands me the bottle and slumps back into the art deco cushions. "I'm simply bushed. All that cleaning can really do a dame in."

She comes over to the five foot long Sturgeon that hangs near the back door and lovingly adjusts the pinstriped tie around its fishy neck. A prize catch she and Ed hauled in years ago. A stuffed fish? I don't get it.

"Sam told me she'd never seen a vacuum cleaner on skis. Then you hauled out the mint green Hoover upright and I didn't know who was giggling more, Lilly or her. I like those old clunkers, you don't need to buy new bags or over-priced filters and—"

"—You should always vacuum *first,* seeing as those machines kick up a regular dust storm. I do like your idea of only dusting *seasonally.* Makes such sense, and if we never move a thing, why— who's to know?"

"Howard and Johnny,"—I sit down beside her—"have someone come once a week and do the heavy cleaning. I don't know if I'd want a stranger cleaning up our messes, besides, I get a certain feeling of pride after snazzing up our place. Then again, coming home to a clean cabin has its advantages."

"Ed and I had a maid for a time," Ruby reflects. "That big brick house we had on Rust Street in Eau Claire was all corners and steps. We used to entertain a lot of the University faculty. I wonder if your parents were ever guests."

"I suppose they *could* have been. God, how insane this world can be. I bet that your Ed and my mom *did* meet at some kind of party. There was all that resentment between my folks—all those years while I was busy trying to grow up. I could feel it in the house like an unwelcome relative and all along it was *me*. Imagine."

"I should hardly think of you as a *resentment,* darling. Really. You can be such a drama queen. I should be the one with my knickers in a twist. Don't forget it was *my* husband having an affair with your mum, getting her pregnant with YOU has turned out to be a blessing in disguise. But nearly everyone involved is dead, except you—and your father—of course. So *many* reasons for therapy. Perhaps I should find someone."

I roll my eyes. *"And you,* let's not forget." Rocky leaps into my lap and just as quickly leaps off and dashes away. "Oh for crying out loud!" I jump to my feet. "He left behind a *mouse bit!*"

Ruby looks up at me, then down onto the floor; then she looks closer. "It's only a *small* bit, darling. A head, I believe." She stands; smoothes her creased slacks and tosses back her sassy bob. "I'll fetch the trusty vegetable tongs. Be a love and pour us some wine, would you, darling?" She heads back up the stoop and through the arched doorway into the kitchen.

I throw back my shoulders, move my head this way and that and try to steady my breathing like Lilly has suggested. It's not that easy when a mouse-head is watching you.

Ella Fitzgerald is softly singing on the hi-fi in the living room. The golden sun slowly dips down, about to slip into Lake Superior for the night. I can nearly hear it sizzle as it hits the water. With full tummies, we're doing the last of our supper dishes.

"This simply *must* be the last of the lot," Ruby hands me a dripping, hot platter. "I *do* so love all this, but eating such rich foods morning noon and night can be—"

"—Dangerous for my waistline." I concur. We've finally eaten through the Chicken Florentine, Swedish meatballs and there's not a piece of wedding cake to be had, thank goodness. "Jesus Ruby, how the hell do you stand the rinse water so hot?"

"Since you *refuse* to allow me to install a proper dishwasher, you've no right fussing. Can't have pesky bacteria clinging to our dishes now can we? You're such a nudge—really."

"Neither one of us likes those machines," I remind her. "Besides, I've always enjoyed hand washing my dishes. What's more—think of all the problems we've solved in the process."

"You've a point there, shall I get that or—?"

"—I'll grab it, my hands need to cool. I bet its Lilly, wondering how I *really* feel about screaming bright yellow feathers bursting from my head." I hand her the still burning hot platter and head toward the phone. "Eve Moss here," I say, cradling the phone on my shoulder while trying to maneuver the curly-cord around Ruby.

"Hello Eve, this is Kate."

I recognize her voice immediately, my stomach clenches. "Hello Kate," For some odd reason, I put my hand over my heart.

Images of my father fly through my mind. How he looked at my mother, his odd distance while she lay dying, and then his bizarre behavior after he married this *Kate,* this Mormon widow with six children. He never looked back, simply left me to live my life, and to be honest, I pretty much did the same. What little there was between us—mom—we let it go. I know in my heart why she's called and I feel faint.

"I wanted you to know that your father has passed away." She snivels and it irritates the hell out of me.

"Was it the lung disease he had? Did he *suffer!*" My chest tightens and I'm feeling light-headed.

"He's buried in Forest Hill cemetery, you'll be happy to know where—"

"—Why wasn't I *told?* I would have come to the funeral, he was my *dad*—I—!" Tears stream down my face; frustration, sadness, anger, floods through my mind like hot mud.

The bottom line is that he *was* my dad. Nothing can change that. I've always felt that no matter who plants the seed, it's the gardener who tends it. Something crowds inside me; there underneath my heart it feels as though another organ is taking shape. With my parents both gone, this new thing is what I'm left with. I imagine this must be where their birth and death settle in after creating me.

"Your father told me, your…um…circumstances and I figured that—"

"—You had no *right* not to tell me my father was dying! Now he's dead—gone forever!"

A fresh wave of emotion hits. I can't find my voice so I hand the phone to Ruby. I feel as though I'm in a dream as I move through the living room. I push open the screened door and all I can think of is getting to the end of the dock. To be by water where I'd always felt safe.

The full moon has turned my world an ugly blue, though the water glistens and shimmers like shards of glass as it burbles around my feet. I imagine them cut to shreds like my heart.

I hear the slap of the porch door.

"Here, have a sip of this, darling," Ruby sweetly says, handing me a goblet as she tenderly wraps my shoulders in an afghan. "I'm so dreadfully sorry about your father, I am." She scoots down beside me.

"The old poop," I lamely offer and half-heartedly laugh. "Sorry to have left you with Kate-the-bitch, but I just couldn't deal…"

Ruby waves my words away. "She was still chatting on about how she didn't feel it proper to ring you, seeing as you two hadn't been on the best of speaking terms. Then I reminded her of how you and your daughter had more or less reconciled with him recently. She realized I wasn't you and got rather pissy, poor dear." She sighs.

The hardness loosens in my chest; my heart goes out to Helen. The mother in me feels a sudden pull and I nearly cry out. I realize that a parent's love is a patchwork collection of all of those you've loved and cared for—even the ones you gave away. Maybe these the very most. Something lifts and I can breathe again.

"Let me have a drag of that," I say and take the glowing orange-tipped cigarette from her. "I hate to say it—but that's much better—thank you. I wonder how...how he went. When Helen and I visited him, it was so hard for him to breathe, God, I can't imagine not being able to breathe—Pulmonary Fibrosis literally *sucks* the life out of you. *From* you."

"Perhaps we're done with this then?" Ruby takes it from me and stubs it out. "He died at Luther Hospital accompanied by, and these are the exact words that child-producing woman used, I swear, *Larry is now in the bosom of Abraham*! Good heavens—a man with a *bosom* is running things on the other side? What next?"

"You wanna stick around and find out?"

"I wouldn't miss it for the world."

Chapter Two

I'm backing my VW van out of the two-story log barn behind the cottage and pulling over to the back porch door. Morning dew-drops glisten in the grass; a mist hovers above as I shiver. My stylish flip-flopped feet are soaked thanks to that dew. I watch as two sparrows dive-bomb over the creek, float in perfect sync over the surface and then zip into the barn's open door only to blast out again as if shot from a cannon. Flying like that, in such perfect harmony, must be so awesome. Nest building, on the other—wing—would be another matter.

Earlier I had given this old baby a bath and tidied the inside up a notch too. It was hard to get the top sprayed off since my head doesn't come close to it and I couldn't reach the ladder in the barn. Howard came over and gave me a hand. I give the yellow balls around the windshield a few pings.

Adjusting my leopard-covered rearview mirror, I check my teeth and give my curls a scrunch. Dressed in black Capri pants and a white frilly blouse, I definitely feel like I'm about to visit a cemetery.

My heart holds a confusing mix. With the loss of my dad, I realize it's the end of my family. Yet what about the family I have here, interesting how the word *family* really means the ones that are there no matter what. I wipe away a lone tear; I swear my eyes have struck a leak. A strong breeze rustles the leaves of the aspen trees and the sound soothes me. Like change rattling in a bowl.

"Sorry, darling," Ruby hops in and slams the door closed.

"*Jesus*—Ruby.

"I don't know that I'll *ever* get used to these dreadfully thin doors. I've just rung off with the girls at your salon. They are *so* excited! That sounds odd, *your* salon. You've been gone for nearly a year—nearly. What are you grinning about over there, you sly cat?"

I tap my iPod and Nina Simon starts carrying on about *sugar in her bowl*. Perfect.

"It does sound odd—*and* I really think it's weird Watts hasn't considered changing the name. I mean, I realize she's been managing it for me..."

"—You've hung on to it in case this Madeline Island madness here—well—drives you *mad*. I hardly blame you." Ruby waves away a blue moth that nearly flew into her mouth.

"Ruby," I say and put the clutch in while carefully choosing my words. "You've been beyond generous offering this place to me to be your roomie. It's been a riot—so far. Hey! Don't you have a birthday coming up soon? How old *will* you be?" I dramatically gasp as I hit the gas. "The big 7—0 ?"

"You're ghastly! I'll *never* be that old—now drive on before my Prada purse becomes a lethal weapon."

"You've read too many murder mysteries."

I head down our winding rutted drive, as it is about to cross the wooden bridge over the creek. A shallow creek about as wide as my van is long, ambles the back of our barn, under this bridge and eventually pitches itself over some rocks, falling into the lake down by the boathouse. It's crazy-beautiful.

"Look—it's them!" I point to the left. "I'm *sure* they're the same ones I've spied around here before and *look,* they have two little fawns along."

The buck lifts his regal head up from drinking creek water; droplets fall from his whiskers like beads of mercury. Our eyes lock. Then, in an instant—gone. Tall ostrich ferns sway in their leaving. We head up the drive to the gate.

"My heavens, if I didn't know better, the one with all those towel racks seemed to *know* you."

"I like to think so, anyway. Would you do the honors?"

"Certainly, if I must." Ruby hops out, opens the gate and I motor through as she pulls it closed behind, then hops back in. "You certainly can tell its spring," Ruby mentions as several cars whiz by. "I recognize the fact that tourist dollars are important, of course, but it's such a bloody drag come summer with lines and lines of people about."

Then a familiar car heads our way, but I can't place the owner and I'm really lame when it comes to brands. It's a big, white gas hog, with rust eating away its once fancy doors. It slows as it passes by. The driver, a man with a dark mustache, dressed in a brilliantly white shirt, glances our way. He hits the gas and rockets away, leaving us in the trail of some twangy country western song.

I turn left onto School House Road and head toward La Pointe. The morning is sunshiny bright; the clouds have rolled away to the edges of the horizon. We automatically put on sunglasses; mine are big black Ray Bans and hers are rhinestone cat-eyes. She's dressed smart in a tailored beige skirt and cream-colored blouse, her auburn hair fluffy in the open window's breeze.

We zoom along, taking in the lake as it peeks through tall white pines only to be blocked by an occasional cottage. Unlike our place, these are perched on the edge of a sliver of land, between the road and Lake Superior. There are some larger homes on the right side of the road, even a few farms.

"Hey, with all the acreage *we* have," I comment, "we should plan a garden. I'd *love* to grow some of our own food. Maybe even can some stuff. My mom used to get a bushel of tomatoes every summer from a farmer north of Eau Claire and then spend the afternoon canning. Made the whole house smell like a tomato for weeks afterwards."

"There's simply a *lovely* plot beside the barn," Ruby adjusts her sunglasses. "Years ago, Ed grew all sorts of things—why—seems to me there were some apple trees next to that little cabin. I recall seeing them in that model up in the loft and you do know I love to can. Should be called *bottling*—I should think."

"Cool, let's give it a peek tomorrow after our belly dancing," I suggest and shift down as we're coming into town. "Hey, look who's outside."

I pull the van over in front of a faded two-story blue building with a screened porch all around the ground floor. A neon sign above the screen door blinks *Al's Place*. A thin woman dressed in a faded housedress and a bright white apron reaches up and tucks her unruly hair under a straw hat while watering festive window boxes bursting with red geraniums. She puts down the hose and walks over.

"Hello ladies," Bonnie leans in Ruby's window. "That sure was a lovely wedding we threw. Howard and Johnny dropped off the chairs earlier, so all I need now are some hungry customers. Where are you two off to, looking all elegant and done up?"

"Eve's father passed away," Ruby reverently offers as an explanation. "So we're headed down to Eau Claire for the day in order to pay our respects."

"Oh Eve," Bonnie comes over to my side and gives me a hug through the window. "I'm *so* sorry—I know you'd mentioned that he's been fighting some terrible disease. But no matter what we think we know, death is so—"

"—Final," I half-whisper. Bonnie takes a flowered hankie out of her apron pocket and wipes my tears away.

She looks deep into my eyes and for a moment I'm sent back to the time when her husband died. Seems like eventually, you reach an age in life when you'll inevitably experience death. But no matter how prepared you think you are, it still feels like having the rug yanked from your life.

"Hang on—I've got just the thing." Bonnie dashes over to the steps that lead into her restaurant and picks up one of the many terra-cotta pots of yellow and blue petunias, "A little something for his grave. I'll put it in the back here."

"Thank you so much," I start to tear up again, then take some calming breaths. In out—much better. "Listen, say hi to Marsha when you see her—the ferry's probably about to dock, so we gotta be on our way."

"I think she's over at Toad Hollow helping Alice Anne," Bonnie steps back from the van. "Have a safe trip—bye ladies!" She waves us off as I head over toward the waiting ferry.

I watch her figure in my rearview mirror. Bonnie turns and looks up at the blinking sign above the door, puts her hand to her heart and shakes her head. I wonder where Al is now. I'm not a believer in the concept of hell, or the devil for that matter, but a drunken, wife-beating louse like him sure makes suffering somewhere really *hot,* awfully tempting to ponder.

"Good *heavens*—look at all the huge trucks coming off the ferry. Must be for that development everyone's talking about—such an abomination to this lovely island."

"No kidding," I pull up behind an old pickup and wait for the ferry to empty. "The really *sad* thing is, those fancy-schmancy places being built will only be occupied a few months out of the year, and I fully understand they'll be adding cash to Ashland County, but—" I sigh. "I hate to admit it—I'm a NIMBY."

"Touché, darling. What's the name of the one by us? Oh yes, *Gilded Sunsets*—really."

"Gilded," I huff out. "Bonnie had the developers in for lunch recently and overheard some of them talking. Apparently, they'd really prefer it if Madeline Island had only residents on it and the hell with all the local businesses, can you imagine? The balls."

"Or lack thereof—perhaps we should organize an occupation of sorts. Why look who's in front of us, I think it's the Tree-Stud."

"Really...I *hardly* noticed," I say with a touch of snark. "Look, there's a woman next to him, probably the wife by the way she's leaning her blonde head onto his shoulder. Johnny said he's got a stand on the island selling fresh vegetables and flowers during the summer."

"How...handy. He did indeed sell us the loveliest Christmas tree last winter and now garden goods come summer." Ruby absently runs her hand through her hair. "We'll have to give him—*it* a look then, hmmm?"

"Here we go!" I follow his truck onto the ferry and pull way up front, then park.

The ferry fills with cars and people as well as a big group on bicycles. With the windows down, the ferry chugs away from the dock and begins its short journey to the mainland.

I'm in a mood of reverence and the overwhelming kind of surrender that only a death can stir up. Even though we spent the last years since my mom died avoiding one another, I knew where he was. He was still my dad—all the history I had left.

I shake my head and watch as seagulls swoop up and around the van, several sailboats skim along in the distance as the outline of the little port town of Bayfield comes slowly into view. I honestly don't imagine I'll ever tire of this magical two-mile trip back and forth. 'Course taking the ferry sure puts a dent in my purse. So I'm glad we have that other, old clunker—my beloved duck. I honestly think everyone on the island should have one parked in their barn ready to either zip down the road or splash into the lake.

"Lilly mentioned," I say, breaking our reverie, "that the bookstore in Bayfield, Apostle Islands Booksellers, is under new ownership. What was his name—Riley I think—she thinks he's single, *around her age, and* I think she might be hot for him."

"Really? The tramp," Ruby spits out and we laugh. Lilly is anything but. "Perhaps next Tuesday we should hit Andy's IGA singles night, just for the hell of it—mind. Maybe see if Lilly's in any danger of being taken advantage of. Besides, never hurts to peruse the proverbial menu. Though up here, the selections are a bit on the slim side."

"Oh so *miss I've had the love of my life why even look* is wanting to, what, *peek?*" I shake my head and she smacks my arm. "Hey, no hitting the driver please."

"Maybe. Oh why *not* have a look, hmmm? Well here we are, darling, let's hit the road!" Ruby proclaims and off the ferry we trundle.

I maneuver the van up and around, hanging a left onto First Street. As we pass the bookstore, I notice a handsome man flipping a wooden sign over to *Open*. I toot the horn; he adjusts his black-rimmed glasses and sends us a wave.

"Oh my, he *is* a hottie," Ruby teases. "If you like the bearded, intelligent-mysterious-looking type, that is."

"Right," I deadpan. "He looks a bit young for Lilly though. Then again, you never know..."

As we pass Greunke's restaurant, the owner, Janelle, is stepping out of her classy red convertible. I hit the horn and she turns to wave. Tall, blonde, strikingly beautiful and reeking of good health; the kind of woman I picture zooming down snowy peaks, climbing a mountain or parachuting out of a plane over Africa. All of which she's done.

"Good heavens, we certainly are the popular ones."

"Ruby, there aren't that many people that *live* up here year around, and I *do* think that we've given the locals all *sorts* of gossip to chew on."

"I should bloody well hope."

I steer us onto highway 13, hit the gas and off we head, back to Eau Claire, where it all began.

We've been flying down highway 63 and as I merge onto 53, which will take us right into Eau Claire, I reach over and switch to the radio, when the announcer says, "This has been Larry Meiller. Thank you for joining us and my guest, Jay Gilbertson, author of *Moon Over Madeline Island...*"

I snap off the radio. "Hmmm, someone's written a book about Madeline Island?"

"Couldn't be very *compelling*" Ruby smirks. "I should have been consulted—*included,* really. A character such as I would lend a certain *class*, not to mention my..."

"...Incredible gift of bullshit," I add. "Let's see if that Riley carries it and give it a read. In the meantime, you want to stop at Norske Nook in Rice Lake, for coffee and to share some pie? I could use a potty break and a stretch. My legs and neck are stiff as hell."

"Sounds—lovely."

"This booth okay?" Our robust waitress raises heavily painted on brows.

"Sure, fine," I say as we slide in. She hands us laminated menus and ambles off, coffee pot in hand. "Did you get a load of her hair? Who would do such a thing, tight perms are so—"

Ruby holds up a manicured hand, her jingling bracelets cause the group of white-haired gals next to us to glance over. "Not one word, and don't you *dare* suggest a makeover to her either. I'm simply not in the mood to save her from her permed-to-death *life* and God only knows what lies beyond those eyes of hers. I mean, she could have a masters degree, written thirteen books and been to prison for heaven's sake."

"I was only commenting. I promise. I won't say a word to her—how she could look ten years younger. And those goggle-glasses!" Ruby clears her throat. "Okay, let's order something really fattening."

"Shouldn't be too difficult."

We settle on a slice of Sour Cream Apple Blueberry, bottomless coffee and top it off with a smoke. Since it's a horrible habit that all of us are honestly trying to quit, I've started counting out six a day. This is my fifth. But just as I'm about to fire up, Ruby taps a painted nail on the *No Smoking* sign above our booth. She snaps her gold cigarette case closed and motions her head in the direction of the door.

"In case you've been asleep, darling," Ruby sighs with the attitude of speaking to a child. "Wisconsin passed a No-smoking law—anywhere. I swear, I can't take *you* anywhere."

"And how are you getting home?"

"Oh for heaven's sake—give me the bill then."

"That hit the spot," I say as I turn back onto highway 53. "I'd like to stop at the salon first and then do the grave thing." Reaching over, I flip down the enormous ashtray. "I restocked this morning, would you do the honors? I realize we just consumed a pound of sugar back there, but these gems settle my nerves. One couldn't hurt."

"Certainly, darling," Ruby reaches in and selects several. "You really should consider investing in this company." She un-wraps a Reese's Peanut Butter Cup and hands it over.

"What do you mean? I guess I do buy enough of these to pay their light bill, I suppose I *should* look into actually buying some stock. Are they investable?"

"I've simply *no* idea," Ruby tries to say, but it comes out all garbled, as she's managed to stuff her mouth with an entire cup.

We pass a bloated raccoon carcass lying along the highway.

"Pretty, *real* pretty," I comment. "Why in the world no one picks those up any more is beyond me."

"Lovely of you to point out," she comments while repairing her lips in the visor mirror. "Should be jolly fun visiting the salon again, don't you think?"

"I'm getting more nervous, the closer we get, excited too. I spent so many years in that place, not to mention living upstairs in my cool apartment."

"It *is* a cool spot." Ruby saying *cool* doesn't quite work.

"Funny," I pause, thinking. "It's not the physical space that I've missed, but my clients. Not to mention all the drama of Dorothy and Watts—then there was *you*! All that *Ruby-drama*."

"Smart alec you! Oh you *are* a bit dodgy, darling, aren't you. You know good and well how dreadfully dull my life was back there. Why now—I simply *drip* drama!"

"That you do."

On we go, down past Chippewa Falls and into the northern part of Eau Claire. It's odd, when you've been away from a place, how it seems smaller somehow. The buildings and homes appear different, foreign almost. I turn onto Main Street. I like to pass by what used to be Boyd School, where I went to grade school.

A little further, on the right side, is what used to be my junior high school, or *Central* as it was referred to. More like Hell, if you ask me. I was overweight, overly endowed and had bright red curly hair (not much has changed). Kids can be so mean and boy were they. I was always the last to be picked for anything *gym-related* and taking a shower in front of everyone was awful. I feel my palms sweat remembering.

"Are you all right, darling?" Ruby asks. "You look so *gloomy.*"

I pull over in front of the school's three-story, red brick building and look up at it. Late morning sun glints off the windows. Many of them have torn shades hanging this way and that, giving off a feeling of neglect and time, like a book whose pages have gone yellow.

"Would you mind if we went in? If it's open, that is," I say in a voice I don't recognize. "I want to see if something is still here, in this rotten old place."

"Let's go!"

I lead the way up the steep concrete steps to the faded and cracked, red wooden double doors and cup my hands around my eyes to see in the dusty window.

"That's odd, the lights are on," I say and give the door a try—it opens. "C'mon, follow me. I had heard it was closed for good and going to be torn down."

We head in. The terrazzo floor is just as I remembered, the musty smell too. I can even hear the echoes of my past here. Kids rushing up and down this staircase; up on the right, down the left. We head down.

"God, it's so freaky to be back," I say, my voice echoing off the walls and cracked tile floor. Our heels make a hollow clacking sound. "It's like time stood still—the lockers are still here, that seems weird."

"I should think,"—Ruby twists the chrome spigot on the white porcelain water fountain. Icky old water arcs out, but soon turns clear. Instead of sipping, she looks around—"This could be a museum, I mean, did they even *have* electricity when you attended school all those years ago, darling?"

I shake my head, grateful for the company. I head over to what used to be my band locker. As I reach to unlatch it, I'm overwhelmed by the memory of several brats grabbing me, shoving me in and locking the door. I had to wait the *longest* time for the janitor to come and let me out, only for an entire class of boys to clap as I struggled to stand up.

I give the locker door a try and it bangs open, the locks having been removed long ago.

"I can't imagine," I lean in and pull up on a back, upper panel. It doesn't move at first, there's a scraping sound and then it gives enough so that I can pull it away. I reach around wondering if by any chance—then my hand touches the bundle.

"So this *is* where these have been hidden—Jesus," I comment to Ruby and she gives me a questioning look. I pull a bunch of letters out of hiding and the panel snaps closed. "This is so bizarre, these are notes, silly love letters really, that Helen's father wrote to me. For the life of me, I couldn't figure out where I'd stashed them. Why the hell didn't I think of this before? But what's even stranger is that they're still here."

"You've simply got to be off your mark—why the chances of these being here are bloody incredible! It certainly seems to be true—things are as they're supposed to be, darling. Perhaps you didn't need them until now."

A man appears around the corner. Dressed in an ill-fitting suit, he has a paper thin comb-over gracing his shiny head. Huge, black-rimmed smeary glasses magnify bloodshot eyes. He huffs over to us, a curtain of Old Spice crowds the hallway. Ruby gives her bob a toss and smoothes her skirt. He notices and grins, there's something green stuck to one of his teeth.

"Can I help you ladies?" Comb-over asks. "This is a private office building and..."

"We were just leaving," Ruby proclaims with tons of attitude while I tuck the letters into my purse. "Our inspection is complete and we'll be in touch. Come along Professor, we must consult with—with the appropriate consulters."

"This is when I wish I had power-steering," I gasp as I wrestle the van into a parallel parking spot on Water Street. "Good thing these spaces are huge, I'd never have been able to swing this in here otherwise."

"Good thing the curb's not too bloody high, the way you ran us up onto the sidewalk. Why I thought that woman passing by was a goner for sure!"

"I only—never mind—c'mon."

I turn to admire my building. It's a simple, two-story brick storefront. Looking back, this was the *ideal* place for me then, but now, I feel so distant from it all. Sighing, I notice a change in myself. I'm not that Eve any longer, I give my curls a fling and pull the glass door open.

A memorable waft of hair spray, perm solution and that old smell that buildings this age never seem to let go of washes over us. Soft jazz is playing and I can hear Dorothy's loud laughter rise and fall in the background. All the years I spent here seem to have lost their, what—sparkle?

I can see myself standing behind my *chair-of-confessionals* as I always fondly called it. My specialty was coloring away pesky gray hair while soothing my client's worries into something they could take from here and feel re-energized. Something that now I realize was simply—love.

Funny, now I can appreciate how it was really me who got the most from my clients. It's so true that you're attracted to people and places that can teach you what you most need to learn. What have I learned so far? That the most important moment is the one in front of you, *this* moment is really all there is. Now, I feel too big for this place, I've become something else—someone else.

"Oh man—you're looking *so* fantastic!" Watts comes around the corner. "It's been too damn long, give me a hug woman!"

Watts's bleached white hair is no longer spiked. Now it's tamed into a choppy, stacked bob, and instead of her standard blue lipstick, she's glossy pink. But the torn-to-shreds jeans live on. Her bright blue eyes sparkle back to me and I realize how much I've missed her. For a twenty-something, she's really got it together—as much as you *can* at that age.

She lets me go and regards me, we both wipe away tears. "You sure look beautiful Eve—must be that island life up there." She turns and notices Ruby. "Give me a hug too you little Brit."

"Lovely to see you, darling," Ruby reaches up to give her a squeeze. "Good heavens Watts, you simply *must* eat—you're as skinny as a pole—I *do* love your hair though, you've got that texture thing down pat."

"Thanks," Watts replies. "You have a face-lift or something? Oh I know, it's your hair color, got an auburn-red thing going. Nice look lady, real nice." Ruby shrugs. "Dorothy's finishing up with Mrs. Gustafson. She complained that her hair wasn't high enough—Jesus. Wait until—"

An older woman in a crisp navy shift sails by, a cloud of Aqua Net trails along. Her hair stands a good half-foot up above her plump face, and boy is it something to regard. She lifts an arm to wave as she proudly tromps out the door.

"Well, look who the cat drug in!" Dorothy follows in Mrs. Gustafson's wake and hugs us both, then steps back, adjusts her glasses and gives her shellacked bangs a push. "I am *so* glad to see you two. Why it's only been since last week at Helen's wedding but—*where* has the time gone? You know, it does seem longer, I suppose because you haven't set foot in here since last year!"

Granted, Dorothy and Lilly are cousins, but why they've ended up with similar swirled-to-the-heavens hairdos is beyond me. The only difference is that Lilly has silver-white hair and Dorothy's is a carrot-red that would make Lucile Ball burn with envy. In a yellow pantsuit and a little too much makeup, she's an original—and perfect.

"We are both done for the day!" Dorothy announces. "We moved our afternoon appointments so we could spend some time with you two. Watts and I thought it'd be fun to have pizza sent over from Sammy's and—"

"—Eve's salon is officially closed!" Watts announces as she flips over the sign in the window. "C'mon upstairs and let's catch up!"

Glancing around my apartment, I take in all the changes. I'm surprised how feminine it is. Watts always struck me as a chrome-and-white type, but this is cool. Lots of wicker and bamboo. I had it done up in more of an English cottage meets fifties look. A knock at the patio door and the pizza has arrived!

"Oh Watts, my favorite," I say, opening the huge box and taking in a big whiff. "Pineapple and shrimp—to die for."

Grouped around her shiny pinewood table, we dig into comfort food turned up loud. I fill the gals in about the Toad Hollow project and the apron business and all the goings on with putting Helen's wedding away. Ruby and I have brought them aprons and they have them on. Dorothy's is covered with dancing yellow ducks and Watts is a simple deep red with a big black button in front. We tidy up and then thump down onto the cozy green sofa I had left behind.

"Thank you, darling, just a touch more,"—Ruby holds out her mug and Dorothy pours—"That was lovely."

We all nod in agreement, sip our coffee and are quiet for a moment. I look from Dorothy to Watts and then pull several envelopes from my black purse.

"I don't know why I didn't do this sooner," I say as I hand one to Watts and the other to Dorothy. Ruby grins. "You can read this stuff later, it needs to be signed and all, but basically this is the deal. I'm selling the building to Watts for a buck, the business will be split in half, making the two of you partners. There's some legal stuff about how to dissolve it, should either of you want out of the partnership, and you *have* to change the name to something you can both agree on."

"A buck, only a buck?" Watts asks as tears flow down her pale cheeks. She runs over and hugs me; I tear up. Dorothy hugs me as well, and we all end up crying—even Ruby, who hands out tissue by the fistful.

After we simmer down—Watts turns to Dorothy. "Can you front me a dollar?"

"My goodness," Ruby adjusts her seatbelt. "I don't know that I've ever seen Dorothy without makeup, the darling cried it all off. She's so much lovelier without it, and I *do* hope Watts has stopped hiccupping, poor dear."

I'm about to pull away from the curb when Watts comes racing out of the salon door.

"I almost forgot to give this to you," she pants out. "Some really uptight woman dropped it off, Kate I think was her name. Said she didn't have your address up north." She opens the back door and puts the box on the floor. "If it hadn't been sealed so damn well, I would have opened it, but, I didn't—I swear." She slams the door and steps back.

"Must be some stuff of my dad's," I offer. "Sure as hell hope Kate didn't put a bomb in there. I'll be sure and give it a good looking into. Now go think up some amazing name for your salon and keep in touch!"

Watts waves us off and then turns back to the van. "Starr's Sister Salon—that's what I'm going to call this joint." Watts steps closer to Ruby's window. "My little sister and I don't see eye to eye—she lives somewhere up north. I miss the little shit."

"That's a splendid name—perhaps Starr will come visit one day and won't that be a surprise for her!" Ruby pats Watt's arm and I pull away.

"Let's go check out my parents' graves," I say and head us in the right direction.

"How does it feel?" Ruby asks. "You've truly cut yourself free of that place, and in such a kind, generous manner. Such a turn for you—*really*."

"Hey! I can be generous. Besides, Watts hasn't got any family to speak of, and Dorothy has that lazy husband. So now they at least have the salon, and Watts will *always* have a home. Just like you've given me—'course you'll have to drop dead before it becomes *my* cottage, but none-the-less, you inspired me."

"I *am* an inspiration, so true, but I really don't care to simply drop dead. Heavens no. I should like to go..."

"—Years and *years* from now," I finish. "Now hand me one of your cigarettes, I only brought the six, and boy do I need a smoke."

"We'll have to split the one I have left." Tapping it on her gold cigarette case, she carefully lights it with the sleek matching lighter. "Lung cancer seems such a wretched thing, don't you think?"

"Hand that thing over," I take a puff and feel myself relax. "My dad—Larry—used to say that *something's* gonna get you. Poor guy had to haul oxygen all over the place, what a major drag." Ruby puts the cigarette out and we roll our windows down a bit farther.

I tool along Water Street, back over the Chippewa River and then on second thought I hang a quick left and head into an area I used to walk through several times a week, marveling at all the beautiful lumber baron mansions. One in particular I became obsessed with; taking pictures of it every season and imagining strolling through its countless hallways, wine glass in hand, admiring all my statues and oodles of tasteful stuff.

"How many times have I dragged you over to this place?" I pull up to the James Barber House. "It's still so amazing to me. This huge place takes up an entire block. To think, all these years, and I've never set foot inside." I drive really slowly all around it, admiring the brick and stucco, the gabled roofs and bargeboards.

"You know I've researched the history of this place a ton," I tell Ruby for the umpteenth time. "James Barber was a lumber baron, he established the American Colonization Company to support the settlement of all the cutover land his company had left. I mean, he got rich taking the lumber, but then the land was open to possibility and he helped get it going. I like that." After I ogle the mansion from the front one more time, we head on to Forest Hill Cemetery.

"Such a lovely spot," Ruby comments as I pull over to a group of gravestones we both know well. "Shall we stop off at Ed's first, then?"

"Sure, why not." We hop out and head over to a rather impressive marker. *"Husband Ed Prevost and Wife Ruby Prevost*—it's kind of creepy that your name is here. Of course your birth date isn't."

"What a *ludicrous* notion. Why in the world does one need to carve, in stone, no less, one's birth and date of death? You're *dead*—end of story for heaven's sake." Ruby bends and pulls a weed. She opens a fresh bottle of Chevas Regal. "Here's to you, my darling *louse* of a man."—She turns to me—"Or would you care to do the honors, seeing as he was not only my husband but your father? Such Oprah-esque complications."

"Knock yourself out."

"We all do the best we can, I would imagine." She pours the Chevas Regal over the grave. "Even though you turned out to be a dirty rotten scoundrel." She empties all of it out except a tiny bit and then tilts back the bottle and finishes it off. "Dreadful stuff, really." She sighs and her usually upright shoulders sag. "I truly shouldn't be such a dreadful bitch, really, I shouldn't. We had an entire lifetime together and all in all, it was jolly lovely. Besides—I've you in the bargain."

She takes a breath, lifts her shoulders up again, then reaches over and gives the marker a soft caress that brings a lump to my throat.

"You're something," I say, shaking my head in awe. "I have such , I don't know…different feelings. I never knew your Ed as anything but how he was the love of your life. Wish things weren't so complicated." Ruby studies me in a way I'd never seen before, like she is seeing something new in my face.

"I know I put on my high airs, darling," Ruby looks up toward a bird as it soars above us, then smoothes her slacks. "But one day you'll reach a turning point and begin to let things go. Perhaps I'll start cussing a bit more, feels bloody damned good."

"C'mon—it's my turn."

Following my instincts and from habit since I came here a lot when my mom first died, I lead us up and over a gentle incline to my mother's gravesite. Interesting how she and Ed are neighbors.

"I really didn't know *what* to expect, Kate could have done anything, I suppose. I mean, she could have buried him in her own plot somewhere else." Carefully I place the pot of petunias on the ground in the center of the grave marker; I turn it and then step back.

"Your parents are together once again and what a lovely touch, Kate must have added all these white geraniums. Odd to have those lights though—wonder if Ed's grave needs them as well?"

"Are you crazy?" Bending down to look them over, I ponder the ridiculous reason why a grave needs a pair of solar powered nightlights.

I stand back up and have a look around. I can see that all sorts of graves are equipped with their very own lights. Who thinks of this stuff? I notice one nearby gravesite is completely ringed with its own set of carefully placed grave-lights in the shape of a rectangle. I suppose it's to represent the fact that six feet down is the occupant's casket. Looks more like a miniature landing pad to me.

"You've had such a dreadfully *emotional* day, how about I leave you with your parents and when you're ready, meet me back at the van, hmmm?" Before I can respond, she heads off.

Looking around, I notice how really beautiful it is here, quiet and everything so tidy, graves all neat as a pin. Many have baskets of flowers suspended from hooks; they sway in the breeze. My folk's cream-colored granite marker is cool to the touch as I reach down and run my fingers inside the inscribed letters.

I sigh as the enormity of all that's past between us—the three of us—is over. I'm truly all grown up now that there are no more parental units around to say things in that *certain way* that smacks of all the history you shared with only them. I used to love/hate hearing my mom proclaim—*well of course I know what button to push in order to get your goat, I installed them!* I have so many unexpressed emotions simmering inside.

"Why didn't you ever tell me about your affair with *Ed* or how *lonely* you were?" I demand from my mother's half of the tombstone as hot, angry child-tears roll down my cheeks. I focus on my dad's half, "And why the hell didn't you ever *once,* stop into my salon and at least say *hi?* Why did you both stay together if you were so damn unhappy? Because of *me?*"

I feel something inside me cut loose. Now I know madness; a bolt of understanding overcomes me. I feel as though I'm standing on a cliff and I can either fly high into the sun—or fall.

Part of me, a part I can't control, grabs Bonnie's pot of flowers. I lift them high above my head and watch in astonishment as in slow motion it falls squarely on their grave. It breaks into two perfect halves—landing at my feet. The sound as the pot broke echoes in my head as something deep inside of me pulls free. I look at my hands and a calmness settles in. The sun seems brighter, sounds of the birds clearer, everything slides into clarity.

Ruby appears, takes in the broken pot and purses her lips. "Perhaps petunias weren't the proper choice after all."

I look her in the eye; she wipes my tear away then pats my arm.

"Would you like to drive by your old house on Rust Street before we leave?" I ask and my voice sounds different.

Ruby links her arm through mine. "Rust Street *used to* be my home—dear friend. Let's go back to Madeline Island—shall we?"

"I was hoping you'd say that."

CHAPTER THREE

"**O**uch!" I helplessly fuss while Lilly pulls yellow fabric around my family-sized rear-end. "Now I know how Helen must have felt when you fit her for her wedding dress. Like a voodoo doll!"

"There. Step down before I *really* stick a pin in you," Lilly says through a mouthful of them as she helps me off the stool. The sewing crew applauds.

"Girrrl," Sam shakes her head. "Ain't gunna be no finer lookin' duck around—no sir. And how that Lilly's making you a *sexy* duck to boot—sure is something."

"Yeah, something," I mumble and move back over to my cutting table. "I shouldn't have eaten so many of Howard's taco-Tuesday tacos. Maybe Lilly would have an easier time fitting me into that thing and she certainly wouldn't need so many bolts of fabric."

Ruby moves the mini-step ladder over to the mint-green fridge and amps up the stereo. Soft marimba music floats through the boathouse.

"How many of these heavy cotton aprons do we have to make?" I ask no one in particular, "This stuff is so stiff it's a pain in the ass to cut."

"They're for a bloke in Rice Lake. All the order says is Thyme Worn Treasures. They're after fifty and it's a bloody *rush* job." Ruby announces reading from the order clip-board. She re-hangs it next to our Chippendale calendar. "Good heavens—has anyone peeked at Mr. May?" We all nod. "I see, well he *is* a hottie, though Mr. April certainly hasn't been a disappointment." She removes her bifocals and heads over to the ringing deer head phone.

Ruby reaches up, pulls down the jaw and the phone glides down a black cord that slides out of the deer's mouth in slow motion. "Ruby's Aprons, this is Ruby." She cradles the phone on her shoulder and quietly gabs while tidying up the kitchen.

"After belly dance class later this afternoon," I mention while zooming my electric shears along the heavy cotton fabric. "I'd like to propose a communal garden idea I'm thinking about."

"Howard and I had a garden out back of our place," Johnny comments. "But I can't *tell* you how many times some animal or another would trample or eat the whole works down to the nubbins. We finally gave up."

"I haven't had much of a vegetable garden for *years*," Lilly adds. "But I *do* love my flower beds and enjoy canning when the gardening bug hits. I still make freezer jam once strawberry season is full tilt in Bayfield."

"Most folks now-a-days in Ashland," Sam says, in her rich voice as she sews several apron pieces together so fast you can almost see smoke. "They's more excited as to whether or not their fancy lawn is the right green. Me—I grow all *sorts* of vegetables. Well I was thinkin' on planting me a *fine* garden, but then I been seeing what Eve's got up her sleeve and I've been waiting for the lady to speak."

I shake my head. It's nearly impossible to get used to having someone around that can read your thoughts. Sam looks up and we catch eyes, and then she winks and off her machine zooms.

Once again I take down the festive postcard Helen and Ryan sent from Hawaii and re-read it. The front is covered with Hawaiian leis of pastel pinks and blues, arranged around an old suitcase.

'Hey Madeline Island Family!

Between the scuba dives, climbing up and around and into the lush rainforest and all this sunshine—we 're having a refreshing, as well as extremely decadent honeymoon, I couldn't be happier. Ryan tells anyone who'll listen how his bride was duck-delivered and then he explains all the details. I just grin. Found out who was behind the 'carry-on incident' and am scheming my revenge. I may have to consult Eve & Ruby

Sure miss you all!

Sending our love,

Helen & Ryan

P.S. We have a surprise to share when we return!'

Tacking it back up, I wonder what Helen means by a surprise. I notice an odd look cross Sam's face, then she goes back to her sewing.

Ruby lets go of the phone and it swings back on up and into the mouth of the deer. Howard comes out from the office in the back where he runs the finances and does computer work for our website.

"You're going to kill me with that blasted thing!" Howard dashes out of the way of the swinging phone. "I'd be more than happy to install a normal, everyday, socially acceptable telephone."

"And take all the fun out of it? *Really,* darling," Ruby admonishes him with a shrug. "That was Bonnie, she and Marsha just had the most interesting customer in for lunch."

"Okay," I say, "Who did they just serve lunch to? No, wait, let me guess, Cher was here on her way to Duluth."

"Oh my," Sam shakes her head. "There's gonna be some trouble for dessert, yes sir."

"It was Helen's father," Ruby replies. "That handsome Italian man—Tony Giamana, Giamonna, *Gia-something* or another."

That's one unusual name and my heart takes a tiny leap. There's only one Tony Giamonna. He was my high school sweetheart. When I was all of seventeen, he left me pregnant with Helen.

I glance over toward Johnny, he has the oddest look on his face.
Like he's shocked.

"Tony *Giamonna?*" Both Johnny and I say at the same time.

Sam, Ruby, Lilly and I are all up in the loft. Above the barn, it
is an incredible space that once was the ballet studio of Ed's great
grandmother. Now we use it for our yoga-belly dancing space. The
yellowed wood floors got a good buffing and now they reflect the
sunlight when it chooses to shine through the big window facing
the lake.

We're dressed in our belly dancing outfits, complete with colorful head scarves, tasteful veils, Zills clanging between our fingers
and coin belts that jingle and jangle like the door of the bookstore
when you head in—only times four! It's wonderfully obnoxious.

The mesmerizing music Lilly plays on an ancient boom-box
evokes an atmosphere of sensuality and I have to admit, the incense
helps too, especially if anyone has gas. Actually, this has turned out
to be a great thing to drop some weight and a fun way to work off
some of those tacos. Our dance instructor extraordinaire, Lilly, is
so fussy about posture and breathing and holding our hips *just so.*

"Good, good," Lilly encourages us from up in front of the wall
of mirrors that reflects all our moves.

"Let's all do our Flamenco Shimmy, then the Envelope Turn—
lift your veil a bit higher Ruby—much better."

The veil, in our case, is a long silky rectangle of fabric that we
either have draped around our waist or sometimes over our shoulders. Then, when belly-dancing-boss-lady tells us, we lift it high
in the air and wave it around. With us crazy ladies in motion and
all this color trailing around, it's really beautiful—and truly nuts.

"One is *limited,*" Ruby puffs out, "simply how *bloody high* one
can lift one's veil, darling woman."

We burst out laughing, then someone farts. Lilly lights more
incense and the lesson for the day is done. Yes, women have gas.
Not Ruby though—never Ruby.

Full Moon Over Madeline Island • *41*

"Maybe,"—instructor Lilly clicks off the CD and the music disappears back into the black box—"We'll skip the yoga portion and resume our lessons come Wednesday."

Filing over to the grouping of furniture in front of the window, we happily plop down.

"Land Lilly," Sam breathlessly utters and swipes her brow, then swigs some water. "Girrrl—you sure out to kill us off, my hips have *never* moved like that."

"At least you've *got* some," Ruby adds.

I roll my eyes wishing I could share mine. "Such a problem, this one—oy vey," I do my best Jewish impression. "Listen," turning to Sam, "I was wondering if—"

"—I know you'd be wantin' to take a look see 'bout your new neighbors wanting to move in on your good thing," Sam waves her hefty arm my way. "Don't mind if I do—c'mon then."

Sam heads over to the far corner of the loft. A beige canvas drop cloth covers a shape the size of a pool table. I lift one end and Sam lifts the other and we fold it together flag-style then lay it on a nearby chair. When I look at it, it always makes me a little dizzy. It's a flawlessly recreated model of Madeline Island that Ruby's Ed made years ago.

There are exact duplicates of each and every cottage and restaurant and barn and—you name it—they have miniature kitchens with tables and chairs; dishes even. Minuscule docks with boats and leaves on the trees and if you flick the switches on the left side, the whole thing lights up. Car lights and porch lights and the tower room right here in our cabin. In a way, it's kind of creepy.

Sam is able to *sense* certain things by focusing on a particular building or place. The first time she looked at the model, she said it's like looking through a history book of what took place and where and sometimes (but not always) why.

"What I'm hoping for,"—I look into each and everyone's eyes—"Is that by some luck of the draw there's an ancient Indian burial or lost treasure or some other historically significant thing in that area down south that's about to be developed into Gilded Sunsets."

"Such a dreadful shame," Ruby says. "Besides the gated communities, so many of the lovely cottages here are being *done over,* into rambling lodges of such *gargantuan* size."

"It's happening,"—Lilly folds her arms over her chest—"up and down the entire Lake Superior shoreline. But back in Eau Claire, my cousin Dot just called me earlier this morning, she said the construction craze has dried up like a prune. You know," Lilly plops her bifocals into her hair; the chain smacking her cheeks as she speaks. "She also mentioned some minor vandalism at Forest Hill Cemetery; nothing major, a broken pot." Ruby and I shrug. "Hey—isn't that where you and Ruby were the other day?"

"Sometimes," Sam lowers her voice and we lean in closer. "Seems we humans jus' gotta learn the *hard* way and the way things is marching on in this world, fast as lightning, trouble is *sure* to follow."

"Oh great," I comment with major sass. "The arctic poles are melting, we're running out of oil and—"

—Sam holds up her arm and I shut my big mouth. "This land you pointed out, there's not a thing...wait...over here." She points to several small buildings in La Pointe. "There's something coming to this..." She straightens up, gazes out the window a moment, then sighs. "It's something around Marsha. Someone means her harm or is it the other way around? Something don't seem to add up there."

We've stopped breathing, waiting for her to finish.

"I can't see if it's...one of them knows of this darkness—it's a secret, more like. But the other doesn't. Like this side of reality is hanging onto something that's long passed on. I jus' can't get more than that."

"Maybe," I suggest, sending a lifted-brow toward Ruby. "Marsha's husband isn't the romantic memory she painted for us when we first met her?"

"It's funny, that romance fantasy we all seem so hard-pressed to find," Sam scoffs. "Always seems to me—that the ones nearest to our hearts—can cut the deepest."

"Good heavens," Ruby says. "Should we warn her?"

"That was Marsha," I say and hang up the phone in the kitchen at the cottage. "She thinks we've lost our minds—which could be true—and more or less told me that her husband would never hurt *a fly,* let alone her."

"Oh dear," Ruby sags onto a stool, "I can still remember that framed poem she has that he wrote. She must feel rather odd, I suppose, an oddness that never leaves you."

"I've honestly never heard of someone disappearing like that, and over the years, I've heard some pretty amazing,"—the phone rings, I put down my well earned cigarette-half—"This is Eve Moss, and this better be good."

"It's Johnny. Listen...I think we need to talk."

"Do I need to bring a gun?" I ask with a half-hearted chuckle. My stomach suddenly takes a leap. It's his voice.

"No, of course not," Johnny replies, half-laughing as well.

I can feel his apprehension prickle over the line. "Maybe Tony happens to be a familiar name and—" I offer feeling strange, like I'm talking underwater.

"Look," Johnny sighs. "I...I *knew* him...*know* him and it was a long time after you and he and... look. Would you just get over here," Johnny demands in a voice I don't like. "Howard won't pester us, and I *really* need to talk to you—*alone.*"

"Okay. Alright. I'll be there in ten minutes." I hang up the phone. "Do I have to do this?" I ask Ruby who's putting away the pasta salad leftovers from our supper.

"Oh darling, you mustn't forget how the past can be so—it can be so bloody—"

"—Complicated," I offer and she nods. "Why am I so scared to find out what this Tony Giamonna thing is all about? I mean, I knew him a long time ago. Thanks to his overly active sperm and hormonal me—I have Helen. But what in the world does this have to do with *Johnny?*"

"I couldn't *begin* to imagine," Ruby offers. "But whatever it may be, you keep in mind Johnny is your friend. Me—I'm your personal chef, housekeeper, counselor, do-dad sewer and dock master. Did I miss anything?"

"Yeah—major pain in the ass!" Ruby snaps a towel at my retreating rear. "Ouch!"

Rocky leaps up onto the stump table, I give him a good scratching, then take him in my arms and head upstairs to change.

"Knock knock," I call out as I walk through the boy's back door.

"I'll be right there," Johnny calls out. "Pour us some wine."

Their place is nothing like our cottage; its sleek, stainless appliances and black granite countertops go on and on. It's a craftsman style with lots of taste and a manly undertone I like. They have a collection of McCoy pottery that's mind blowing. Dean Martin is crooning softly in the background.

Taking down several tall stems in the midst of the back-lit crystal collection, I pry open one side of their fancy fridge and gasp at all the stuff crammed in there. Selecting an open bottle, I pour and then carry the goblets into the living room—Great Room—actually.

Wood beams criss-cross high above, the floor-to-ceiling windows look through a stand of birch and then on out to the lake. Normally white-barked, they're awash in shimmering orange and yellows as the sun slowly slides into the lake.

"Hey Eve," Johnny crosses the room and gives me a friendly peck. "Howard's working on our personal finances in his office. Pull up a couch and take a load off."

I slide onto a plush tweed love seat cozy with throw pillows made of soft cotton. We clink our goblets and sip. I look down, into an old photo album with the cover flung open.

It's my Tony; only he's got his arm draped around a much younger Johnny, with permed hair, no less. By the tight white pants Tony wears and those ridiculous sideburns, this must be from the early eighties. I sit back and process this. Sipping more wine.

"With the wonders of the internet," Johnny crosses and uncrosses his legs. "Tony and I got back in touch not too long ago and he told me this amazing story about a long lost daughter. The pieces more or less fell together. I did the math and the damn lightbulb above my head burned on."

I feel odd, exposed for some stupid reason. I set my empty wine glass down. "Am I about to have a *Brokeback moment* here? I mean…" I lean forward and flip through the photo album. It's filled with mostly pictures of the two of them. Holding hands here, making goofy faces in this one, an entire series of them in various poses wearing matching red skimpy bathing suits. So skinny. A blown-up photo, your typical eight-by-ten glamour shot, takes up one entire page—of them kissing! I slam the book closed and sink back into the coziness of his designer sofa. I lift my goblet and hand it to Johnny.

He re-fills it and hands it to me faster than I've ever seen him move. I sip and imagine Tony back then. "The thing I remember most about him was how wonderfully shaped his hands were. When he held mine, I felt as though I was the safest girl alive—"

"—Eve, I don't know what to say," Johnny's voice is so small. Boyish. "It was years *and years* ago, but I had to tell you. Especially now that you and Helen…" Her name hangs in the air like an odd smell.

I drink my wine down in one gulp. "Does *she* know too? And not *me,* not until *what?*"

My mind races back in time to when Tony came to the cottage the day after Helen's wedding and there he was in his UPS uniform as if time had stood still. Well, time had taken all his beautiful, curly hair, but he still looked damn fine in those shorts.

"I haven't said anything to—only Howard—of course."

"Look, this is a lot to swallow, you know? I need some time to figure out what to do, or not—that…just what to…I can't explain what this feels like."

"I understand, I do. I'm so sorry to tell you like this—of course I had no *idea,* I mean, he never mentioned a kid back then."

"Well, he and I *were* only kids, after all." I feel foolish remembering him and I squirming in his backseat, the windows steamed up. "From what I know about sexuality, which isn't a whole hell of a lot, mind you, I doubt he even *knew* he was attracted to guys. I can see why you were attracted to him, what a grin he—this is too weird."

"He's had a hard time with it," Johnny offers, his eyes pleading. "Being raised in a Catholic-Italian family with all the macho stuff. He was married for a while too—didn't work out is what he had said."

"Eventually you have to be true to what you are," I consider my empty glass. "Look—I know logically that this is all history, old stuff that happened years ago—"

"—Eve...I honestly..." Johnny says, his hands open, pleading.

I stand to leave. Running is what I *really* feel like. "I need some air and to put this in some kind of perspective. Um, goodnight." I bolt.

Johnny says something, but I'm halfway down the path between our places and don't *want* to know. I don't want to know *any* of this. What would have been wrong if he'd never told me? What's a little ignorance once in a *full fucking moon?*

The tightness I had felt earlier in my chest loosens with the wind blowing in my hair. The windows from our cottage cast yellow squares over the yard offering, what? I'm not the same person who only minutes ago, left that place. Yet, what's changed? The twinkle of fireflies against the darkening woods, crickets and those noisy toads surround me with their night sounds—my mind calms down to a low buzz.

So many times I've had this dream of running round and round the outside of my parent's house, trying to find a way in, while they stand apart from one another, framed inside the living room window—waving. That's how I feel, like my dad must have felt about me. Like I'm watching me fumble around in the dark with this new section of my history; I no longer can imagine Tony married with kids. He must have had a lousy time for a while, not being honest with himself as well as those around him.

Clamoring up the wooden stairs, I cross over the verandah, pull open the screen door and head into the warmth I know is waiting inside.

"Thank *heavens,*" Ruby tries to say but it comes out garbled; chocolate stuck to her gums. "I laid in a good supply of these B. T. McElrath chocolates, seeing as you've managed to consume your entire supply of Reese's."

We're sitting opposite one another in one of the window seats in the library. A half-drunk bottle of wine sits on a silver tray; we're surrounded with letters and empty colorful chocolate wrappers lying against cushy red velvet pillows. Rocky is leaping into the air, chasing his tail and then he dashes out the door.

I open yet another yellowed envelope and read aloud. "Eve Moss, how I love the name Eve. Your bright red hair and green, green eyes are the only eyes for me. Let's run away and be together forever and ever and ever and ever and ever. You are my forever and ever, Tony G. The O in Tony is a big red heart. That becomes his signature in all the rest of the letters I have."

"Such a poetic fellow," Ruby says with awe and sarcasm mixed in equal parts. "After reading this entire lot of love-sick letters, how does it make you feel, hmmm, darling? I mean, now that you know how it turns out—and all."

I finish folding yet another one into an airplane and sail it across the room, Rocky races back into the library and pounces on it.

"Oh—I don't know. It's funny...I mean...for such a long time, *especially* when I was pregnant with Helen, I felt so alone, more than anything. I knew there wasn't much he really could have done, seeing as I was giving up the baby. Geez, what the hell do you know when you're barely a teenager?"

"What do you know when you're—when you're," Ruby stammers. "A *mature* woman, such as myself? Life keeps changing around you and things truly are never quite what we think they are."

"You sure as hell can say that again."

And, of course, she does.

CHAPTER FOUR

April becomes May and the flowers poking through last year's leaves and pine needles are gorgeous. After hauling several books from the Madeline Island library out here to the creek, I figured it's time to learn some of their names.

The clumps of bright yellow flowers with ear-shaped green leaves that are popping up along the creek bank are Marsh Marigolds. There are several Jack-in-the-Pulpits that are really cool looking. Bloodroot is what I had pulled up by the root earlier in order to check out the sap. I wanted to see if indeed it's really blood red—it is. Then, of course, I sat on it by mistake. Explains why my jeans are now splotched with dark red. With my luck it's permanent.

Since it's early morning, the dew is soaking into the bottoms of my jeans and my feet are deliciously wet. Rocky's been fussing about getting his coat all wet, but he still follows me, *meowing* the entire time. I spot an odd blue-ish-purple flower growing on the end of a stalk of grass and am curious; it's got little flowers growing at odd angles all the way up the stem.

"Oh here it is, under Iris," I mention to Rocky whose busy burying his do-do in a little mound he created. "Blue-eyed Grass."

All over are these unusual long-stemmed plants with the faintest white flower in the shape of little cotton puffs or caps. Paging through my handy-dandy book, I find a similar picture of it.

"Miterwort or Naked Bishop's cap. Who comes up with these names anyway?" Apparently the name comes from the fact that it's shaped like a bishop's cap. It's really beautiful, kind of reminds me of Lily of the Valley. Rocky looks as though he could use a blow dryer.

We've reached the wooden bridge that crosses over the creek; I close the book and take in the beauty of this heavily wooded valley. All around me are the sounds of spring, of things beginning to rustle back to life; so energizing. Several swallows swoop up and around us. Rocky lets out a limp growl in case someone's looking, I guess, the weirdo. Must be why he never allows anyone to pick him up outside. I mean, God forbid some mouse is watching!

Since the brush hasn't started its race with the surrounding tree canopy to see who will block out the sun first, I figure a peek at the little cabin back there would be perfect. Besides, it's broad daylight and I don't *want* to believe in ghosts.

By keeping the circle of white pine trees surrounding the cabin in my line of sight, I meander up the old trail. It's still somewhat visible, even though several poplar trees have taken root smack in the middle of the path here and there. And they grow like weeds up here and when the wind blows through their leaves it sounds like running water and I either smile or run to pee.

The log cabin was once home to Ed's grandfather, Gustave. He and Adeline lived there until the cottage Ruby and I live in was built. Since it was constructed so soundly, it may outlast even *me*. Walking around to the front, I remember the last visit here and shudder. The heavy locks on the front door are still secure, and I sigh with relief. What happened here basically involved some really old bones and a spirit that needed some guidance. Life can really be bonkers.

What happened was that while we were snooping around here, we found an old hatbox way up on a shelf and inside was the skeleton of a tiny baby. Some really bizarre things took place and we ended up burying the bones in our local graveyard next to one of her parent's, Adeline. The locks are for our peace of mind.

"Wow, what's that smell?" I take in another breath of the spicy-sweet aroma, and then spy a blossom-coated branch reaching around the far corner of the cabin.

Rocky and I head over to investigate. "Holy cow—look at this—there's an orchard hidden back here. Ruby was right."

I count thirteen apple trees in various stages of bloom, the air is *thick* with sweetness. I page through several sections in the book until I find one that has fruit trees and walk around to see if I can figure out who is what, from the pictures. One I'm pretty sure is a Ginger Gold. There are several actually. Three more seem to be closest to the picture of McIntosh and I figure another is Grimes Golden and some Granny Smith too. Good grief, what in the world will we do with all the apples? I suppose for years they've ripened and then fallen to the ground for some happy critters to enjoy.

Way off, at the edge of the orchard, I see a deer and realize *that's* whose been eating all these apples. "Well, it's time to share!" I yell over toward it. The deer lifts its head from where it was munching on something, looks me over good, then turns and strolls away into the woods.

As Rocky and I wander back to the cottage, I can't help but rehash last night's conversation with Johnny. It only freaked me out for a while that Johnny and Tony used to be an *item*. Wonder who he'd been married to, most likely someone from high school. Maybe he's already told Helen about it all when he came by after her wedding. Nah, she would have mentioned. Wouldn't she? She's too wise to get all bent out of shape.

It was a long time ago and the old adage sure is true, people change. I grin, he and Johnny looked kind of cute in their little matching Speedos. Really though, does anyone look good in one of those? Sometimes a little less is really more, or is it the other way around? More coffee might help.

"There are my lovely charges," Ruby bubbles as we walk in the back door. "Oh those are *divine*—thank you, darling." I offer her a bouquet of flowers I picked on the way back.

"If you'd like," I fill a mug of coffee and sit down on a stool at the stump table. "I can tell you all their names, what they like to grow in, and about their sex lives too"

"Ooo, *do* tell." Ruby pulls two bowls of yogurt covered with granola and sliced banana from the fridge.

"This is perfect."

"Well of course it is, darling. Hand me my coffee, would you? Now tell me all about this one here with the spindly stalk."

"It's called Miterwort and—"

"—I want the sex part, start with that and work backwards, for heaven's sake."

"Good morning Ladies," I comment to Sam and Lilly. "Hey—where's Johnny?" They shrug their shoulders, share a glance and go back to sewing.

"Perhaps he's in the back?" Ruby offers with a questioning voice. "With Howard."

I peek into the office. "Hey Howard, where's Johnny at?"

"I think,"—Howard leans back in his swivel chair and puts his hands behind his head—"He's feeling that maybe you're angry with him and don't want him around for awhile. He feels awkward, I would surmise."

"Oh for the love of—" I throw my arms up and head back into the sewing room, pull down the phone and dial.

"Hello—you've reached Johnny and Howard, please leave a message and we'll call you back."

"I know you're standing there listening, get your skinny little ass over here right this minute and I mean it!" Then in a nicer voice I purr, "Besides, who else can I tell all my secrets to and not get yelled at?" I glance toward Ruby and she shakes her head.

John Mayer's new music is pumping inspiring rhythm into the sewing room. Howard installed an iPod station on top of the fridge where the boom box used to sit and I think I've got the swing of it. All that music in that little thing—pretty cool. With the French doors open, a crisp spring breeze is fluffing any left-over stale winter air right out. We're getting together an apron order for Wild Rice, a fancy restaurant right outside of Bayfield that wants a classier apron for their servers.

"I've never made apple sauce," I offer, and hand Johnny black satin apron parts. "A couple of pies and *tons* of apple crisp, but there's so many apples—you all have to make sure and help yourselves."

"Such a *lovely* find," Ruby says while threading a needle. "Ed and I used to get *more* than enough apples from the few trees over by the barn. We were honestly more interested in the grapes that hang off the side. What *divine* wine they make. Had no idea there were all those trees back there. That model certainly has come in handy."

" S'pose you all could make hard cider," Sam suggests. "Got a mighty kick—it's the *real* reason we got all these apple trees across America. Don't have *nothin'* to do with keeping doctors away—no sir." She adjusts a hoop earring and adds her machine's whine to the room.

"I remember reading about that," Lilly offers. "What was that book called? Oh yes, *The Botany of Desire*. Interesting premise and I think Pollan wrote about marijuana too."

"It's so bizarre," Johnny says through clenched teeth as he bites off a thread. Clearing my throat, I hand him a pair of scissors. "You can grow the stuff anywhere! I can't tell you how many of our sick friends would never have lived as long if they couldn't smoke it in order to simply *eat*."

"Imagine if farmers were allowed to grow hemp!" I say for the hundredth time.

Ruby rolls her eyes. "Oh good heavens, here we go again."

We literally zoom through the day, once again solving some of the world's problems and we got a hell of a lot of aprons done too. The boys head back home, armed with a few gardening books from our library. They're going to pour over them in order to begin the planning of our community garden plot. I'm excited; the only thing I used to grow was mold in my fridge's crisper drawer.

Ruby and I plan to take a picnic supper to another island, so she's busy throwing together something *smashingly yummy.* Everyone's gone for the day here at the boathouse. But I like to hang around a while after we're done, enjoying the sound of the waves and winding down. I review the day and also make sure we're set up for tomorrow. I'm in charge of a lot of stuff, but the main thing I focus on is keeping us stocked with enough bolts of fabric for our orders; I *love* fabric, so it never really feels like a job at all.

Running my fingers across the neatly stacked bolts, I can't help but feel this overwhelming gratitude to be here, in this magical and often crazy-as-hell place. Howard and Johnny had made shelving out of old, white shutters we found in the barn. One entire wall is lined with bolts and bolts of material all standing upright. It goes from white through the color wheel all the way to black way at the other end. Mostly cotton and some patterned and prints in the middle. It's a wall of color I get such a kick out of looking at; a wall of possibilities.

Rocky is lounging on top of Sam's sewing table; I give his ears a good scratching and then reach down to snap off the light on her machine she never can seem to remember to do. Unlike Lilly and Johnny's tidy areas, Sam's sewing machine is covered with colorful Post-It notes hanging this way and that.

'Course, I give them a read, who wouldn't? *Get Lilly's jam-bar recipe, Remember Marlene's birthday—send funny card, Remind Howard to renew swipe-cards for the ferry, Keep your nosy self outa my business Miss Eve!'* I jump back feeling as though someone had popped into the room, and then laugh. Lifting off my personalized Post-It and then realizing she'll know—then realizing she *does* know now—oh hell, I zip it off and toss it into the trash bin. Pulling all the doors closed, I snap off the overhead lights, scoop up Rocky and head out the door and on up to the cottage.

"It's a bit more drab," Ruby remarks as I back out. "Without all the flowers we had looped about for Helen's wedding, but it still looks grand with the new red awning."

We're sitting high in our amphibious duck which I keep parked in the barn. The first time I laid eyes on this baby I thought of all the rides I had taken on one down in the Dell's as a kid. It's the best way to zoom around up here in the summertime *and* we save a bundle on ferry fees too.

"Let's head over to the island we went to with Charlie and the boys last summer," I suggest while finding some jazz.

"Let's do."

I steer down the drive, across the wooden bridge and on up toward the gate and hang a right onto North Shore Drive. The winding road is lined with towering white pine, yellow and white birch and maple trees that stand shoulder to shoulder competing for the sun. On either side, mysterious lanes disappear down and around, leading to other cabins and cottages.

Many have festive signs, painted or carved at the entrances with the names of the families, often listing all the kids too. I love the one next to our gate—a big yellow sun announcing *Eve & Ruby's* in bright red letters, compliments of Howard and Johnny.

I notice the entrance to the Gilded Sunsets development and slow the duck down. Looking through Ruby's side, I can see they've begun to clear the woods away. Newly carved lanes have been dug and there's a big sign with all the different shaped lots they'll be offering. I hit the gas and off we go.

We pass several mobile homes; in one of them the front yard is filled with fancy painted, complicated birdhouses seeming to float on tall poles. You can barely make out the corner of a pink trailer. A clump of weeping willow trees slumps over one entire side making it look like its slowly swallowing it.

"Oh shoot," Ruby smacks the dash and the glove box flings open. "I should have thought of inviting him along."

"Oh hell," I say as I swing into his driveway and head down the lane.

It's a rutted dirt road with grass starting to grow in the middle, like most driveways here. Charlie Bruns lives alone here. He's tall and slim, with a sinewy build and a long, long gray braid that hangs way down his back. His weathered skin and trimmed moustache make him look like a sea captain or an old movie star. Originally I imagined he and Ruby would be a *hot item* but Ruby has no interest in another relationship and I for one can't blame her. And honestly, friends with benefits only seem to work in novels.

I pull up in front of his stoop and we clamber down the ladder and head to his door. It's an older, art deco inspired trailer that has 50's-style chrome fins and a circular window in the front door.

I reach up to knock, but before my hand touches the door—it's pulled open. "Eve and Ruby," Charlie's smiling face announces. "What an immense surprise." His blue eyes twinkle as we each get a hug. "What brings you two over here, and in that old tugboat no less?" He points beyond us.

"Charlie, darling," Ruby gushes. "So sorry we didn't ring you first, but have you had your supper?"

"Well—no. I haven't thought that far as of yet," he gives his head a scratch. "What'd you have in mind?"

"Care to join us," I chide, "for a duck-ride-wine-and-food-cruise?"

"Well now—don't mind if I *do* long as it includes an island in the mix and who can refuse one of your picnic suppers? Let me grab my hat and a jacket."

He disappears inside and we head back over toward the duck and climb in. I take in the fact that Ruby *does* have on a rather snug sweater set and is that a new lipstick? I glance down at my baggy jeans and over-sized cat-covered sweatshirt and shrug. Charlie scuttles up and into the duck, thumping down into the seat next to Ruby. His brown fedora and spicy-earthy cologne remind me of my dad when he was much younger.

Turning back onto his drive, I move us along slowly to enjoy the miniature bird-house mansions and cabins and cruise boats Charlie built over the years.

I head us back onto North Shore, at the bend in the road, instead of veering left, I steer us straight onto a long sandy beach, then I crank the wheel a hard right and we're facing the lake. I hit the gas and we splash in. Seconds later, I switch to the propeller and—we're off!

The sun is still not ready to set; now that we're heading into summer and nights are so much longer. I pull down my visor and direct us over toward a tiny little island we often sneak off to.

"This is simply *lovely,*" Ruby pours wine into our colorful aluminum tumblers. "I'm *so* glad you could come along, darling." She adjusts the red and white gingham cloth we're seated on.

"Me to," Charlie wipes his hand over his moustache. "Thanks for the invite and *boy,* you sure can make a mean egg salad sandwich."

"She can be plain mean, too," I add. "We're just happy to finally be done with all the wedding leftovers."

"Hey—speaking of," Charlie says. "What have you heard from the newlyweds?"

"*Well*—" Ruby delves into the airport-sex-toy story and due to her naughty embellishments it becomes such a riot that we laugh until our sides hurt.

The two of them get engrossed in a discussion about whether or not Thoreau was *truly* a great writer or just a keen observer lacking the proper adjectives, this according to Ruby. So I decide to take a stroll along the edge of the island in order to do some thinking.

Sometimes I forget what I left behind in Eau Claire. The familiar streets and buildings, all the history I had there; recognizing everyone who passed by my shop's door, belonging, knowing who you could count on and who you couldn't. Now it's happening here on the island. Now—*this* is where I belong.

Something green reflects the sun's colors and catches my eye. As I pull it out of the cool water, a lone seagull passes overhead; its shadow flutters a beautiful bird-shape design on top of the lake's surface. For a moment, I can make out the outline of someone I once knew. I hold the chilled piece of lake glass in my hand and suddenly smell my mother's perfume waft over me—then—it's gone.

Yet it leaves behind the wonderful feeling of everything warm and kind that my mother was.

I miss her.

CHAPTER FIVE

"This is really shaping up," I comment to Alice Anne. "I can't get over how much has changed here."

She has the same pretty face as her mother, Marsha, even the turned up nose, but that's where it ends. Working as an ER nurse in downtown Detroit has obviously taken its toll and explains why she's so dang tough. Maybe it's the blonde spiked hair and what is it with rings coming out of your eyebrow?

"We've gotten some really,"—a jazzy tune zips out of her jeans and obviously interrupts her train of thought—"That's my cell, 'scuze me a sec. Hey—Boo, what's up?"

I stroll off into the main living room. What, or who, is a *Boo?* I am so out of it, I have yet to figure out how to change the greeting on *my* cell, let alone how to turn down the sound so everyone around me isn't forced to listen to Ruby rant on and on. Funny, phones don't even *ring* anymore.

Maybe I've gone a tad off my rocker, but by creating Toad Hollow here in this old farmhouse, I hope to help others who were like me—pregnant and alone. I'm a board member too because it's really become important to me. Oh I know we've got choices now and this is one more. There wasn't an option for me and we women need all the options we can get!

Not only will pregnant women be able to come here to have their babies, but if a mom and her kids need a safe place to be—this is that place. I have to remind myself that it was dear old dad who helped with the down payment. Life is an amazing ride and it seems to always head back to where it began. The endless circles of life can sometimes make you dizzy.

The house is nothing fancy; gathering areas will be on the first floor, big, roomy kitchen in the back and four comfortable bedrooms upstairs with the possibility of adding on should the need arise since the house sits on twenty acres. I do need to build up my cash reserve, hence the Ducky Derby competition and whatever else we can think up. Restoring an old place that's sat empty for a while can be a major money-pit and also, in the end, (hopefully) a great investment.

Underneath the stairs that lead to the second floor, is the make-shift office area where Alice Anne has set herself up. Eventually we'll have a more elaborate examination room so she can do her work properly. I'm relieved as hell she's agreed to run this place. I don't know when she'll move in permanently, but with all that hammering and sawing going on up there, it should be soon. We're having the third floor attic, which has only been used for storage in the past, converted into a cozy apartment for her.

Alice Anne is playing some music I honestly don't even think is from this planet. I like it though and the little movie playing on her teeny tiny screen is kind of cool too. I sigh, realizing the second you step away (say move to an island), technology is liable to fly right by you.

Alice Anne struts in. "I'll hit you up on the hip later—bye." She touches the screen of her mini-phone-tv gizmo and then shoves it into one of her bazillion pants pockets.

Should I even ask *whose* hip? "You must be anxious to move in here, the carriage house you're sharing with your mom is—"

"—Cramped as hell!" Alice Anne thumps into her office chair. "I'm twenty-six and living with your mom can really put a fucking damper on, well...*everything.* And besides, she's been acting really schizoid lately—not that she wasn't always a little crazy growing up."

"Really—like in what way?" I ask as casually as possible. I sit down opposite her, so maybe she'll be more comfortable and shed some light on what Sam saw in the model.

"Oh I don't know, she's really edgy and I've noticed when she goes to bed at night, she locks her door; and she's recently added a dead bolt—on the *inside* of her bedroom door!"

"Maybe she's paranoid about living on an island or..." I suggest and realize this may be more than I want to know.

Alice Anne sighs, then glances out the window. "I've never really *known* my mom, not really, you know? I mean, she's always kind of been a shadow of someone, like she's there, but not all of her. Hard to explain—I've tried and tried to find my dad—to ask him why he left us and find out the other side of all the bits and pieces that mom's told me. To know the guy—you know?"

"He walked out on you both—right?" She nods. "That would sure set *me* back ...a *lot* actually. But to be honest—though it was a lot later in my life—my dad left the second my mom died and we really never spoke again. I didn't reach out to him, either. Just stewed like the spoiled brat that I was. Maybe your mom's never gotten over it, being abandoned like that."

"Sorry about your old man. I suppose it *could* explain her weird ways. But don't you think it's odd I can't find even a *trace* of him? It's like he never was. I mean...I've never fucking *seen* him—*ever!*" She says with an anger that I can see runs deep.

"That *is* peculiar," Ruby says. She motions me over to the stove with a wooden spoon. "Be a love and give this sauce a good stir, would you?"

I take the spoon from her. Steam rises from the green porcelain pot and the kitchen fills with oregano, rich tomato and garlic. A loaf of rosemary bread is baking in the oven and hot pasta noodles are heaped in a chrome colander over in the sink, waiting for this yummy sauce.

We always make extra food so we can either freeze it for later or have enough to take down to the boathouse and share with the crew. I hum along with *This Can't Be Love* playing on the hi-fi in the living room.

"What would make someone leave their newborn baby and young wife?" I pause, thinking. "I mean, how could you do such a rotten thing and then—on top of it all—he's gone forever. No child support, no visits to see the kid, not even a card at Christmas from *Mexico* or something."

"Does seem a bit *odd*," Ruby concurs. She takes a sip of wine and straightens a dangly earring of tiny silver balls. "Perhaps there's more to Marsha than meets the eye."

"Whad'ya mean? Like he never *left*...that maybe Marsha—"

"—Put something *special* in his soup, chopped him up and put him under her rhododendrons. Perhaps she composted him along with the table scraps and then grew the loveliest tomatoes *ever* that year. Then canned them and on the label she could have written *Don's Delicious* and bloody well meant it!"

"You are really twisted," I shake my head. "I think reading all those murder mysteries is warping your mind."

"I should think *something's* warping it a bit." She raises her arched brows in my direction.

"This sauce isn't from Marsha, by any chance, is it?" I lift an aromatic spoonful up and then let it flow back into the pot. "You're not missing *a finger,* are you?" I chuckle and she smacks my arm.

"People are an odd lot, darling. The moment you think you've got the game all figured out, someone goes and changes the rules."

"Speaking of odd." I pull two dinner plates from the cupboard; one is china, covered with an intricate gold and blue pattern, the other is Blue Willow, a favorite of mine. I set out two place settings, turning a plate right, adding mismatched silverware and carefully folded paper napkins. These are vintage fifties, laughing salt and pepper shakers dance along the edges in bright reds and yellows.

"I know odd," I say as I slice the bread and we pull up stools. "It's rather incredible how the actions of *one* person can screw up so many lives."

"We're also jumping to conclusions," Ruby says around a mouthful of pasta. "There could be so much more that led up to this Donald Kelven's disappearance and as you know, sometimes you never *do* know all the facts."

"True. Hey—you should see all the work that's been done over at Toad Hollow. Alice Anne is doing a great job and I bet we can throw a grand opening party soon."

"That would be quite lovely, darling."

We hear a crash somewhere upstairs. Seconds later, Rocky zooms down the stairs, leaps up onto the countertop that separates the kitchen from the living room and plops down a mouse. It scurries off the edge and we hear more banging off toward the library.

"Be a dear and pass me the bread," Ruby says cool as a dead mouse.

After tidying up the kitchen we snap close, and then label several containers of pasta and sauce. We head downstairs to see if we can cram these into the freezer.

"There, that should do it," Ruby quickly slams the door closed. "Enough in there to get us through several winters, I should think."

"Maybe it's high time to take a look into the ominous box of my dad's," I say as we head back upstairs.

"I can't *believe* you've not opened it yet."

"Sometimes it's better imagining a thing than actually seeing it and besides, what more could there possibly be to my family secret?"

"I'll put the kettle on and meet you in the living room."

We're all cozy facing the river-rock fireplace, working on a box of chocolates, sipping tea, with the box between us and a scissors lying on the coffee table glinting in a mocking way.

"Here goes nothing," I say as I slip the blade along several hunks of cellophane tape. "She certainly used enough tape—good God."

"Too small of a box," Ruby adds, "to contain anything like, oh, say a fur coat or perhaps your late father's gold bar collection."

I toss the brown crumpled paper aside. "There's a note from my dad. Must have written it right before he died. The writing is shaky and his used to be very up and down—full of pride. I smooth the note out on my lap and read it to Ruby.

"Dear Evie, a few things I thought you might enjoy having." A tear lands on the note with a plop. *"So glad to have met your daughter—I bet the wedding was a sight to behold and—so is she. It's time to try and let go of the past, it's just that—the past. Be as happy as you can and for goodness sake, quit smoking! Love, dad."* I sigh.

"Short and sweet, that," Ruby points out, "What *else* have you got in there, hmmm?"

I lift out several books, a file folder stuffed with papers and a framed picture.

"It's of the three of us," I pass it to Ruby. "He had it in his office at the university, God, I must be all of thirteen. We had a little tiny house on Summer Street, gray with a pink front door. Later we moved to a much larger place—I've shown you—over by the university."

"Yes, I recall. My my, you do look like your mum in this picture. I think it belongs over here." She strolls over to the wall leading up and along the staircase to hang it on the first nail in a line of empty nails that wind up the stairs and down the hallway. "It's perfect—and high time we get busy putting up other pictures of our lives, don't you think?"

"I do. Wow, get a load of this, a beautiful book of poetry called *Place,* by Maxine Moss—what in the world? That's mom!" I flip to the back of the yellowed dust jacket. "Look, she must have been— what—twenty? Man...she was so beautiful. Why didn't she ever show this to me?"

"Read me something, darling, would you?"

I flip to a yellow tinted photo of a cascading spring that winds down and around flowing into what looks to be the ocean. The water is calm as it laps onto a sandy beach; a mist makes the horizon hard to make out, it looks like a dream. After I show it to Ruby, who *ooooo's* and *ahhhh's* I read the passage on the opposite page:

> *"What does the ocean sound like?*
> *Listen, it's there in the wind as*
> *it rushes through leaves, the rumbling*
> *of a street car; the crowded streets have*
> *ocean sounds too. It's there in your head*
> *when you hurry into the world, a heartbeat*
> *of life is the ocean and it's always there for*
> *you to dream. The ocean is life and flows into*
> *all those I love; its tide a blanket to warm you."*

"Lovely...simply lovely," Ruby sighs. "Your mum—such *divine* passion. Makes you wonder just why it went off the boil for your father and her."

"Off the boil—sounds so much better than walking by their bedroom and taking in the two twin beds, side-by side."

"Such on *odd* custom for grown-ups, hmmm? Nothing Ed and I ever managed, we only had the one bed. Double louse that he was."

"The file is filled with—oh, for God's sake—it's all sorts of stuff I drew years ago. I used to want to be an artist. Funny, but almost all of these are of islands. And look at this one."

"Oh dear me, you've drawn the cottage here. Why look—there's the boathouse—and isn't that the barn in the back there? My word."

"It sure looks like it, but there's no *way* I could have known about this place. This is really creepy."

"Oh goodness no. It's not creepy at all, darling, just *telling*. I think perhaps sometimes what we dream of as children often becomes what is."

Rocky and I are snuggled, cozy together, upstairs in my bed. As my Felix-the-Cat clock informs me, it's half-past midnight and I'm engrossed in my mom's book. A *her* I never knew, the deep way she looked at life from an angle you'd only imagine someone much older would. So profound and yet clear—crystal clear.

It's funny how sometimes a story can take you away, or in this case, bring you closer. I miss her, our home. I think that where you live is so important in defining who you are and what you become. Some places are really not the best for certain things. Like big cities don't necessarily mean you have tons of friends any more than if you live on an island. But there are places that can bring you out, that can nurture you in a way that's hard to explain; yet you feel it in your soul.

I glance around my bedroom. Faded wallpaper of tiny roses, dark stained wooden arched doors, the narrow passage up to the tower room. How in the world *couldn't* I be home? Rocky stretches and turns onto his side, I give him a good scratching and he softly purrs.

Wonder if I really *did* know about this cottage way up here; that this is where I'd find myself. Life is like standing in front of a mirror and yet there's another directly behind you...

I wonder myself to sleep.

CHAPTER SIX

"It's just like anything," I say handing Johnny faded denim apron parts. "Once you get people interested, things take on a life of their own."

"We all been talkin'," Sam slows her sewing machine to a low growl. "Seeing as this here Ducky Derby is to help folks and now you tellin' us there's going to be all them booths with youth organizations, we don't expect pay from you ladies when we're helping out."

"It's not up for discussion," Lilly quickly adds and off she sews.

"Close that mouth," Johnny chides me. "All that room in there, the flies buzzing around here could just move right in." He puts his machine on high and the room is alive with the thrilling sounds of things being created right here.

My world used to be filled with my client and I trying to have a conversation over the obnoxious blast of my blow-dryer; the air around us a hair-spray haze mixed with the myriad of perfumes some of my client's practically bathed in—and coffee.

I look toward Ruby and she grins, seeming to read my mind. She reaches to fiddle with the tunes and Gnarls Barkley growls his addictive tune, *Crazy*. Ruby ups the volume more and then I go over, give it one more tap.

I start to do a little dance underneath the deer head and before I get too *crazy,* Sam and Johnny come over and start to shake their groove thing. Then Ruby and Lilly do the same. Howard smiles from the sidelines, snapping his fingers. We play the song and boo-gie one more time, then get back to work.

"That was bloody fun!" Ruby huffs, while starting to set lunch out. "Who brought this *divine* smelling pesto-pasta dish?"

"Howard and I," Johnny offers as he unwraps the foil top. "We grew a horde of basil last year and had to do *something* with it, so we made pesto, it freezes great."

"Everyone best have a good helping," Ruby says. "Otherwise my garlic breath could simply kill you all."

"Of course we'll numb it down," I remind her, "with a short cigarette break afterwards."

"With all we know nowadays about the *disgusting* habit of smoking," Johnny says with loads of sarcasm, sliding onto a chair at the yellow and chrome kitchen table."I don't know why *any* of you still do it."

"*Really* Johnny," Ruby utters dramatically sitting down next to him. "If we didn't have this one *horrid* little habit, why—we'd be practically perfect!"

"Alice Anne is doing *so* much," I say between bites. "Organizing this derby event and getting Toad Hollow put together. We've met with several guys over at the fish hatchery south of Bayfield, oh shoot, what did they keep reminding me it's called?"

"The Les Voigt State Fish Hatchery," Howard offers with his regal voice. "It's really an amazing place, built in the late eighteen hundreds."

"And the best part," I add. "Is that we can use the grounds in back, which is where Pike's Creek flows through. After all, we need a moving body of water to float all these rubber ducks down."

"Could you give us an overview?" Lilly asks dabbing a napkin on her mouth with surgical-precision. "Exactly how *does* this whole thing work?"

"Sure," I say. "Basically, this is the deal. With the ducks that Lilly has given us *and* we just ordered five thousand more—we have to think big here—we'll ask folks to adopt a duck for five bucks. They in turn will have the chance to win some cool prizes, should their duck float through the finish line first or second, on up to tenth. It will depend on the amount of prizes we get donated. Oh, and we'll give something fun for the last one too. Always being the last to get picked growing up, this is my revenge. The money goes to Toad Hollow and several other non-profit youth organizations."

"What *kinda* prizes?" Sam wonders out loud. "I don't need no more junk to add to my junk I already have, no sir, seeing as I always win something or other. I am one *lucky* charmed lady," Sam bursts out laughing. "You should see you all's faces, I am just *pulling* your leg—sorta..." She says the *sorta* part real low.

"Prizes can be anything." I think for a moment. "I mean, this lady in Colorado who I've been emailing, she's done this kind of thing for years. She suggests local things. I was thinking a trip to one of the lighthouses, a fill your cart in 10 minutes at Andy's IGA, an apron collection, dinner certificates—use your imagination."

"Which reminds me," Ruby says. "It's the first Tuesday of May. You know what *that* means?"

Lilly shakes her head. "Oh now, who hasn't heard of singles night at Andy's and what a *ridiculous* idea at that." Her lisping *ridiculous* makes me grin.

"*We* haven't," Howard and Johnny say at the same time.

"Well I don't suppose you two *need* it either," I playfully taunt." Oh, another thing about the derby and then I'll shut up about it."

"That'll be the day," Ruby says under her breath.

"We're trying to get some bands together," I add. "So during the day the derby we can have a little festival going on. More ways to make some money, and there's so much musical talent up here, why the hell not?"

"That Ric Gillman," Sam suggests while helping clear the table. "He sure knows his way around a guitar, and I bet Charlie'd blow some jazz out of that clarinet of his, for a good cause and I'll check with my all-purpose agent—see if I might be able to sing some blues for y'all."

"You're available," I say and we laugh.

"Ruby, you can't be *serious,*" I admonish as I waltz into her bedroom and slide onto her cozy window seat.

Her room, at the end of the open hallway upstairs, has the most unusual willow-twig bed. There's a dreamy canopy of off-white cotton draped around the frame that puddles onto the floor in loose circles of fabric that Rocky often naps in. A lily-pad shaped rag rug graces the floor. The frog in the center of it closely resembles Ed. I notice that the book he had left lying on this seat before his death has been finally put away. Good. After a time, you really do need to get on with things.

"It's a *simple* outfit, really, darling." She turns this way and that in front of the full length mirror next to her bathroom door. "I'm only doing this to keep any undesirables away."

"I say—loose the leopard pants, put away the pearls and let's go!"

Rocky *meows* in agreement. Ruby quickly re-dresses more casual, and we head down and out to the barn. May is giving us days that are a tad longer, so the sun is still semi-up in the sky, and boy does the air smell fresh and wonderful.

Ruby hits the big green button and the barn doors accordion-fold into one another revealing the duck. We clamber in. I head us around the porch and down the path, past the boathouse and then splash into Lake Superior. I expertly tap the screen and Stacy Kent croons *More Than You Know*. I switch to the propeller and off we go!

We have dinner reservations at Greunke's, but plan on peeking in at Andy's, just to see all those desperate *single shoppers*. Besides, I'm practically out of Reese's Peanut Butter Cups and I've bought all Lori's Grocery Store in La Pointe had. Peanuts contain oodles of nutrition and I'm making sure not to run out. Of nutrition, of course.

Ruby reaches over and turns down the music. "Bonnie rang up earlier,"—she fidgets with her leopard pattern clutch— "Just wanting to catch up on goings on, what with the Ducky Derby being the talk of the town and all, but she *did* mention that Marsha's been on edge and wondered if we'd chatted her up lately."

"Funny," I add. "I keep thinking about what I told you, that Alice Anne had said something to that effect too. She's getting really paranoid—all those locks on her bedroom door is pretty darn weird, if you ask me."

"You know, we *really* don't know her all that well," Ruby says with a question in her voice. She settles back in her seat. "I can still see the immaculate house she had in Rice Lake. Felt as though time had stood still in there, you know. Even her shined-up kitchen appliances, all from another era."

"Ruby—we have a stove that was probably brought over on the *Mayflower* and one of the very first electric fridges invented! But—I do think maybe we should stop in at Al's Place next time she's waitressing and talk to her."

"Good thinking," Ruby says, ignoring my other comment.

We float on toward the shoreline of Bayfield. Passing the ferry headed the same way, I pull down the mike, flip the switch and say, "It's a beautiful spring day in Wisconsin!" Then give the horn a good blasting.

The packed ferry is suddenly alive with frantic wavers as we pass by; we wave back, leaving them in our wake. I steer us toward the City Marina. As we drift toward the landing, I click off the outboard, engage the wheels and up we head toward Rittenhouse Avenue.

"Since this baby is so long I'll park it in my usual spot in front of the library," I say and drive around the corner pulling all the way up to the corner so no one will park in front of us. "Now—we're only here to do a quick shop and then off to supper."

"I'm simply *dying* to see what desperate singles up here *look* like." Ruby re-applies lipstick and then kisses a tissue.

I reach over, pull down her visor and face it her way and then snap on the little light. "Take a look sister!" She smacks me with her clutch.

"You can be such a nudge, *really*."

"Let's keep in mind that we are just *looking*, no crime in that. I give my curls a quick scrunch and we head into the fluorescent-lit grocery store.

Instead of the normal country tunes, soft jazz wafts down from the speakers. I grab a cart and we head in. One of the front wheels is not cooperating, so steering is tricky and since the aisles are pretty narrow, this should prove interesting.

"Good evening *single* shoppers," a familiar voice booms over the loudspeakers, trying her best to be *way* too sexy. "Be sure and stop by our wine display for free tasting, we have an extensive local cheese selection *and* all lines are (dramatic pause) *open*." The mike clicks and pings and in her normally cranky voice Darlene says, "Looks like most the town's here on the prowl. Oh shit, where's the button on this..." The music comes back up fully jazz'd.

There are more *shoppers* out than I would have imagined, the women outnumber the men by a long shot; no surprise there. As I edge my way around the first aisle, something catches my eye over by the frozen foods. A black man—long narrow nose, piercing eyes and hair flowing down his shoulders like water. Our eyes meet; he bows his head. A chill runs down my back.

"Eve, darling—*watch out!*" Ruby warns me, but it's too late.

My damn cart slams into a tower of Pringles and the canisters go clunking down around me in a percussive mix of *pings* and *pangs*. A hand-lettered sign spinning above, reminds shoppers to *Pack Your Picnic With Pringles!* The mysterious dark man has vanished.

A pimply young fellow pops over and begins re-stacking my shopping-cart disaster.

"Sorry. My cart has a mind of its own."

"No problem—gives me something to do," he loads his arms full of multi-colored canisters and sends me an impish wink.

I maneuver around a grinning Ruby and head down the snack isle. My mind still reeling. If only I could twitch my nose and be sitting over at Greunke's sipping wine. The thought of finding true love while picking out a roast seems pretty lame.

"Hey lady," Pringles calls after me. I turn back; he ambles toward me, his gate reminds me of a rooster. He pushes his thick glasses up his impressive nose and I can see things being considered in his big, brown eyes. Lashes to die for. "Would you, um, like to maybe—"

—Shaking my head, maybe those glasses of his need cleaning. "How old *are* you?"

"Twenty four," he coyly replies while passing a canister back and forth like a football.

Mid-toss, I snatch it from him. "As much as I'd *love* to pack up my picnic with you and these ever-so-tempting Pringles, I'm going to have to pass." I toss it back to him.

There's a loud snapping sound, "Mitch Miller to check-out aisle three please. Get your cute butt up here and quit your flurtin'!" More clicking and then in her cranky voice, "Damn—I broke one of my nails!"

He heads toward the front of the store. Halfway down the aisle, he turns back, "If you ever change your mind, well you know where to find me!" He struts away, hormones and all.

"Well," Ruby says with her well-timed flourish. "Perhaps you should run into something *else*!"

"Let's find the candy section," I suggest and shove on.

We shop our way up and down several more aisles than necessary, but hey, I want to see who might be doing the same. It never hurts to look and in the meantime we've found buckwheat waffle mix, popcorn, a lipstick color I like, two six-packs of Reese's Peanut Butter Cups and some Earl Grey tea for when Helen visits.

Standing in the checkout line, I notice a handsome bearded man out of the corner of my eye.

"Hey," I half-whisper to Ruby. "Isn't that the Tree-Stud guy over there?"

Ruby turns ever so slightly his direction. At the same time, a pretty blonde woman dressed in a faded flowered dress hands him a box and they turn down an aisle.

"Paper or plastic?" Darlene-the-gossip asks in a rather bored voice. "Hey—Eve and Ruby, funny seeing you two out tonight."

She raises both of her *Joan Crawford* brows extra high. I wonder if all that foundation leaves a face-print on her pillowcase. Her chocolate brown hair color *is* rather pretty. I can spy white roots marching down her part, and boy did she put on the perfume.

Peering over the rims of her bright pink bifocals, Darlene says, "You would not *believe* who I just checked out," she glances both ways to make sure the coast is clear of spies. "Riley Blatty, the fella who owns the bookstore in town and you would not *believe* who was all hot to trot on to him like a dog to a stick." She purses her dark lips for dramatic effect. "That Lilly Thompson, you should have *seen* how fast she flew over to my check-out when Riley got in line, why, she practically *burned rubber!*" Darlene begins to ring up our stuff—finally.

"Perhaps," Ruby offers, "Lilly was only in a rush to get home before her favorite TV program began." Ruby, forever the sensible one.

Darlene shrugs a bony shoulder. "It *is* singles night, you know, besides, he's a looker. I'd bet you half the women of this town would like to *turn his page.*" She says *turn his page* with big shakes of her head and I know who's in front of that line!

"Oh dear," Ruby mutters and we dash out the door.

"Thanks for stopping," Pringles says after us. I glance over my shoulder and he waves me off with a cucumber in his hand.

We're seated at our favorite table at Greunke's restaurant. Since the forties this memorabilia-crammed joint has been serving up great vittles and the owner is a hoot. Janelle Vickerson single-handedly operates this place year around and how she has time to climb mountains and go on safari is the stuff of legend around here.

"My goodness," Ruby says, and then takes a sip of wine. "Perhaps Marsha's simply a few peas short of a casserole, a lap behind the field, a teapot with a cracked lid—hmmm?"

I raise an eyebrow and think for a beat. "A few fries short of a happy meal, no hay in the loft," I warm to the clichés. "Never misses an episode of her screensaver." Howard told me that one and it still makes me chuckle, and we do.

"One clue short of a solution," Ruby adds, "Plays solitaire—for cash, won't eat eggs because she believes the *this is your brain* ads."

I stifle a cackle, several people look our way, I lift my newspaper-menu up higher and so does Ruby. The menus here are printed in the style, as well as the paper, of an actual newspaper. We *are* being mean, but honestly, it's just to let off some steam and Marsha will never know.

"Thinks cheerios are doughnut seeds," I add, my menu shakes with laughter. "Teflon brain—nothing sticks, studied for a blood test—and failed, runs squares around the competition." The mascara's running, I'm sure of it. My stomach hurts but we can't seem to stop.

Janelle heads over from the kitchen to take our order. "While you two are having all this fun,"—she points over her shoulder— "I'm going crazy trying to train in a new cook who's obviously not worth hen-shit on a pump handle when it comes to making my white fish liver dish right!"

Janelle shrugs her shoulders and pulls up a chair. "I should have seen this coming," Janelle shakes her blonde bob in frustration. "Under education she'd put *Hooked on Phonics*. Shit, I'm screwed."

"I imagine you are—darling—wine then?"

CHAPTER SEVEN

A big wind off the lake yanks my straw hat and it goes flying away. I race across the sandy beach and chase it down. Plopping it back on, I stand on the dock and admire the sparkling clean duck lashed to its side.

I've spent the last couple of hours giving the boat a good spring tidying and now the white painted sides gleam. Rocky curls around my ankles, purring like crazy. Ruby's off to town, so it's all this glorious sunshine—just me and Rocky.

I take a final puff; since I'm down to three a day, I make this sucker count and then I put it out in the sand. The butt goes in my pocket. I read on the web that it takes a hundred years for a filter to disintegrate. When I'm behind another car and watch a cigarette fly out the window, I want to slam on the gas and go yell at the liter-bug. Wisconsinites don't do that, we stew instead.

The waves make a great sloshing sound against the shore; it's a rhythm I don't imagine I could live without. Bending down over the cool sand, I start to build my dream castle, it's become a tradition. Rocky wants to help, so he digs right next to what *would have been* the sculpture garden and takes a dump. I smooth it over and re-imagine it as the family's private burial ground. A shadow blocks the sun; I glance over my shoulder, thinking it must be a bank of clouds.

"Bon jour Madame," the black man from IGA says. "Hello monsieur Rocky," he bends down and scoops him up.

The weird thing is, Rocky lets him. *Nobody* picks him up when he's outside.

I stand. "Where'd you come from—how'd you know his name? You're the guy from IGA, huh?" I step back and a wave of panic whips through me but it melts away when he smiles.

His long glossy-black hair ripples in the wind, he gives Rocky's head a scratching then puts him back down on the sand. He's dressed in a tightly tailored white collared shirt and dark pants, several leather necklaces sit in the middle of his smooth chest. One is a silver piece in the shape of an eye; the other a small leather pouch. The scent of musk and earthy-spice wafts from him in the breeze awakening my senses in a way that makes me feel odd—vulnerable. His accent lingers in my head like faraway music, a tune I can barely recall.

"I come from Niger," he offers as if reading my mind and I notice his eyes are the lightest brown, maybe it's because they're against his dark skin. I would kill for his cheekbones. "Walk with me and I shall explain why I've come to you." He takes my hand in his; its warm and dry and about twice the size of mine.

Weird, but there's something so familiar about him, maybe some photographs Ruby showed me? I can't put my finger on it, but I feel safe with him and that too is totally odd.

We head up the path and around toward the old cabin in back—stroll—more like. Funny, but this all seems as if I'm dreaming *him*. Am I? The little bridge that crosses over the creek seems newer, as though all the old, mismatched wood has been replaced. Howard only yesterday mentioned that he thought there was wood-rot going on, and now it seems so new. He must have re-done it, but wouldn't he have mentioned?

Something *else* is odd too; the woods back here don't seem as crowded. The towering white pines aren't nearly as, well, towering.

I glance back toward the cottage and can't see it anymore. Doesn't *seem* like we've walked that far; maybe it's hidden by this small hill we're heading down where the creek crosses the road. Could I be sleeping back there in the sunshine? God, I hope I put on enough sunscreen, you would not believe how this skin of mine can go from deathly pale to lobster red.

"Where are you taking me?" I finally find my voice. "I mean, I don't even *know* you and yet—"

He turns, regarding me, as a lopsided grin crosses his generous lips. "I came out of gratitude—come."

We float up the steps of the cabin, the door is open, and all the locks that used to hold it closed, have disappeared. And then I notice what's so different. Everything is new and clean inside, like we've stepped into a picture. The grime and spider-webs—gone— the little bed in the corner that had a faded and dusty quilt is now bright and comfy looking. Fresh daises burst from a vase on the kitchen table.

"It's only May, where'd you find these?" I touch a flower, to make sure it's real. "What's going on here anyway? I mean, this place was all closed up and abandoned long ago, and now it looks like Martha Stewart lives here! Look buster—who the hell are you?"

"My name is Leandre and as I informed you, I am from Niger," he gestures for me to sit in one of the two chairs that flank the fireplace. "My parents were of French and Nigerien heritage, as a young man, we traveled a great deal and this is how I came upon Adeline Prevost. You read of her terrible sadness and did a most kind and noble thing."

"This can't be!" I stammer, trying to make sense of all this. "You knew," I shake my head in disbelief. "Ruby's husband—Ed's grandfather, that would be Gustave. His wife, Adeline, had an affair with *you?* I mean we're talking nineteen-O-six or so here, how in the world?" I try to put the pieces together. "So it was *your* child in the hatbox? Tied with a ribbon and I cut through it. Then—later—when we came back to take the remains over to the graveyard, the ribbon had mysteriously re-tied itself. Scared us half to death. Speaking of death, I need to get the hell out of here." I stand up and move toward the door. "This is too bizarre and I need to wake up or at least get a fricking grip!"

"Please do not be alarmed, Eve," Leandre rises from his chair. In a different, softer voice he says, "While in France I saw her dance at the ballet and fell completely in love. The power of love is so strong it cannot be denied." Tears pour from his eyes; the hurt in them is so thick I stop in my tracks. "Her husband, that impossible man—Gustave—he brought her here and it is here that she bore our child. Our dead child..." His shoulders shake with grief.

There are times when the clarity of a situation hits you in the heart like a stone breaking free and rolling away. For whatever reason this is happening, though I must be dreaming, this moment feels important. Crucial.

"I'm so very sorry—I know about your child." I reach up and wipe away a tear. "We found your little girl's bones—*remains*," I quickly add, "and the note and, well *you* must know all that stuff. Hey, do you know Sam too?"

He nods, "It is through her that I have been able to come. To thank you for helping both Adeline as well as our child. She's free now and no longer bound to this place."

"That's really wonderful," I offer, feeling relief that we'd done the right thing. "Aren't you supposed to be on the other side—with them?"

He smiles and it's brilliant."I am now free, now that I have thanked you properly."

He pulls me close and I can feel his heart beat, then he bends and kisses me so gently it's like a whisper. Then he's gone.

I look around and the cabin is back to its dusty self, except for the vase of yellow daises.

"Hello dear—such *dodgy pests,* those bloody deer have managed to eat all my Hostas and they were *barely* out of the ground."—Ruby comes into the kitchen and sets down several sacks—"Why you look simply *radiant,* darling."

"Must be all this spring air," I reply feeling totally off balance. "You want me to fix up your color later?"

"Well if the gratuities were notched up a bit," she hands me a head of broccoli. "How about giving that a rinse and I'll whip us up something *divine* for supper."

I pour some wine and get rinsing. "You want to come with me to the cemetery where Adeline and her baby are buried? Since I can't take the time and zoom down to Eau Claire and plant my folks' graves, I thought it'd be nice to fix up theirs, seeing as its Memorial Day tomorrow."

"That would be lovely," she takes the broccoli from me. "They're half-related to you and Gustave is there as well, you know seeing as Ed is your father. Let's see, what would that make Gustave anyway? I suppose he'd be your great grandfather. You sure you're all right, darling? You seem a bit off the boil."

"It's probably post-menopausal lingerings," I say with too much enthusiasm. "By the way, Alice Anne's almost ready to move into the apartment at Toad Hollow and then it's just a matter of weeks before the first floor is done. We should plan a party of some sort."

The phone rings. "Eve and Ruby's, Eve speaking."

"Hello Eve, Howard here."

"Well good evening, neighbor," I reply and sit down onto a wicker stool. I mouth *Howard* to Ruby. She starts slicing up the broccoli. "What's up?"

"We've fired up the grill for the first time this spring and felt it appropriate to invite you two over for,"—I hear him say something to Johnny—"herb-stuffed trout, skewered veggies and wine. I realize its last minute, but we serve a mean trout."

I relay the invite to Ruby, who quickly agrees. "We'll be bringing a delicious cold broccoli hors d'oeuvres item *and* a pan of Ruby's famous strawberry jam bars. 'Course these are the ones that are completely fat free—long as you don't swallow."

"Wonderful! Since it's a touch chilly, we'll dine indoors," Howard chuckles. "We'll gather around the window in order to make sure Johnny grills everything just right. See you in a bit then." We goodbye. I unravel the yellow cord from around Ruby and replace the phone.

"Smart alec—fat free? Really, how *horrid* would that be? There's absolutely nothing in the world wrong with a bit *of real* butter now and again."

"It's the again part that's got my hips all *hipped out*," I reply and she sticks her tongue out. "How is it that cats never seem to gain an inch and eat all day long?" I scoop up Rocky and give his belly a good rubbing.

"Mind," Ruby hips closed the fridge. "He does seem to put on a bit of a pouch come winter."

"I just continue to add to mine," I comment.

Ruby breezes by, giving him a pat on the way. "Be a love and grate this up a bit, would you. I'm going to whip up a parmesan-garlic dipping sauce for the chilled broccoli—now where in heaven's name has my grater gone off to?"

A huge, howling blast of thunder shakes the cottage, followed by the lights dimming and then going out altogether. Rocky scratches the hell out of me as he leaps off into the darkness. A powerful rain pelts the roof, its roar deafening. Lightning crackles, lighting up all the windows in brief snaps and pops that have my ears all messed up.

"A storm must have blown in!" I yell the obvious toward where Ruby stood last. "Sounds like a whopper!"

I hear a crash somewhere outside. Ruby's face becomes illuminated by a candle's eerie glow. We light several more and then I root around in the junk drawer for our big yellow flashlights. I click one on, hand a matching one to Ruby and we head into the living room.

"You take the upstairs," I yell over the deafening rain. "I'm going to roll down the shades on the verandah."

I fling open the French doors, they smack on either side, one pane flies off, smashing to bits on the wooden floor. Rushing from one end to the other of the L-shaped porch, I wrestle the heavy reed shades down and secure them, then head back in, quickly cross through the living room, and head down the hallway toward the library.

"Oh shit!"

The floor-to-ceiling drapes that surround both window seats are billowing far out into the room and have managed to push over several chairs. And a table holding the Tiffany dragonfly lamp is about to fall over! I rush over—hefting it up and onto all four legs again. I struggle the fussy window latches closed. The room suddenly falls silent. The rain has let up, leaving behind an odd electrical smell.

"Eve darling?" A bouncing, seemingly suspended, light-beam dances into the room. "Are you alright, dear?"

"Soaked to the skin," I reply taking in my wet jeans and t-shirt. "And if you don't stop shining that damn thing into my eyes—I might be about to go blind as well! Jesus Ruby."

"Sorry love."

The lights abruptly pop on. We take a look at each other and burst out laughing.

"You look bloody awful, really."

"The wet look never really took off."

A slimy creature slinks around the corner, its slick black fur shimmering in the light. We scream like *bloody* hell!

"It's a God damn rat!" I shriek, and leap up onto the window seat; Ruby follows.

"I've seen a good many rats in my day," Ruby pants out, "but this one is simply *gargantuan*!"

Instead of racing to find a corner, it comes over, sits down on the floor in front of us and meows.

I look at Ruby, "If you don't tell—"

"—Deal."

A lively fire crackles in our fireplace; Louis Armstrong has started singing *What A Wonderful World* from the hi-fi in the corner.

We've taken a rain check on having a grill-out with the boys seeing as there's now a fallen tree where the grill used to live and Howard's chainsaw is nowhere to be found. But they're going to join us for dessert.

I glide a broccoli spear through the sinful cheese dip and pop it into my mouth. "Nothing like hors d'oeuvres for supper," I say, and then lean back into the cushy red sofa. "I did manage to chat briefly with Marsha earlier today."

Ruby leans forward, "Do tell, darling. I already told you how Bonnie's been trying to get her to open up a bit as to what's making her such a nervous wreck—she won't budge."

"It is about her long ago missing husband," I leap up and sweep a glowing coal back into the fireplace. "Talk about snappy wood, must be the sap that makes it pop and crackle like hell."

"Perhaps the bloke's bribing her," Ruby suggests and I shrug.

"I think she's afraid of him, like he's dangerous or knows something. I can't quite put my finger on it. Wonder what Sam—what did she say? Something about darkness."

"Simply *no* telling," she sighs into her cozy afghan. "I'm forever amazed at the things people harbor deep in their souls. The secrets we cling to and choose to carry with us, like a chain and ball—imagine."

Rocky curls into my lap, I give his head a soft scratching and he purrs. Did I honestly dream Leandre? Is this how people go mad? Oh for God's sake, this is ridiculous. I give the sofa's arm a frustrated smack and a puff of dust leaps into the air, making me sneeze! Rocky leaps off and zooms down the hallway toward the library. When I sneeze, I imagine the neighbors looking up from whatever they're doing and wondering what kind of animal *was that?*

"Bless you, dear. I do hope you're not coming down with anything, but I highly recommend you *not* beat the furniture. What in heaven's name has that sofa ever done to *you?*"

There's a knock at the back door just as the phone decides to ring as well. I head over to answer the phone. Ruby waves the boys into the living room; they fling their wet yellow slickers over my outstretched arm on the way. At least I get a peck on the cheek for the effort.

"Good evening—this is Eve," I sing into the mouthpiece as I head over to the wall of doorknobs and hang their coats up. Why didn't *they* do this? Men.

"Eve, this is Ryan, Helen's in the hospital—bleeding and—" Ryan's voice is shrill and riddled with panic.

"—Hospital!" I screech and everyone gathers in the kitchen. "What's happened? I only just *spoke* with her and—is she all *right?* What hospital? Oh for Christ's sake no! It's Ryan—Helen's in the hospital," I quickly explain to the kitchen group. I look from Howard to Johnny, feeling helpless. Ruby's eyes tear up.

"We didn't want to tell anyone we were pregnant until we could be sure,"—Ryan gasps and then starts to sob—"She got these horrible cramps and then all this *blood* and—"

"—Where Ryan? Where the **hell is she?**"

"St. Luke's in Duluth, St. Luke's on First Street. She's still with the doctor, she was so pale," Ryan whispers the last word and then snivels.

"Hang in there—we're on our way," I announce and hang up the phone. "Grab something warm, because the ferry's not running this late, but the duck sure as hell is!"

Slinging my purse over my shoulder, I smack the green button and rush over to the duck. The accordion doors seem to be taking forever to open. Revving the engine to life, snapping on the lights, I head into the night. Pulling up to the stoop, Ruby, followed by Johnny, and then Howard, clamber up and in.

"Hey! Watch it!" Howard yells, nearly being catapulted down the aisle as I take off down the hill. He struggles into the seat next to Johnny.

"Sorry!" I yell back.

"Do let's try and get there alive—shall we?" Ruby says with obvious control.

I'm hardly listening; all I know is that I have to get to her, to make sure she's all right. I don't know where this need is coming from, I can't explain this powerful feeling to be near her, touch her arm, see that nose of mine. I only just found her and now *this*! I feel frantic inside, like everything is reeling, about to topple.

"Look out, darling!" Ruby cries out as two deer leap out of our way!

My mouth drops open in awe, just as the second deer flies by a hair's breath away from hitting the bow and disappears into the night. A beat later I hit the gas and we continue down the hill and zoom on into Lake Superior. I head toward the lights of Bayfield—to Helen.

I remember how the nun had to pry her hand off of my fingers, how she didn't want to let go. I was so afraid and alone, having just gone through hours of horrible labor pain. The actual birthing wasn't all *that* bad. Part of me—the mother ingrained in my very molecules—didn't *want* it to end. Yet I knew it would, and I couldn't see anything beyond. Then I heard that first cry, and I was lost—in love—and lost. That love for your own flesh and blood, you never lose it. Not ever.

Slowing down, I switch into wheel-drive and maneuver up the road next to the City Marina toward highway thirteen.

"Who in the world?"

Sam and Lilly are standing along the side of the highway, waving us down like the crazy women they are; I pull over.

"Thought you all was either gonna run us down," Sam gasps out, "or 'jus fly on by, way you drivin' this buggy."

"Sam and I were having pizza while watching a Carol Burnett re-run when she got all up in arms and told me we had to **run**!" Lilly explains while reaching up to cinch her pleated rain bonnet.

"Way I saw you movin'," Sam says hefting herself up the ladder. "Girl—I *knew* we didn't have much time. Evenin' boys, hey Ruby." Sam sits opposite the boys and Lilly slides in beside her. "Now before you get us killed, hang on one sec—here she come."

The sound of a siren is getting closer. "Lady owes me a favor and we wouldn't get far before bein' pulled over in this thing."

A police car, flashing lights pulsing like a heart-beat, pulls in front of us. A long, slender arm reaches out and waves us to follow; my eyes zoom in on the fingernails—painted bright pink. I nearly sob with relief as the enormity of what possibly lies ahead nearly knocks me sideways. Ruby rubs my arm, bringing me back to the surface.

"Let's go, darling."

The yellow dotted line in the highway began pulling us on—pulling us forward—our headlights dancing in rhythm with the swirling blue and red flashes, seeming to pulse the mantra *she's going to be fine,* over and over. My mind dulled down to a powerful need to see her, fearing the worst for her unborn child. Onward we speed toward uncertainty like a moth to flame, and in my heart, I know the truth.

I pull us over toward the emergency entrance, hog several parking spaces and shut off the engine. For a brief moment I wonder where the hell we are—then it all slams into focus. The cop car pulls in alongside; she taps the horn several times and heads off into the darkness. I lead the group over in the direction of the hospital's bright lights; we hurry through glass doors that silently swoosh closed behind.

"Can you direct us to Helen Kearney's room?" I hurriedly ask as Ryan comes around the corner, shirttail hanging out.

He takes me into his arms and says in a voice I don't recognize, "She's going to be fine now. They had to do a transfusion and a minor surgery to stop the bleeding." He pulls away and hugs everyone.

We follow him down sparkling corridors, in a procession of hope.

As we round a bend, a tall, slender woman with severely pulled-back blonde hair in a tailored raincoat, stands and walks nervously our direction. I notice the sparkle of a diamond brooch perched on her collar, and then see the fear in her tired blue eyes.

She weakly offers a hand; I look down at it—at her—then take her into my arms.

"She's going to be fine," I say as the thin woman shakes. "I'm sure of it."

"My grandbaby's gone," Saundra pulls away. She gathers herself up, seeming to gain an inch or two in the process. "But the doctor has assured me that,"—she glances at Ryan—*"Us,* he's assured *us* that she should be able to conceive again. Thank God."

"Or Allah," Sam adds and we all sigh with the kind of relief you'll remember forever.

"She's really too weak to speak," Ryan offers. "There's really—"

"—Just for a second," I plead. "If I could see her for a second… alone."

I look back at all the expectant faces. Sam shoots me a wink, the boys are shoulder-to-shoulder and Ruby and Saundra nod. I pat my mess of curls and push open the door. It closes in slow motion behind me. I head over to the shape tucked into the whitest sheets I've ever seen. A soft yellow light glows across her pale, serene face. I reach down and swipe a wisp of hair off her forehead. She stirs, then slowly opens her eyes,

"Hey, you look like hell, you know that?" I say and then snivel.

"Thanks," she croaks out. Then in a softer voice she whispers, "I lost my baby." A stream of tears pours from her eyes.

"Oh honey," I sit down and gently pull her into my arms. We sit there for a moment and I rock her. In a soft voice I say, "It just wasn't the right time—hell—maybe there was a last minute re-call of the spiritual kind. I had a client…she was a midwife," I carefully choose my words. "She explained the loss of a young pregnancy like that, and it *could make* sense. Like maybe the little spirit who was about to cross over into life, wasn't quite ready to take the plunge."

"I like that—I think," Helen scrunches up her nose and considers. "I always *did* figure you had a pretty deep understanding of life."

"Oh, maybe it's just that as you move through it—gathering up more experiences, you start to realize—the possibilities are endless."

"I'm so sad, "Helen blows her nose and then carefully lays back into the pillows.

"It's okay to be sad," I pat her arm like Ruby does to me sometimes. "Actually, it's important to let yourself feel whatever you need—but I'm just so relieved you're okay," I tear up and Helen hands me the tissue box.

"I wanted—*we* wanted the baby so much. God, you should have seen my mother. You'd have thought it was *hers*!"

I glance out the window, then back toward Helen's sorrowful face, "Right now, there are no words that seem right. I was so worried about you—all I could think of was getting here—to see your pretty face." I brush her tears away. "To know you were okay. I'm so sorry my dear Helen."

"Thank you. Thank you so much for coming." Helen's pale face brightens a tiny bit.

I hold her hand and my heart swells. This is one of those moments I'll never be able to put aside. Not ever will I be able to take this pain and for a fleeting moment I want to scream! If only I could take all the hurt away from my child, and fling it out into Lake Superior. Where is the sense in all this? Sometimes life—death—doesn't make any God damn sense at all.

I gently rub Helen's arm, she turns her head and we lock eyes. Now I know the meaning of unconditional love.

The door opens a crack and Ruby's head pops in, "Must you be such a dreadful *hog* of the patient?"

Ruby moves forward into the room and then it's suddenly filled with all of us. I look into Helen's eyes and for a moment it's just the two of us again. I mouth, *I love you* and she smiles. I look up—Saundra beams back.

Dawn greets us as I back the duck into the barn. The boys slowly stroll home; hand-in-hand they walk away, the mist wafting off the lawn swallows them up like a dream.

"I'm simply bushed," Ruby says as we head into the warmth of the kitchen. "Lovely of Saundra to have taken us out to breakfast, but I'm not used to being spun about while eating my lox."

"Revolving restaurants should be everywhere," I offer as I take down the coffee pot to fill it with water. "I couldn't help laughing when Saundra kept passing by," I start to chuckle, then burst out laughing. The kind of laugh that's only funny when you're this bone tired.

We had eaten at the Radisson in Duluth; on the top floor of the hotel there's one of those kitschy revolving restaurants that used to be so popular. The center doesn't move, which is where the kitchen, elevator and restrooms are. The outer ring, where the tables are, continually moves around and around so that as you eat, you can look out the curved windows and take in the view of Duluth in 360 degrees of panoramic gastronomic pleasure. Why more of these places aren't being built is beyond me.

"Finally Sam tells her," Ruby says, wiping a laugh-tear away then lowering her voice, "Girrrl, you jus' stand still and the little ladies room's 'bout to smack you in the butt."

"Sure enough"—I gasp out— "seconds later it sails into view. She raises her head high, lifts an elegant arm and waves as she heads in." Ruby and I *wave* to each other like she did and dive into peals of laughter.

"Poor Saundra didn't see the waiter," Ruby sputters out, "and there went our breakfast, all down the front of her Prada!" She smacks her hand down and Rocky leaps off the stool and makes it spin like a top.

We laugh ourselves silly. Not really because of what happened to Saundra. Underneath, deep in our hearts, there lies the truth that when something like this happens, something that involves the death of a possibility.

What's left is what counts.

CHAPTER EIGHT

A warm morning breeze flutters my bedroom drapes like a ghost dancing in the wind. As I lie here, in that half-dream state, stretch my arms and legs—there's suddenly so much damn snapping and popping you'd think I was a bowl of Rice Krispies! Rocky, now literally *snapped* awake, takes one look at me and leaps off my bed and heads out the door.

"Cheap date!"

My cat clock tells me it's only six in the morning, but I'm wide-awake and a hot mug-o-java is crucial. As I slip out of bed, I make it as I go. Like never leaving dirty dishes until morning, I can't stand an unmade bed.

I pull my yellow terrycloth robe around me and slide my feet into my morning-cool bunny slippers. Instead of heading downstairs, I walk over to the small door that leads up to the tower room. A draft of chilly morning air slips around me as I pull it open. I must have left a window open up there. Rocky suddenly appears and scoots around my ankles, then zips up the narrow stairs. I follow, minus the zip.

At the top of the landing, I stop to admire the huge compass rose. The intricately painted design covers the entire middle of the hardwood floor. It shows me exactly where the hell north is. Since this square room has windows all around with built-in benches underneath, it's a perfect place to admire the lake, not to mention being able to see a part of the boys' place next door. This was used as a lookout back during prohibition. What folks did for a slug of booze.

Rocky has his front paws up on the window sill; together we watch a cluster of gulls flutter by the boathouse. He growls and snaps his tail. Lifting him into my arms, we settle into—I glance to the floor—the northeast corner bench and stare out toward the lake and all that water. Giving Rocky's head a soft rub, I gaze as he purrs and pushes up against my chin.

"Look at that," I say and startle myself, my voice echoing off the walls.

"Can you believe how fast they move in those things?" I stand up and use one of Rocky's paws to wave down at the line of kayaks quickly slipping by the end of the dock. A single person mans each one; I count eleven as they race by at record speed. They're bright yellows, blues and reds, with white bottoms and everyone's wearing some kind of yellow vest. The paddles have blades at both ends and everyone dips and lifts at the same time so it's like a perfect dance. And from way up here, it's silent, like an old-time movie. Whoever's in the last one suddenly looks up and spies us. His muscular arm lifts the paddle high into the air and he gives us a big wave.

"Oh for God's sake—it's the Pringles guy. Nice arms dude." Rocky and I wave back as he disappears around the corner behind the birch trees.

A loud buzzing sound nearly gives me a heart-attack—Rocky flies out of my arms. I head over to the small green box hung directly behind the door, open it and take up the black ear-piece, then stand on my tippy toes and say into the mouth-piece inside, "Tower room, Eve here."

"Good morning, darling," Ruby's voice crackles into my ear. "Thought I'd find you up there. Oh my, Rocky's just meowing hello down here—where coffee's on the boil, I might add." I hear the familiar sound of her exhaling most likely a smoke ring. I picture it sailing up and away.

"I hear that and I don't mean Rocky."

"I'm putting it out. There. Only two bloody puffs—really, you can be such a nudge and it's only six in the morning."

"Sorry," I offer and realize I'm holding a pencil like a cigarette. "I haven't had my morning fix yet."

"Rocky and I will put together a tray and be up directly." She clicks off and the phone goes dead.

Slowly I close the small green door and glance at my image reflected in the mirror that hangs next to it. If I hold my chin way up, you'd never notice the bags under my blood-shot eyes. Still don't have too many wrinkles to speak of.

Pulling my robe tighter, I drift back to the windows facing the lake. All that water out there, it goes on and on. Being Memorial Day, it's certain to rain. I remember my mom always said that the raindrops were tears of the dead and that it *had to* rain. I always figured it was because we usually didn't have school and it was some kind of punishment or something stupid like that. God, I'm glad I don't have that to dread every day any longer.

"Here we are, then," Ruby bustles into the room. She's wearing a teal kimono with matching headband. "Give me a hand, would you, darling?"

I set the handled silver tray down on the bench and we sit on either side. She *loves* her kimonos, on me they have more of a muu-muu effect. I wonder if muumuu is a farm-related term? Ruby pours hot coffee into a china cup, places it onto its matching saucer and hands it over.

"Fancy," I comment as I sip the delicious brew. "I wonder if it's—wow, look at that!"

We watch as rays of sunshine begin to fill the room. The thick lavender clouds have rolled back letting golden, warming sun into the room.

"So much for your yearly dead-people-tears concept, hmmm?" Ruby lifts her eyebrows and I chuckle.

"Sometimes you know me too well." I pour us more Java. "Let's buzz into La Pointe after a quick breakfast and see if we can find some flowering plants for the cemetery—if you're not too busy, that is."

"Seems to me, we've given ourselves the day off—but perhaps we should give Helen a ring first, see how the poor dear is faring and all."

"Good idea and honestly, I would have called when I got up, but it's still so early and she needs all the rest she can get."

"You certainly are the worry-wart," Ruby raises her brows. "Oh don't give me that look, we're all concerned about her, darling."

"She's tough, but this is different." I say then think for a moment. "Sure hope they don't give up on having children. This kind of thing can be so hard on couples, but it's really not that uncommon."

"Oh heavens," Ruby sets her cup carefully onto its saucer. "I'd nearly forgotten that your mum lost a child before you."

"It's weird to imagine that I might have had an older brother, you know?" I shrug. "Mom and dad never talked about it—it just slipped out of my mom's mouth one day when I'd driven her to her wit's end."

"Something I would imagine you were quite gifted at—*are*."

"Hey, somebody's got to test the proverbial boundaries."

"There's the phone, and we're out of coffee—shall we push off and start our day, darling?"

"Let's."

I put a dab more powder onto my oily forehead, brush up my lashes with mascara, and then swoop my curls up into a soft do, held in place with a two-pronged black antique comb Ruby gave me years ago. Turning this way and that, I roll on light pink gloss and mosey out to my bedroom in order to find the perfect outfit for a day of cemetery planting.

Not *petunia pot-breaking* like I pulled in Eau Claire. I have to admit though, it really felt good and think of all the money I saved on therapy! Rocky lifts his head and sends me a big yawn from his perch up on top of my headboard, then goes back to napping; something the guy is really good at.

I slip into favorite jeans, pull on a yellow peasant-top, and step into a pair of comfy green Crocs. While tromping down the stairs, I admire the spots of sun bouncing from mirror to mirror, a daily thrill when the sun is out.

I stop midway to adjust the mirror Dorothy gave me. I imagine that maybe it once sat on top of a vanity that held a bottle of Chanel and an ivory brush and comb set. I run my hand over the mirror's scalloped edge. Then I remember an old habit of mine at my salon and leave a pair of pink lips imprinted smack in the middle.

"There you are, darling," Ruby looks up from her cutting board.

I notice a cloud of smoke over by the sink but decide not to mention it. She's decked out in a snappy fitted red sweater, the cowl neck neatly *arranged*, perfect makeup with her rhinestone bifocals perched on the very tip of her up-turned nose. The crystal eye-glass chain glows with sunshine, little specs of light pop around the kitchen making me dizzy.

"You have such flair with food," I comment as I head over to the cupboard and start setting the stump table for us.

"So true—I mean it takes a great deal of *flair* to slice up a banana properly, let alone plop the slices artfully onto one's granola."

"While you plop, I'm going to give Helen a ring on her cell, see if she's up now." I head over, lift the yellow receiver off the hook and dial.

"Hello Eve. I'm back at my condo—our condo—Ryan's at the library, studying for a class, and if he calls me one more time I'm going to *kill* him," she says in a rush and I'm relieved she sounds so *sunny.*

"Who the hell needs hello anyway, but for the record—*hi.*"

"Sorry," Helen sighs. "It seems like he's taking it so much harder than I am."

"You have nothing to be sorry for, besides—you both need time to grieve before you even consider trying again. I know this maybe isn't what you want to hear, but this isn't *that* unusual, you know, especially for the first." I say this last past more gently and decide not to mention that my mom had a miscarriage too.

"I know, but I also know that my being thirty means the eggs I have are thirty years old as well. And to be honest with you," she sighs. "I'm just not sure if I can, *you* know, go through this again."

"You don't have to make any decisions right now, just focus on healing and getting back to teaching. How long are you supposed to be—"

"—Resting? Going stir crazy is more like it. But my gynecologist informed me it's more or less up to me when I can go back to teaching and I wasn't planning on doing too many classes for summer term since I was *planning* on being pregnant..." Helen sniffles and I do too.

"Oh, honey. Look, why don't you and Ryan come over to the island and stay with us this weekend. Ruby'd love to have more than me to cook for and maybe you can help us stop smoking!" I glance over toward Ruby and her face is all lit up.

"That sounds wonderful—thank you."

"Come around four and you can join our belly-yoga class—if you're up to it. Otherwise, it'd be good for a laugh."

"Or ten," Ruby adds.

We good-bye.

"We'll make up the spare room across from the library," Ruby says as she pours milk into our granola bowls. "She'll be right as rain in no time 'tall, darling. Just you wait and see. *Why* my cooking *alone* has been known to cure all *sorts* of things."

Rocky meows to be let out the back door. I follow him down the stoop and over to the side porch door and let him outside. With spring here we can leave all the doors leading to the porch wide open and enjoy the moving air as it carries the smells of spring right into the cottage.

I turn and admire Ruby's huge, stuffed sturgeon and shake my head.

"I honestly think I've the hang of it," Ruby offers in a voice riddled with something verging on sarcasm. "I simply have to learn my timing a bit more, don't you think?"

"Timing?" My voice rises an octave. "You hardly even *shift* when you're supposed to." I clamber in the passenger side of my VW van and Ruby gets behind the wheel. She turns the key, lets out the clutch and off we go—sort of. She tries again and this time we shimmy and shake and then we're moving toward the driveway at a steady, but cautious pace. I open the ashtray, check my supply of Reese's Peanut Butter Cups and hope for the best. When the pressure's on, it's good to know there's something there waiting to lean on.

Ruby glances at the fuchsia-pink Post-It with the 'H' diagram I made for her on how to shift. We make our way down the lane and over the wooden bridge. So far so—well—we're moving.

"How am I doing?" Ruby asks.

"Not bad," I say and mean it. "Have you been practicing?" Just as I finish asking we begin to lurch up the hill toward the gate.

"Of course not, "Ruby retorts with gusto. "Who has time to practice something as simple as knowing when to *shift*—for heaven's sake? Now if you'd be so kind as to hop out and undo the gate, why—we'll be on our way then, won't we."

I smile and do as I'm told. Pulling the metal gate open, I remember the first time we came here and how this old gate was so overgrown with weeds we had to struggle to get it undone from their stubborn hold. Now the two ruts that lead down, into the dark wooded tunnel are worn and familiar.

"Okay, sister," I say with a renewed oomph and thump back into my seat. "Let's get on over to La Pointe and get us some plants!"

"Bang on!" She turns onto North Shore Drive. "How 'bout something jazzy? You're not going to simply sit there and comment on my driving abilities."

"'Course not, what was I thinking?" I tap around the screen and find some Adele I had downloaded earlier. "Thought I'd never get the hang of this. Texting is next and then I'll have finally entered the—what—next level, I guess."

"I'll leave texting to you, darling. *Ridiculous* waste of time and what a phone call ever did to anyone is *beyond* me."

I un-wrap a double Reese's Peanut Butter Cup, needed for energy. Ruby puts her hand out.

As we zoom by Charlie's birdhouse collection, Ruby gives the horn several good toots. I notice how the Poplar and Birch trees are starting to leaf out again and the Oaks have finally let go of last year's leaves and new ones have begun to unfold. But the tall, stately White Pine trees are always dressed in green and add such permanence to the hilly landscape. They're definitely my favorite.

Birds are everywhere. As if they all came in on one flight and can't seem to decide what branch to land on. They swoop and sail every which way and, the colors—brilliant Blue Jays, Indigo Buntings and Yellow Goldfinch. Weird, even the Swallows seem brighter somehow. Spring is such a snappy time of year. The refreshing, crisp air is catchy; like peeling away a layer of winter that you no longer need or have a use for. It'd be great if you could do that with these thighs.

"You know," I say with a conviction that makes me sit up. "I'm thinking…it's going to be one helluva summer!"

"Girrrl," Ruby offers in her best *Sam* voice. "You know *that's* right."

I try not to look at the Gilded Sunsets sign as we zip by, but knowing it's there is enough to give me some major pissyness.

"Sure are a lot more cars," I say trying to take my mind off the looming development. "I better get used to it, summer's coming full steam ahead and everyone and their mother's opening up their cabins, cottages and what not—oh boy."

"Oh boy, is right!" Ruby slams on the brakes just as a black dog leaps across the road, disappearing into the woods, "Bloody dog, nearly got us *killed*!"

"Great save and thanks to Sam, the brakes on this old crate are dog-leaping safe."

"Let's see now," Ruby slows, as she turns onto Main Street. "Just where *was* that stand going to be anyway, do you recall, darling?"

"It's right down the street from Al's Place—hey, let's stop in and shoot the breeze with Bonnie and Marsha."

"Good idea, I'll pull up behind—why this is Marsha's car right here. Who else would have a bumper sticker that says that, hmmm?"

"*Norske Nook does it butter*—so true. Is that something to be proud of, do you think? 'Course it's a ton better than using something with hydrogenated fat or some other fake crap."

"My goodness," Ruby proclaims while checking her makeup in the visor mirror. "There certainly are droves of folks about today." She snaps her visor up and I do the same.

We cross Main Street and stroll up the sidewalk. Several of the cafe tables at *Al's Place* outside on the wide front porch are filled with tourists chatting over plates of yummy looking breakfasts. I spy one with eggs Benedict; the telling yellow hollandaise sauce makes me want to pull up a chair and dive in.

I follow Ruby through the screen door. It announces us as it slams into my rear and I yelp out loud, "Damn it!"

"Look what the cat drug in!" Bonnie lifts up the bar's countertop and comes over to greet us. "I thought about closing today, being a holiday and all, but folks gotta eat and that includes *me*." She chuckles at her own joke and leads us over to a booth.

"Just a coffee for me, darling," Ruby says, scooting over. "Unless you've a bit of that simply sinful apple pie of yours."

"I believe Marsha's pulling one out of the oven as we speak—lucky you. How 'bout you Eve, care for some pie? Or—I *know* you have a weakness for my eggs Benedict."

I am so busted. "Actually coffee and a fork is all I need," I lean toward Bonnie and lower my voice. "How is she anyway? We've been hearing some weird stuff—but you know how hard up for gossip everyone is around here."

"I can't put my finger on it," Bonnie offers. She puts her pen behind an ear and hugs her round tray, thinking. "Sometimes she's just *Marsha*, and then other times, she's—it's like she's *on* something, spaced out kinda but real edgy. I also don't know if I'd believe everything, *anything* that Darlene Kravitz—queen of gossip has been spreading around."

Marsha comes out from the kitchen and walks over toward us. She looks great. Both she and Bonnie have matching long blue and yellow striped aprons on (Lilly's design) and even though the eyeliner's a tad thick, her blue eyes are clear and her lipstick matches her red top.

I read somewhere that clear eyes are a sign of good health, that and a nice set of white choppers. My teeth would be more *movie star-like* if I didn't have an occasional smoke, drink gallons of coffee and eat chocolate. So it's a one-out-of-two thing for me. Or is that three times and you're out?

"Hello, Eve and Ruby," Marsha says wiping flour onto her apron. "I just baked four delicious pies and am about to dig into four more—how's the apron business going?"

Bonnie excuses herself and goes over to seat several more customers, while Marsha heads over to the bar, grabs the coffee pot and some mugs and comes back to pour us several steaming helpings.

"We're crazy busy," I blow on my teeth-staining brew. "I sure am glad that daughter of yours is here, or rather there in Bayfield, what a trooper."

A strange look comes over Marsha, like she's realized something. "Yes…she is…" Marsha says slowly, like she's in a dream. "You have a lovely day now." She moves away and goes back into the kitchen.

"I'm not a doctor, mind," Ruby leans in so no one around can hear. "But there's a bit of a screw loose in that one—don't you think?"

"I think *something's* not right—oh, I don't know. Listen to us. She seems a little distracted is all. I think that we're being paranoid."

We devour the enormous slice of apple pie, with an even *more* enormous scoop of ice cream and slug down more coffee than necessary. I slip a ten-spot under my saucer and we head on out along the sidewalk. Bonnie waves at us from the door, having happily informed us she was closing after lunch for the rest of the day.

Seems she's come full circle and is planning on giving her late husband Al's cemetery plot a royal makeover. She laughingly mentioned that for the first time since they married she knows where he is at night. I was tempted to tell her that not all dead folks are hanging in their assigned graves these days, but I didn't.

"*Woods Hall Craft Shop,*" Ruby comments as we pass by the place. "I've given them simply *heaps* of money over the years—for such lovely things—let's take a peek, shall we?"

"Why not?"

I follow her into the shop, and become immediately drawn to a pile of rag rugs and start searching for colors I like—and rugs I don't need. Yanking out a bright orange one with green stripes, I'm thinking it'd be nice to stand on in my bathroom upstairs. I roll it up, tuck it under my arm and go to find Ruby. And so we shop like this, just get us in the door and off we go in whatever direction suits us.

"That is so you," I comment to her. She models the wide-brimmed hat slanting it this way and that on her little head.

"Says it's made of real hemp. Wonder if you could tear off a corner and get stoned—what do you think?" Ruby sends me a wink.

"I'd say if you could smoke this thing and get a buzz, they'd be sold out in no time."

Several women milling around gather closer to us and casually give these particular hats a going over. I shake my head. It's so interesting how, when I'm out shopping and show an interest in something, people group around and want whatever it is. I call it the banana factor. People seem to come and go in bunches.

"Oh heavens, I simply *must* have this hat. Shall we go, darling?"

"*Madeline Island Candles?*" I show her a beige candle and she smells it.

"*Woods-Hall Tall Pillar Candle,* good heavens that smells exactly like something the boys should have, shall we?"

After giving the nice lady with the not-so-attractive mustache, our checks, we head next door to the charming organic food stand. A hand-painted sign hung helter-skelter proclaims that *Andersons Farm has the best produce—guaranteed.*

Off to the side are all sorts of potted plants and flowers and hanging baskets with trailing vines of the most brilliant colors. I think we're going to go a little nuts here. We both give our purses an extra toss over our shoulders; I lay down the rug next to a terracotta pot bursting with a beautiful dark green ivy vine, its leaves variegated with white stripes. This one's definitely coming home. Ruby plops her hat on top of it and we start exploring.

The Tree-Stud comes around the corner of the stand with a big grin on his bearded face; suddenly I feel self-conscious, hoping I don't have apple skin stuck to my teeth.

"Well hello ladies," his deep voice warm and friendly. "I remember you two from Christmas. You bought me out of every last garland I had!"

Ruby gives her hair a pat. "Well hell—O darling." The Brit has thickened her accent and out pours the charm. "My name's Ruby Prevost, by the way—and this is Eve, Eve Moss. We live here on the island—year 'round."

"*You're*—the apron ladies! I'm Eric Levine." He runs a thick hand through his salt and peppered hair. "My wife bought a slew of your aprons and gave one to about everyone in our family last year. You guys were a hoot in the Bayfield Apple Festival—that black woman sure can sing."

I shade my eyes from the sun to give him a going over. Why not, Ruby's got him occupied and since he's married and all—doesn't hurt to *look.*

Grey T-shirt with the smallest hint of a belly; perfectly faded jeans, not too tight, not too loose and *not* those hip-huggers some guys around my age are trying to fill. He turns my direction and his gray eyes lock with mine. He winks.

Eventually, after having moved the van nearer, we load our hoard of plants, rug, smoke-able hat and several sacks of produce into the back of my van and head off in search of a cemetery. I direct Ruby to get on County Highway H and follow it for awhile.

"Would love to muck about with that bloke," Ruby Brits it up and we laugh."Shouldn't wonder how most ladies that buy from him—overbuy—like we did."

"*We?* You're the one that couldn't stop handing him things just to see him bend over and put it in that sack. You are really something, woman."

"It's *spring*—love—stirs up the hormones. Don't give me that look, I still have some *somewhere.*"

"I think we're coming to it, on the corner here."

"Here we are, Greenwood Cemetery," Ruby proclaims. She shifts up instead of down so we shudder to a rolling stop right in front of the entrance. "Well then, shall we?"

The sun is still high in the sky; rays of gold and yellow struggle through the tall white pine that loom here and there among the solemn grave markers. Like gentle giants, they stand in silence here, where there's a comforting quiet. A silence, but a peaceful-calm that makes you feel reverent and safe.

I don't know what it is about cemeteries, but I've always been drawn to them. We stroll beneath the *Greenwood* sign, its metal letters arching above between two metal poles. We enter the hushed world of the passed-on.

I reach down and brush away pine needles from a tombstone, "*Andrew Hickenlooper Blackmore, eighteen-ninety-seven.* And he's still alive? *Drew. Loving and beloved husband of Madeline, investment banker for gold, gumption and lagniappe*—what's that?"

"It means, dear child—something extra. As I recall, keep in mind my Ed was a professor, it's an old Cajun word for that thirteenth donut you *certainly* no longer get."

"Right." I read the rest of the stone's inscription, "*Madeline Callingham Blackmore, eighteen-ninety-six, died in nineteen-seventy-four. Mina. Loving and beloved wife of Andrew. Mother, grandmother, playwright and teacher. She loved laughter.* That's nice, don't you think?"

"I think I should like to be buried here, somewhere off in a corner perhaps."

"Really? I thought for sure you'd want to be buried right next to that Ed of yours in Eau Claire." We continue on walking.

"As you know, I *do* have a plot there and a marker desperate to know my birth! Seems odd to have one's plot all set and ready to go. Ed always took such a joy in all those details. But you know, I jolly well think that you and I should get our very *own* plots right here on the island." Ruby reaches over and closes my mouth.

"Why the hell not?"

"Let's try and find Ed's grandfather, shall we?"

"Are Ed's parents buried here or—"

"—His mum, that would be Thelma, died giving birth to Ed, and his father, the dashing, yet-always-in-his-cups, Thomas, died two weeks after Ed and I married. They're side-by-side not too far from where Ed is buried."

"Thanks for the history of Ed. It's weird, but you're the end of an era."

"I intend to go out with *quite* a bang. I believe we're getting close. The Hultquist plot, that would be Victor and Flora, were next to Gustave and Adeline's graves, as I recall."

"What in the world?" I reach down and pick up a necklace looped over the corner of Adeline's tombstone. "It's Leandre's necklace," I fall down onto the grassy gravesite and feel as though I'm about to fall through the earth. Instantly I'm covered in sweat. I wipe away a tear and show the silver-eye amulet to Ruby. She helps me to a sitting position—I lean against the cool stone for support.

"Oh, my dear child—are you alright? You look as though you've seen a ghost!"

I nod and let the cool air calm my beating heart. Ruby sits down next to me on the pine-needled floor.

"This was Leandre's necklace!"

"Why, Eve Moss, how could you *possibly* know about Leandre?"

"How about we haul all our planting stuff over here and I'll tell you about this *thing* that happened to me."

"Do you think he'll be back?" I ask while applying hair color to Ruby's roots in my salon that Howard helped create on the first floor of the cottage. "That's if you can believe my crazy story, and to be honest, I'm not so sure myself."

"Oh now, darling," Ruby regards me in the round mirror. "I've come to the conclusion that anything is possible—*everything.*"

"I realize and totally agree. But..." I think for a moment, remembering his pleading eyes. "It was so real, and yet...it wasn't. I can't explain how it felt—how *he* felt."

"Try, darling—I'm listening." Ruby pats my hand.

"Well...it felt like—like I was watching myself in a movie. I felt faraway. Like being underwater or how you feel after waking up from a really real-feeling dream, thick with wonder. I honestly thought that that's what it had been—a crazy dream. That's why I hadn't mentioned it. Then I see his necklace and—*shit*! Does menopause make you a little crazy?"

"Good heavens darling, *life* will do that to a woman." Ruby sighs. A flicker of light passes over her eyes. "Perhaps he was remembering and the power of it all pulled you in somehow." A shudder runs through my body.

"It's something I'll never, *ever* forget. I know in my very core that I'll not see him again and that he's where he should be—with them. I only wonder why—of all the redhead's in the world—why me?"

"Well, that's simple, darling. Really," Ruby grins. "You were there from the very start—here—I should say. Or at least you *could* have been...I'm realizing you never know. And perhaps that's the rub."

I look into our mirrored reflections. Ruby's hair is poking out here and there, with color slowly oxidizing around her hairline making it look as though she's wearing a hat. I'm in the same shape—my gray roots being re-colored their rightful red. I have a flashback of being back at my salon, meeting Ruby for the very first time and all the hundreds of times, thousands even, that I've colored her hair. And all along we were headed here, to this place of *possibilities*.

"Do you think about dying?" I ask as I pour us more coffee.

"You know, darling," Ruby cups her chin with a hand, thinking. "You'd think at my age I would be. But it seems to me, the older I get, the more I think about the bloody joy of *living*!"

"I like that."

CHAPTER NINE

Before you can say—*Helen and Ryan are coming for the weekend*—
it's Friday. The five of us are busy cutting and sewing away on
an apron order from a dude in Las Vegas who runs a strip joint. He
sent along an interesting drawing of what he had in mind, I have
no idea how he found out about us—our website maybe? These are
some of the skimpiest aprons yet and the fabrics we're using are a
riot. Johnny created a station for us on something called *Pandora*
and now Latin guitar is keeping us zooming along.

"Girrrl" Sam slows her sewing machine to a growl. "I never
knew what a pain in the neck this here satin was to sew together.
Damn stuff's slippery as an eel. Now who in their right mind would
wear this?" She holds up the scanty evidence.

Lilly lifts her bifocals up into her hairdo for a good look. "I
think Ruby would look rather snappy in one of those." She lisps
snappy.

Ruby takes it from Sam and models it. "It's simply *screaming* for
bling—don't you think?"

"If anyone knows her bling," Johnny says and Ruby shoots him
a look. "It's our bling-queen Ruby!" He sings like a TV announcer.

"You know," I say turning Ruby this way and that, thinking. "It would jazz it up a notch if we sewed on some glittery *something's*. See what you can find in our growing collection of accessories and just go—"

"—Crazy!" Lilly adds and we chuckle.

"I'm a little worried about Helen," I offer to the room, my in-house therapy group. "Last time we spoke, she almost seemed *too* happy, you know? I mean she has just lost the very beginnings of—"

"—The way I see it," Sam offers in her wise voice and we listen closely. "Sometimes the soul-baby jus' wasn't all fired up to take this life on and does a quick exit. Could be the body wasn't takin' on the right form or...who-all-knows?" She reaches out and takes the fabric pieces from me.

"Do you think we *have* a choice?" Johnny asks. "I mean, in all honesty, I really don't think I would have wanted to come into a world where I was different—like being gay—where you'd be choosing to be called names, get spit on and beat up. Not to mention all the gossip in high school. Makes me *crazy* when some expert claims being homosexual is a choice. Trust me, it's not."

"I'm sorry you suffered, child," Sam says kindly. "I know the way folks can be when they're lookin' at something that's not like them. Fear is a *nasty* thing and can turn people into mean sons o' bitches." We chuckle. "But look how you turned out. A *fine* man with love in your heart and someone to share it with."

"Why weren't you around in my therapy years?" Johnny asks.

"If everyone," I add, "would just listen to each other—I mean really listen—we wouldn't *need* therapists."

"Oh—some folks will *always* need therapists," Sam counters. "When my first and *only* husband—Ricky—would get all coked-up-crazy and he'd be chasing me through our vermin-infested apartment in Detroit—child—nobody on the *earth* needed therapy more than this lady—no lie."

"I thought," I say carefully, "you once said you never married and—"

"—'Fraid I lied," Sam replies with a candor only she can get away with. "Pains me to associate the word married with that bastard."

"Did this Ricky bloke," Ruby comes to stand near Sam. "Did he ever *hurt* you, darling?" We hold our breath.

Sam's strong shoulders start to shake, her lips quiver and a lone tear rolls down her beautiful dark cheek. "That man," Sam half-whispers. "He did things to me I'll nevah speak of. But I found me an attorney-lady who helped me put him away for good. May he rot in hell."

I put my electric shears down and head over to her."No one," I say with a strength I'm sure Sam feels. "Will *ever* hurt you again."

"Hurt me?" Sam regains her oomph. "Most men don't know the first thing 'bout the likes of me. That being said—you all have become the salve I been so in need of."

"Imagine," Ruby says with drama, "all the cold cash we've saved by being our *own* therapists—now Sam, darling—will you be paying us with credit or check?" Sam grins.

Howard strolls into the room from the office. "I think Johnny and I met someone who *could* use some therapy." He adds an order to our clipboard and comes around my cutting table crossing his arms. "We were over to Tom's Burned Down Cafe last night, having a drink at the bar—"

"—That's right!" Johnny says. "There was this guy with a big moustache sitting by himself at a corner table and he was—well—he seemed to be having a pretty major discussion."

"Well, that *is* bloody bizarre! Perhaps we're all headed to the loony bin having been victims of *discussion* most of our adult lives!"

"Um—the guy was by himself," Johnny says.

"Oh good heavens."

"That particular establishment is known to attract, shall we say, a more *colorful* crowd." Lilly says in her instructor voice. "I'm not surprised in the least."

"Perhaps it's worth looking into," Ruby says. "I've never been, it always looks rather forlorn and *very* burned-down indeed."

"I'll get it," I walk over to the deer head, reach up and pull the phone down. "Ruby's Aprons, Eve here."

"It's me, Helen," her voice crackles in my ear.

"Hello, Helen—how're you feeling?"

"Pretty good, thanks. Listen, Ryan and I are just leaving Duluth, so we should be there a little after four."

"Sounds great. Now you don't have to join us for belly dancing—only if you're sure you're up to it. I don't want you pushing yourself."

"I'll give it a try, why not? Might be good for me."

"We're *so* looking forward to seeing you two. Now drive safely."

We *good-bye* and I let the phone go and it slides up and snaps into the deer's mouth. Why is it that we tell everyone to *drive safely* or *have a safe trip now?* Where the hell does that come from anyway? Maybe next time I'm about to utter those words I'll try something new like—*see if you can get here alive* or for really *close* friends, *try not to kill anyone on the way.*

I need lunch.

We're out on the boathouse deck. The sun is high above, shining down its afternoon warmth. A gentle breeze curls our cigarette smoke up and around the roof, keeping it a safe distance from Howard and Johnny and the newly non-smoking Lilly. I'm personally jealous. This stupid habit of ours is harder to quit than I thought when I first started about a hundred years ago.

"Such a *divine* lunch," Ruby sighs, stretching her arms above her. "How you ever found such bloody huge tomatoes this early in the season is *beyond* me."

"An acquaintance of mine starts them very early in his greenhouse," Lilly reluctantly admits."

"Could this be the bloke who owns the bookstore over in Bayfield?"

"As a matter of fact"—Lilly unrolls a potato chip bag and begins to munch—"He's one and the same. Nice enough man."

I send Ruby a *don't embarrass her* look and say, "His bookstore has got to be the *epitome* of what I think of as the most perfect place for tea and a good read."

"Way you behavin'," Sam points out, "all squirmy and like you's in *heat*—girrrl—you so busy getting hot for that man—you can't *see* straight, no sir."

"We're just *friends,*" Lilly counters. "Besides—I get a great discount on books. The afternoon is nearly over—it's time to put the pedal to the metal and get cracking—*ladies.*"

We all stand, stretch and file back into the sewing area. It's a kaleidoscope of colors today, with fuchsia pink material piled on my cutting table. Lilly and Johnny's sewing machines are heaped with neon yellows, sexy blues and greens. Sam is working on parts for some deep red ones all for the strippers. Should I post pictures of this line on our website? Hell yeah!

"Wonder what else they wear with these things," I hold one up and wrap it around my head. "I think I prefer the cotton ones we were working on yesterday."

"If I got a bit tarted up," Ruby comments from the kitchen area. "Well, perhaps *more* than a bit, I could see the attraction—and if it were dark enough."

"Yeah, like *lights out,*" Sam offers and then revs her machine for emphasis.

The afternoon winds down and we gladly hand over the finished *sexual allurements*, as Lilly put it, to Howard who does most of the packing and shipping when we're too busy and lately it's been really crazy. The boys head home and the four of us women shut down the boathouse, pull the doors closed, and then head up the path toward the barn for some serious exercise.

Halfway up, Helen and Ryan's silver Saturn pulls alongside the back porch and comes to a stop. Ryan's red kayak is latched to the top and I wonder if they ever found the keys. I hope so. Ryan had lost them a while ago and Helen has told me several times how tired she is driving around everywhere with a kayak on the roof.

After watching Pringles zoom by the other day, I think I'd like to try riding in one of those. We wave them over.

Its hugs all around, everyone very careful not to squeeze Helen too much, she's pale in a soft grey workout outfit. Ryan's a little wrinkled in jeans and a *Forensics Rule* sweatshirt. They're both being very gentle with each other and its heart-breaking seeing the sad look behind their smiles. Being here away from everything is just the ticket—I hope it is—anyway.

"I mentioned to Howard and Johnny," I say to Ryan, "that you probably won't be joining us up in the loft, so they've laid in the brew and told me to send you right over—pronto!"

Actually, the boys are also going to feed him gourmet pizza, as well as all sorts of fancy hors d'oeuvres. Johnny and I have secretly planned this *boys-with-the-boys* and *girls-with-the-girls* afternoon. Even with Helen at five-ten and Ryan well over six feet, suddenly it hits me how this experience was literally making them seem so small all of a sudden. Even Ryan's blonde hair looks drab.

"I'll just toss our luggage into the cottage," Ryan says as he hefts several bags over his broad shoulders. "And head over there— thanks so much." He looks deeply into my eyes and I nod. He kisses Helen on her forehead, and turns away toward the porch door.

"Such a dear," Ruby says and we move toward the bam.

I open the green-painted Dutch door to the right side of the main one, flip on several lights and lead us over toward the staircase—up we go!

"Now I *know* I've mentioned," Sam huffs into a chair over by the window. "That you all are in *desperate* need of an elevator in this barn of yours."

"It's the perfect warm-up," Lilly chides and isn't the least bit out of breath.

She starts handing out our skirt scarves and coin belts, from her round , mint-green suitcase. We change into them, and then in the midst of the haunting Asian music, we swoop over and around Helen, trailing our different colored silk scarves. We're being silly in order to make her feel more at ease.

"Come over here, darling," Ruby takes Helen by the hand and pulls her over so that she's facing the wall of mirrors. "Lilly, hand me that—won't you—dear?"

We step closer to Helen. Ruby puts a coin belt around her slender waist and carefully cinches it. She gives her arm a pat and steps away.

I have her bend down a touch in order to wrap her long blonde hair with a lavender colored silk headscarf—lavender is her favorite color. Sam helps me in the back, she's an expert when it comes to headbands. Then Lilly shows her how to hold the Zills in her fingers. Helen clangs the small cymbals and then beams us the loveliest smile.

"We'll warm-up with some very basic yoga moves," Lilly says, more gently then usual. "Let's begin from the Mountain Pose and slowly we'll form the Five-Pointed Star. Good—very good."

With Lilly in the middle, Sam and Ruby on her left and Helen and I on the right, we stretch and move with the beautiful music of Fairuz, her haunting voice surrounding us in this wonderful old place. Lilly is making sure to only do some very basic belly-dancing moves and is keeping to a subdued pace. I catch Helen's eye reflected in the mirror and we grin.

Look at us now.

We're gathered in the circle of ancient chairs and the sofa, over by the huge loft window with Lake Superior in the background.

"What did you think, darling, hmmm?" Ruby asks while patting her forehead with a tissue. "Did that make your blood move about a bit?"

"Nearly *kills* me," Sam offers with a chuckle. "Every time—and I even have my girls up and secured with my fine new *hold up, hold them please*—sports bra. I ain't telling the size—so don't ask."

"We're still getting our moves down," Lilly waves away Sam's comment. "But you've got potential—I can see it."

"Do we look as *crazy* as *Helen* does?" I have to ask.

"Eve, darling," Ruby says and I can tell I'm in trouble. "With red curls spilling all about that blue scarf, not to mention your choice in shoes." Everyone looks down at my red high-tops. "I think it fair to say you've got *crazy* wrapped up tight."

"Oh my land," Sam says and takes a big swig from her water bottle. "Lilly girl—you think it's safe leaving poor Miss Helen here with these cats? I know it's time for me to get on home."

"I think it's perfectly alright," Lilly offers and I couldn't agree more.

We change and head downstairs over toward Lilly's enormous white Lincoln. Sam and Lilly hop in. As they're about to drive away, Sam's window slides down.

"Girrrl," Sam looks toward Helen. "If either of them *hormonally deranged women* give you grief—you call us *straight off*—you hear?"

"I will, I promise," Helen says and we wave the huge car off as it disappears down the drive and out of sight.

"How 'bout we all go in and freshen up a bit, hmmm?" Ruby asks as she links her arm through mine as well as Helen's and we head toward the cottage.

Helen brought along a stack of LPs, as she remembered the quality of our hi-fi and really—the sound can't be beat. So some lovely Strauss is soaring out of the living room. We each have a different apron tied on.

Mine is covered with black cats leaping this way and that. Ruby's is basic black with pearls sewn around the outside and a huge brooch in the upper corner. We've put Helen in what we refer to as the *contemporary look*, heavy white cotton with big seventies flowers all over. You can't help but smirk when you look at it.

"Honestly, Helen," Ruby says, "I truly wonder if we should worry about how Ryan's getting on with the boys next door—they can have such a *dreadful* influence."

I role my eyes and Helen grins, then I pour some more red wine into her ruby red goblet.

"Ryan's a big boy, he can handle himself," Helen says. "Thanks. He's really been amazing. Not once has he complained about all my complaining. He deserves some time away from me. I just hope he can relax a little and not worry about *me* so much—I hate to be a pain in the—"

"—I can't imagine you as a pain in the ass," I say in my classy way. "You both need to chill and I figured being somewhere besides *home* might be helpful."

"The drive over," Helen adds, "is *so* beautiful and my gosh—the ferry ride is absolutely breathtaking. Not to mention crowded, how do you all manage?"

"We've the duck, darling—don't you remember being a bride-on-board?"

"That's right, I'd love to take a ride on it sometime this weekend."

"Consider it done," I add as I take down plates and hand them to Helen. "If you think we're just going to wait on you hand and foot—"

"—Oh geez, no. Anyway, I'm too independent, I can't *stand* not being able to do things on my own," Helen says with determination, turning a Blue Willow plate. "Maybe I'm not *supposed* to be a mother—I mean, I *am* really busy with my teaching and all, but…" She heaves a sigh and the kitchen seems suddenly crowded.

Ruby and I exchange a look. "Don't be absurd, darling—*really,*" Ruby says. "You're going to be a lovely mum, you'll see."

"I suppose…" Helen plops down onto a wicker stool and spins. "I did some research and learned that the odds of a miscarriage in a woman's first pregnancy are relatively high. Some women don't even realize they've miscarried and think they've just experienced a heavier than normal period."

"You certainly got my brains," I say and Ruby clucks her tongue. "And trust me, we have fertile ground and you'll have no problem should you two decide to—you know—*do* the deed."

"Soon enough you'll have the proverbial *bun,*"—Ruby adds while pulling open the oven—"in the oven."

"A little tax deduction on the way," I say and we all chuckle and something in the air lightens.

"You two are really something," Helen comments. "Speaking *of something,* what in the world have you got baking in that oven of yours?"

"For your dining pleasure," Ruby puts on her best Julia Child accent, which cracks me up. "Inside my *classic* cooker—you'll find I've taken great pains to stuff a *lovely* chicken with wild rice, slices of orange and lemon, as well as several cloves of the most deee-lec-table garlic. Then—if my culinary efforts haven't blown your bloody top off, I've coated the scrumptious lass with a luscious concoction of olive oil, sea salt and chopped rosemary." She waves her wooden spoon and finishes with a hefty slug of wine.

"I made a simple tossed salad with pumpkin seed oil dressing and mashed parsnips should round things out," I add, not to be outdone. "Oh, and we're re-heating some crescent rolls Ruby made yesterday. Dessert will be chocolate, unless *someone* has eaten it all." Ruby suddenly finds something in the fridge awfully interesting.

Rocky leaps up onto the stump table—grabs a chunk of blue cheese off the cheese and cracker platter, then flies off and out toward the living room.

"Well then," Ruby says, "anyone for a refill?"

"That was such a *delicious* dinner," Helen says, taking a steaming plate from Ruby and drying it. "It was so sweet of you, arranging for Ryan to go over to the boys so we could be alone. It's funny. I honestly don't have that many close girlfriends of my own."

"*Really*, darling?" Ruby gives the roasting pot a good scrubbing. "I took you to be quite the social one."

"We're more and more alike," I comment, taking a plate from Helen to put away. "I've always had such a *social* job—running a salon. All day long I'm entertaining, and by the end of the day, all I ever wanted to do was un-plug. And I bet teaching is really similar, takes a lot of energy, and you're *on* the whole time."

"I never thought of it that way," Helen considers this. "My parents were *constantly* entertaining. Always having over the *right* people, fancy dinner parties with all the trimmings. She's *still* trying to keep up appearances, but—"

"—What, darling?"

"I just wish—I wish she could be my *mother* and not this perfectly coiffed woman *acting* like my mother. I wish we did things like this."

I pull the stepstool over and load the rest of the plates into the cupboard. "You're pulling my leg—right? You and Saundra never did the dishes together? Chewed the proverbial fat?"

"We had—we had *help*," Helen admits, the embarrassment heavy on her shoulders.

"You had *servants?*" I ask and my voice gives me away. "Wow."

Ruby pulls the plug and the sink makes a satisfying sucking sound as dishwater swirls away.

"Here—we help one another," Ruby says and sends me a wink. As she heads over to the fridge she rubs the top of Helen's hand. "Ring the boys and let's have sherry and chocolate by a nice crackling fire, shall we?"

The French doors are open; there's a good fire pulsing golden-yellow flames in the grate and we're all gathered around it. Billy Holiday sings softly on a scratchy old record.

"What a *lovely* day," Ruby says and we all nod. "Pass me that dreadful box of McElrath truffles—that's if *Miss Eve* hasn't inhaled them all."

I take one more and reluctantly hand it down the line. "Lavender, black pepper and dark chocolate? I'm such a goner and can you believe this stuff is *legal?*"

Howard's baritone chuckle says it all. "I think it's a fantastic art—fine chocolates. And the addiction part is every chocolatier's dream."

"I think Mister Ryan here,"—Johnny adds as he lifts up Howard's arm and pulls it around his shoulder like a scarf—"Is addicted to *pizza*—the guy chowed down almost as much as Howard."

"You should have seen them," Ryan says with conviction. "Homemade pizzas—one had fresh basil, blue cheese, pine nuts and tomato, with olive oil drizzled over the top and the other—"

"—Stop!" Helen orders, holding up a hand. *"Nothing* can compare with the fancy baked chicken *and* homemade crescent rolls."

"Our pizzas were homemade," Johnny says, then looks around the room. "Well, the dough may have come from the freezer section and who around *here* makes olive oil or pine nuts, for that matter. But I *did* chop the basil by hand."

"Well then," Ruby heads over toward the kitchen. "Perhaps some sherry and I *hand* around the chocolate." She turns and we all hear her mutter. *Good Heavens already.*

As I put the poker back into its holder, I look from one face to another, grouped around the fireplace, and feel the most peaceful quiet in my heart.

The anger I had felt toward my Dad seems a tiny ember now, a thing to let go out.

Rocky and I are lying in bed, reading. I'm totally engrossed in an wonderfully musty volume I found in our library of Marjorie Kinnan Rawlings', *South Moon Under* and it's taken me away to a long ago time in south Florida. So I hardly hear the soft rapping on my door.

"If that's room service—where the hell's my mint?" I ask, thinking it *must* be Ruby.

The door slowly opens and there stands Helen. She's wearing a conservative gray terrycloth robe; her long blonde hair is pulled back into a ponytail. "I can't sleep and—"

"—Wait right there!" I say with gusto and toss the book onto the bed, nearly missing Rocky's head.

We're outside on the dock, wrapped in blankets with pillows heaped around us; the bright moonlight illuminates the lake making it appear as though we're on an enormous mirror. As we lie back and look up toward the stars, I feel like I could float away. Has to be the sherry.

"How can I *ever* thank you, Eve?" Helen asks in a hushed voice. "All you and Ruby and all of your friends do—is give and give—I've never *met* people like you before."

"Honey—I'm not *a fancy* person, like your mom, and God *know's* I've never had servants. But what I've learned—*still* learning—is that there's nothing more important than taking care of the ones you give a rip about. Funny thing is—it's easy as *shit*! To be honest though," I sigh feeling old and wise and full of it. "The ones you call family don't have to be one iota related to you. Hell, not having all that history of growing up together can have its advantages, let me tell you."

It's Helen's turn to sigh. "What's that strange sound?"

We both sit up and watch as the duck comes flying down the hill, splashes into the lake and floats over toward us.

The mike clicks on. "Hello loves—the full moon over Madeline Island is high in the sky and there's a bottle of bubbly in need of opening—any takers?"

The duck idles over alongside of us.

"Ruby," Helen asks as she steps onto the duck. "Do you need a license to drive this thing?"

I slide into the front bench next to Helen, opposite Ruby.

"I've no bloody Idea!"

CHAPTER TEN

"Let me finish one more,"—Ruby spatulas a flawless *sunny-side-up* egg onto Ryan's plate—"My heavens—you certainly can eat!"

I notice that Ruby has a touch of extra makeup on this morning and I swear she's flirting with that poor man.

"So, what would you two like to do today?" I ask while slicing into a perfectly browned sausage link. "There's actually a pretty decent day shaping up out there. Oh—you need to stop in at the boathouse and check out these aprons we're working on right now."

Ruby turns from the stove and shows off the one she has on, I hadn't even noticed she was wearing one. It's see-through tulle with tons of sparkling beads all over it, very edgy and hardly useful; but hey, that's what the man wants!

"Giving it a bit of a *road test*," Ruby offers, sipping coffee. "I must say, despite this being my *own* design, I don't think I'd want to be caught dead in this vile thing." She unties it and it swirls into a heap of sparkles onto the countertop. "It's too Las Vegas for here, don't you think?"

"Have you two found your kayak keys?" I ask through toast crunching. "I've wanted to explore the sea-caves around the islands near here, it could be great fun. We'll have to find another one— maybe the boys have one we could borrow."

"We did and—they do," Ryan replies. "But, I looked into it myself since I find it fascinating. Most of the sea caves are pretty far away, over around Devil's Island. But we're game for a short exploration of Madeline Island."

I notice how Helen and Ryan seem so quiet with one another. I realize it's morning, but there's this *something* between them. Maybe being out in the fresh air and paddling around will loosen them up a bit.

"Don't forget, darling," Ruby says as she starts to clear the dishes. "We've that fundraiser meeting later this afternoon for Toad Hollow—"

"—Hey," Helen interrupts. "We'd like to attend that meeting too, if that'd be alright, besides, my mother is known throughout Edina as the *queen of fundraising,* so it must have rubbed off some." She tucks her blonde hair behind her ear and gives her half-eaten bowl of granola a poke and then sets her spoon down.

"You two scoot," Ruby says. "Now that everyone has finished eating. Eve and I will tidy up, then we'll head down to the boathouse—we'll simply take it from there. Go on now."

They go out into the living room, and Ruby and I sigh at the same time.

"The poor dears," Ruby says, and I nod.

"Well, there you are,"—I scoop up Rocky into my arms— "Whatever—or *who* ever—he was munching away yesterday, oh man—was his breath *something.*"

"Rocky? Have bad breath? You must be thinking of some *other* cat. Now get over here and let's put breakfast away."

"Isn't she bossy?" I set him down by his re-filled bowls and then answer the ringing phone.

"Ruby's Cafe—sorry, we've just shut down the grill," I say into the mouthpiece all snappy and full of caffeine.

"Eve—it's Bonnie over at the restaurant—something has happened to Marsha, she never showed up for her shift—I need your help with all these orders!"

"I'm not exactly sure," I say as I slam closed my van door, then rev the motor to life. "She wants us over there to help out with the big breakfast crowd—she's in the weeds and we're off to sling some hash!"

"You two loves—just relax," Ruby says to Helen and Ryan who are standing on the back stoop looking all of twelve. "We'll be back in no time."

"Maybe they could help?" I put the van in reverse. "Would you want to come, could be crazy? But I'm sure we could use the help," I yell out of my window.

They both shrug, hop in the back and off we go! In the rush, I threw on Capris and a teal blouse. Ruby nearly matches me, only a trillion sizes smaller and in yellow. Helen and Ryan are in polo shirts and khakis . I like that Ryan wears those slim-line jeans. He can get away with it and it shows things off—but not too much.

Maybe this is good they're coming along. I mean, it'll certainly take their mind off themselves and I wonder— "Have you two ever waited tables before?"

"I haven't," Helen replies. "But—"

"—I worked for a banquet department in college," Ryan offers from behind me. "But to be honest, I wasn't the best at it."

"You just keep an eye on me, darling," Ruby advises adjusting her lace collar. "Wonder whatever's up with that Marsha, not showing up for Bonnie's biggest shift—her Sunday brunch is always a smashing success."

"Bonnie's been trying to reach her all morning," I say as we fly across the wooden bridge and start up the hill. "She even went over there, but said her place was locked up tight. And besides, she didn't have much time before opening."

As we drive by Charlie's place, I toot the horn and sail on. Wonder what he's been up to?

"So Ryan," I ask his eyes in my rearview mirror. "What are you working on at the University over in Duluth?"

"Actually, it's really interesting," he comments. "I'm going over some older, unsolved cases in order to see if we can have them re-opened. It's the final project for my doctoral thesis and once it's wrapped up, as well as written up, I'll become a bona fide Professor of Forensic Psychology."

"Sounds simply *divine, really,*" Ruby gushes. "I can't tell you how I enjoy reading about all those clever criminals who *usually* get caught in the end—but not always."

"It's pretty incredible how many crimes go unsolved." Ryan adds in a confident voice I like. "And the ones that get all the publicity are only a handful of what are being committed—or have *been* committed. I also have some files on suicides under rather peculiar circumstances."

"Ryan's researched some pretty gruesome unsolved crimes," Helen jumps in. " Some were committed in northern Wisconsin—so he's decided to make those his focus."

"Oh, this *is jolly* good luck," Ruby is practically bursting. "I would *so* love to give what you've dug up so far a bit of a going over—hmmm? You wouldn't have brought anything with you, now, would you, darling?"

"Are you kidding?" Helen says with a laugh and I feel my heart un-clench. "He's been carting around this cardboard box of papers for months. I'm surprised he didn't bring it with him to the restaurant."

"Here we are," I say pulling the van up to the curb on Main Street. "It *does* look busy today."

We get out and head over to *Al's Place*. I lead the way, and from all the commotion seeping through the screen door, it sounds like the place is full of hungry tourists. The door smacks closed behind us, and Bonnie, hair half-hanging in her sweaty face, sends us a glorious smile of relief. Dolly Parton is thumping

Nine to Five on the jukebox in the corner and I'm grateful for the rhythm.

"Okay team," I turn to my group of helpers. "Here's how we're going to catch up. Everyone throw on an apron. Ruby and I will fill the orders waiting in the back, and you all are going to deliver. There's a table-map right next to the door on the way into the kitchen that will reflect what's on the tickets in the kitchen. First thing is to make sure everyone's coffee-ed and watered—any questions?"

"Just *when's* our bloody cigarette break?" Ruby demands—hands on narrow hips.

The morning swims by with Ryan only breaking a few water glasses. Helen makes the most in tips and is considering a career change, though she'd most likely rather be behind the bar. Bonnie shows her how to make a few drinks and I can tell she's enjoying the process. I'm sorry, but a Bloody Mary with an egg in it? Maybe explains the beer chaser and if that's what the lady ordered—voila!

The five of us are now sitting in the front booth, the place has all but emptied out and boy are we bushed! I can't get over how cheap some folks are, leaving mere change for a tip, when other tables visiting from bigger cities like Madison or Milwaukee leave fifteen—twenty percent. Maybe those cheapo's don't realize that most, if not all, wait-staff are paid less than the paltry minimum wage. I'll suggest a tasteful sign to Bonnie— something like: *Could you live on $7.25 an hour? See chart for proper tipping!* Or: *They can't shop at your place if you don't tip 'em at ours!* Subtle is not my style.

"How in the world," I ask one more time. "Do you and Marsha handle this place all by yourselves? I mean, granted, we're not the most experienced lot, but we were moving like crazy!"

"You walked in on a mess," Bonnie replies with a grin, tucking up a loose strand of hair. "And cleaned it right up—you've earned some *major* credit here. Normally folks wander in, order, and on it goes. But once you get your ass dragging in the weeds—there's not a lot of hope until you climb on out again. I just couldn't *climb* anywhere this morning—damn her anyway."

"We had a lovely time," Ruby gives Bonnie's hand a pat. "Eve here had a challenge with the garnish, but *eventually* caught on."

"Chef-du-jour *here*," I cock my head Ruby's way. "Wouldn't let a single plate out unless it had its fancy little garnish she insisted I make. The carrot-flower item with a sprig of rosemary *did* add some class."

"I saw some of the plates that flew out the kitchen door," Bonnie chuckles. "You two know how to dress up a plate. Before you go, I'd like you to show me a few of your creations. And Helen," Bonnie sends her a serious look. "So sorry to hear about your loss, I lost my first and only child. But I was more relieved than sad—some men just aren't made to be dads. And at the time I couldn't have handled a baby—my late husband was a—"

"—Dreadful louse," Ruby finishes for her.

"I'm so sorry," Helen finds her voice. "And thank you. I'm learning it's not that abnormal for a first pregnancy and—*somehow* that seems to make it a little easier."

"That and hanging out here," Ryan adds putting an arm around Helen and pulling her close. "Is it always this crazy?"

"Well, that depends on what in *heaven's* you call crazy," Ruby says with punch. "I for one think of this little rock as a piece of heaven."

"With a dash of crazy."

CHAPTER ELEVEN

The group decision is to rent three kayaks from a local place in La Pointe called Apostle Island kayaks. The boys wanted to come with, and since the ones they own are single-man kayaks, we all thought it would be a hoot to try a new model called the Seadart Double. Howard found out about it while researching how to buy kayak parts on the web.

"Johnny said to pack a *small* lunch," I remind Ruby. "We're *not* going to need a week's supply of gourmet goods!"

The bounty we have stored in our cupboards and food pantry could easily feed the entire island—for a year—and Ruby's concept of a small lunch is hard to define.

"Did you remember to ring Alice Anne?" Ruby asks with her head in the freezer so she sounds as if she's got a cold.

"I did, we're going over to chat fundraising at Toad Hollow." A familiar odor sneaks into the kitchen and my stomach flip-flops. "You smell anything—where's Rocky?" Damn, damn, damn.

We hear an odd *meow* as the smell builds around us like a thick cloud of green.

"Skunk!" Ruby and I yell in unison.

Helen comes flying around the corner from the living room. "Oh, *there's* an odor I know all too well—where *is* the little stinker?"

Ruby and I point toward the back door with our other hands pinching our noses. I reach over the sink and slide open the window. Ruby lights up and for once, I think it's a *brilliant* idea.

The three of us stand on the porch stoop considering smelly Rocky. He's cowering next to the screen door looking truly mortified and making a mournful sound. I resist taking him into my arms. Would a rinse cycle in the washer be all that horrible?

"I know that most people suggest rubbing the poor guy all over with tomato juice," Helen advises from our perch. "But I learned of a much more successful treatment. I bet you've got hydrogen peroxide in your cottage-salon here?"

Ryan makes a quick retreat to the boys' house, claiming they need his help with something kayak-related. Coward. He did put Vladimir playing a soft Brahms's piano sonata on the hi-fi in hopes of calming Rocky—*and us.*

Ruby, Helen and I are grouped around my red shampoo bowl, all three of us have our sleeves rolled up and are wearing black plastic hair-coloring gloves. Ruby, ever the clever one, puts a dab of Chanel No. 5 under our noses, so it's not *that* bad. Okay, it's god-awful, but in a pricy way.

"I can't believe how cooperative Mr. Rocky is being,"—Helen mentions while mixing her concoction in a small mixing bowl—"I figure he wants this to be over soon as possible too, poor little man."

Rocky turns and looks up toward me—staring into my eyes from the sink—I give his furry head a pat and I swear he winks.

"Good gracious, prince-of-England," Ruby pronounces with disdain. "What in the *world* do you think Rocky, darling was doing with the likes of a *skunk?* He's a plucky little fellow, but why in the *world* would he choose such a smelly comrade, hmmm?"

"Oh, I think he's just a curious cat," I say and he meows so feebly we all chuckle. "So you add baking soda and some of my expensive shampoo?"

"A quart of hydrogen peroxide," Helen explains, "a quarter cup of baking soda and a teaspoon of dish soap—or in our case—rosemary mint shampoo. Mix it a good while, then we'll try to rub it on the poor guy."

"Should we have worn raincoats?" Ruby asks with a tinge of alarm. "I could run and fetch—"

"—Hold on Ruby," I implore, carefully holding Rocky's head in order to protect his eyes.

Ever-so-gently Helen pours the liquid onto his furry little back. He meows with that sound that tells me *This is not going well—mom!* I begin to massage the mixture into his fur and can feel his muscles tense—all hands are holding him in the sink and I try to be quick about it.

"That looks good," Helen says, "Just rub it in a little more while I get the water going." Helen tests the temperature on her wrist (smart woman), then hands me the water hose. Since it's normally used for human shampoos, there's a small shower-like head that is perfect for our operation. Rocky has started to give out his warning growl, and pretty soon I'd say all bets are off on him *not* clawing all of us to death!

"Okay, he's rinsed," I cautiously announce to the six gloved hands. "I'll shut the water off and if we all step back—"

"—OH SHIT!" We all yell as Rocky has shaken and sprayed us all! He gives us a final shake—then leaps out of the sink and shoots out the door leaving sudsy prints in his wake.

"You said *shit?*" I ask a soaking Helen and she shrugs.

"A most descriptive noun," Ruby primly pats her dripping hair. "Under the circumstances—*shitty* is spot on for describing this *dreadful* experience, don't you think?"

We burst out laughing, all of us looking slightly melted with our gloves and dripping hair. An idea takes shape. I un-roll my latex gloves, dramatically tossing them into the shampoo bowl, take up the hose, turn on the water—careful to test it for proper warmth—and begin to squirt my de-skunking-assistants. I end up chasing them out of the room all to the lovely music of Brahms—so soothing...

We're in my van heading toward La Pointe. The late morning sky flecked with gold and pink is the perfect backdrop for our kayaking adventure.

"Eve Moss should be put away," Ruby suggests. "We're there to help her with that *miserable reeking feline* and *what* does she do?"

"It was only a *minor* squirting," I say in my defense. "I didn't want Rocky to feel left out, and you both needed a rinse—you should be grateful."

I spy in my leopard-covered rearview mirror Helen's leaning into Ryan, his arm around her shoulders. Howard and Johnny are way in the back, in the third seat, talking softly. I eye-signal to Ruby to look behind her, she discreetly lowers her visor and uses the mirror. A satisfying grin crosses her face.

Ruby has changed into beige stirrup pants and a fitted matching top, rhinestone sunglasses cover half her face. I'm trying something new, a *not-baggy* top of soft yellow and (of course) Capri jeans.

I'm focusing on how to *not* obsess about my weight. I can't seem to change my shape without going into some kind of diet-obsession-starvation, which has only ever been a *temporary* remedy anyway. I'm not using the fat word any longer either—I'm voluptuous—and that's that. What did one of my clients say once? Oh yeah, more to love. Nice.

I glance around me. The scenery of Madeline Island passes by our windows as we head down Big Bay Road toward the marina of La Pointe. Every so often, silvery-bright reflections of Lake Superior dance into the van. And what with the trees and all the fantastic beauty of the island coming to life around us, it's comforting to share today with Helen and Ryan.

"The kayak guy said that their rental place is across from Joni's Beach Memorial Park." I mention as I slow the van.

"You just passed it, darling," Ruby offers with a touch of sarcasm. "If you weren't driving so *bloody* fast—"

I stop, shift into reverse, do a quick U-turn and pull over to a building opposite the park and lake beyond. It's a small structure, crafted from rough-hewn wood festooned with ropes and anchors hung here and there. Off to the left are rows and rows of colorful kayaks, and along the side of the building stand a row of paddles, lined up fin-to-fin.

"Hello there," an athletic man pops around the corner.

His suntanned face shows off sparkling white teeth. He beams us a friendly smile. Could he be a *natural* blond?

"I'm Eve. I called you earlier about—"

"—I'm Fred Nelson, that's right. You wanted to rent three doubles—that's awesome."

"Some of us," Ruby comes forward adjusting her movie-star glasses. "Are rather *new* to this. Perhaps *private* lessons are in order?"

The hussy.

"Um, well,"—Fred fidgets with his wrap-around white sunglasses—"Three Seadart Tandems will be a perfect fit for you all. The kayak's designed for two and you don't have to be certified, or take one of those classes where you get wet." He leads us over to the array of kayaks.

"Wet?" Ruby says with a dash of panic.

"We weren't planning a *huge* trip," I add. "Just wanted to paddle over to Big Bay and have a picnic."

"That's a perfect journey," Fred crosses his sinewy arms, taking in Howard with his admiring blue eyes. "For beginners and—"

"Actually,"—Howard steps over and stands next to Fred—"Most of us have been in a kayak, so we'll split into groups so at least one person per kayak will know what to do."

Something shifts in Fred's face as he looks into Howards eyes. Johnny steps forward and Fred nods his head ever so slightly. I roll my eyes at Ruby. Johnny hasn't a thing in the world to worry about when it comes to Howard. That man's crazy about him.

We're a sleek group. Helen and Howard are in a violet kayak, Ruby and Ryan's is red, a white scarf streams from her giant straw hat. Johnny and I zip along in this cool mango-colored one. Even though we're wearing lifejacket vests, we've managed to look *dashing*. It took us a bit of ingenuity to fit our rather lavish lunch into the little storage bins, but we did—even the wine.

With the wind to our backs and being so close to the water's surface, I can carefully lean over and spy the rocky lake-scape below. All three boats have found the rhythm of lifting and lowering our paddles at the same time as our boat mates in order to move more effortlessly. It's really kind of sensual.

"We sure got a kick out of having Ryan over the other night," Johnny says from behind me. "What a great guy and *smart*. He and Howard got into this whole discussion about human motivation versus action. Like how so many—most really—people only *dream* of doing something different with their lives, but never take action."

I stop paddling a second and we drift; I turn around slightly. "Did he say anything, about—*you know*—I'm just worried is all." I say the last part in a half-whisper, even though they're pretty far ahead.

"Actually," Johnny pauses a moment. "I wasn't sure if I should say anything to you, but"—he chuckles—"I knew I would. He admitted that it's been really hard—for both of them. But coming up to visit you two, all of us, has shown them what's significant. What really matters is that they have each other."

"God, that's a relief," I sigh and feel my shoulders relax. "Sometimes you men are so hard to crack open to let the hurt out—especially with each other."

"You're telling *me!*"

"There are no breaks," Ruby shouts from the head of the line. "Until we pull these bloody things ashore!"

I overhear her asking Ryan if there have been arrangements for them to be *properly escorted back to Captain Fred's establishment*, or if she's expected to paddle that *dreadful excuse for a boat all the way back?* Ryan laughs.

Since a kayak can float on very shallow water, we're keeping close to the shore; it also keeps us out of the comings and goings of all the bigger boats that are zooming around further out. Being able to look the island over from here, it's easy to see how solid it is, all the different stone ledges and stunning outcroppings. Some of the cliffs have pine trees growing on them that seem to be holding on for dear life! Clouds of sea gulls swoop down and then soar up into the brilliant afternoon sky in mysterious formations that make you wonder how they don't all bash into one another.

We round a bend in the shoreline and a long expanse of sandy beach appears, but it *also* appears that we're not the only ones who had a picnic at the beach in mind. There are clusters of umbrellas with people, kids and dogs scattered up and down the length of the beach. Ruby and Ryan, who are still in the lead, slow down and then we all do, so that now we're alongside one another to discuss the situation of the beaches over-crowding.

"You sure can tell it's nearly summer," I comment, slightly mesmerized watching a dog leap into the air and perfectly catch a blue Frisbee.

"I suggest we head that way,"—Howard points with his paddle—"There seems to be a tiny island over there and I don't see anyone on it—yet."

"Let's make a mad dash for it, shall we?" Ruby says re-tying her hat. "Perhaps you can pick it up a bit back there, hmmm darlings?" She pokes Ryan with her paddle.

"I'm game," Helen adds.

And we're off!

With Madeline Island behind us, we slip across the wide expanse of water toward a clump of rocks with a smattering of trees—perfect. We're once again side-by-side heading toward a small half-circle of sand surrounded on either side by huge boulders, one with a clump of birch trees that are beginning to leaf out. Everyone climbs out and pulls up the kayaks onto the sand, roping them loosely to some rocks. Good thing everyone wore flip-flops or the like.

"Oh, this is lovely, isn't it?" Ruby unfurls the huge gingham red and white checked tablecloth onto the sand. "Will someone lend me a hand—as well as everyone's shoes? This bloody thing will simply *not* cooperate."

Ryan and Helen help by putting one of their fancy sandals on each corner, then we all do the same.

"This is truly grand," Howard says, leaning back on the cloth. "An island all to ourselves."

"Here, darling, would you be a love and open this?" Ruby hands Johnny a bottle and an opener. "That's a special vintage, you know. I was *thrilled* to find white wine with a toad on the label."

Johnny pours a few glugs into the colorful aluminum tumblers we brought and we all raise our cups and clink.

"To the soul of our child," Helen says, looking all around at us. "May it come back again one day." A lone tear slips down Ryan's cheek.

Everyone stops—we glance from Ryan and then back to Helen, unsure of what to do. Then we slowly raise our tumblers up and clink again.

"Good heavens, darling," Ruby says as I plop onto her bed. She closes the door. "I simply couldn't *believe* the queer feeling I got when Helen made that toast, could you?" She stands in front of her armoire's mirror, smoothing down her fitted black jacket and giving her hair a final brush.

"It was a wonderful gesture," I say, standing up. "She seems to have really resilient coping skills. I'd be a wreck for weeks, eat too much chocolate and then—"

"—You'd get cracking—let's be off, shall we?"

Following Ruby down the stairs, I see Rocky sprawled out on top of the cabana bar. He gives us a friendly *meow* and then continues cleaning his rear end. Has he no pride? Ruby heads into the kitchen and I wander down the hallway to see if Helen and Ryan are ready to roll. The human-sized, stained-glass toad at the end of the hall has begun to light up with late afternoon sun. His green eyes always give me the willies—they look so real.

The guest room is empty, so I turn to peek into the library; Helen and Ryan are sitting in the window seat, opposite each other, reading.

"You guys sure you wouldn't rather hang out here?" I ask and move closer into the room. "All we've done all day is haul you hither and yon—you don't *have* to come, you know."

"And miss out on seeing the soon to be famous Toad Hollow?" Helen asks as they stand. "You've got to be kidding."

"Yeah," Ryan adds. "We also have to report back to the *Saundra.*"—Helen jabs him in the ribs—"We have to make sure her dollars are being well spent."

"I think she'll be impressed," I answer and we file down the hallway in search of Ruby. She looks up from the cutting board, then chops a perfect line of cigarettes in two, deftly swipes the ends into the trash bin and slides the severed-cigarettes into her gold cigarette case. She snaps it closed with a *don't ask* look on her face.

Since the temperature can drop as low as fifty-five in the evenings, we take coats and jackets from the doorknobs lining the wall in the kitchen.

I pull the duck out, and drive over to the back porch door where the three of them are standing with their thumbs in the air, hitchhiker-style. I toss caution to the wind, and pick 'em up!

I tap around and in seconds Dean Martin belts out, *Fly Me to the Moon* (their wedding song). I turn us around, hit the gas and we fly down the hill and splash into the lake. I switch on the outboard and head toward Bayfield. The sky is unfurling shades of orange and yellows, a damp air sweeps through my hair, and I shiver.

Passing the ferry packed with people, cars and several big trucks, I click on the mike, "It's a beautiful evening in Bayfield!" Then I honk, and the ferry toots its really LOUD horn back and most everyone onboard sends us a wave. I'll never tire of that.

As the lights of Bayfield begin to come on, I drive up the City Marina boat ramp and head us toward Washington. The streets are busy with folks out looking for a good place to eat or perhaps do some evening shopping. The air is filled with delicious food smells.

I turn onto Tenth and go all the way to the very end. Before turning down the rutted lane, I point to the small wooden sign. It proclaims in happy green letters: Toad Hollow. Along the right side is a toad with a small smile crossing its mouth and if you look close you'll see that this toad is wearing a tiara instead of a crown, like the one at the cottage.

"Those boys," I say and turn down the drive.

It curves off to the right and ends abruptly along-side a freshly painted, white clapboard two-story farmhouse. We climb down the ladder and step toward the wooden stoop.

"Seems rather odd," Ruby says, "Wonder why Alice Anne has all the lights burning? Mustn't mention *that* to your mum."

"Or the music she has blasting—hope the neighbors are far enough away so as not to hear all that cussing. Maybe that's why she has such a potty mouth." We cross the verandah. "That's really weird—Marsha's car is here as well. Maybe she spaced out her breakfast shift earlier this morning or wasn't feeling well."

"Hello?" I call out as we enter the foyer. "I doubt anyone could hear me. Hang on a second."

The wooden floors have been sanded, plastic tarps lie in heaps in the corners of the living room and the smell of fresh paint fills the air. I head into Alice Anne's office and turn off the music, if that's what you'd call it.

Helen and Ryan explore the first floor and just as Ruby and I are about to start up the stairs, we hear the familiar clomp of heavy boots heading down.

"What in the hell is going on here, Alice Anne?" I ask in the most controlled voice I can dig up. "We could hear your music half a mile down the driveway!"

Alice Anne comes all the way down and sits on the bottom step. She pushes her blue-white hair out of her face and shakes her head. She lifts her thick, dark eyebrows several times obviously trying to find the right words.

"Honestly, I think maybe I'm going a little insane here. I came home from taking a jog and Mom's car is parked outside, plain as day, music is going *full-fucking* tilt and for the life of me, I can't find her in the god damn house *anywhere!*"

The sound of a door somewhere opening and then closing echoes to the four of us gathered around Alice Anne. Footsteps cross the kitchen in the back.

"Well, there you are," Marsha says as she comes down the hallway.

She's dressed in jeans with a powder blue hoodie zipped up tight and with her hair all tucked up underneath a ratty old baseball cap. She looks so young. I imagine her at Alice Anne's age raising a child all her own and wonder how in the world she managed.

"I was outside back by the shed admiring the most incredible bird nest—look what I found." She takes Alice Anne's hand and puts something into it and then closes it. "I'm going to head home—ga'night all."

The front screen door bangs closed. Alice Anne unfolds her hand and we peer into it.

"Three robin's eggs?"

Chapter Twelve

May slips by and becomes June, bringing all the glory of summer that comes with—and all those damn tourists too! Everywhere you go, either in town here on the island or over at Bayfield, lines of humans coming and going *and* spending like crazy. That part we like.

Even though it's Monday and we're all normally creating aprons, I've asked everyone to put on their grubs and meet over at Toad Hollow for a crash-clean. We've got to get things together for a pizza and beer open house this Friday.

"Ruby," Sam says tightening her bright yellow headband. "You the only woman I *know* who can wear a leopard outfit like that and not get a lick'ah dirt on you."

"Darling,"—Ruby puts hands on her hips—"Dirt and I simply *don't* see eye to eye—besides—I see no reason fashion can't be a part of your every moment. I only wish I could get Eve out of those dreadful bib-overalls she seems so attached to."

I shake my head, adjust my bra strap and address the small group gathered on the yard facing Toad Hollow's porch. "Thank you all for changing your schedules and meeting over here today. What the—"

A sleek black car polished to a shimmering gloss, purrs up the driveway and then parks behind the duck. Helen and her mother, Saundra, hop out. Well actually, Saundra kind of slithers out.

I wave them over and continue, "There's nothing left as far as any heavy construction to finish up, thank God. We just need to pick up all the crap the guys left behind, and hopefully get the oven running." I check my clipboard and try to read all my notes I made late last night instead of sleeping. "Fill the dumpsters that are parked in the back with all the trash you find, and let me know when they're full—check the basement too. Every floor needs to be swept, windows washed, and make some kind of a list of anything that isn't working properly as you go. We're looking for a relatively quick—overall—tidy job. *Not a* deep cleaning—any questions?"

"Howard and I will get the oven going," Johnny says with a certain man-tool confidence. "And I think we need to figure out the issue of the constantly blowing fuse-box."

"Let's give it a look," Howard says and Johnny and Alice Anne clomp up the porch steps.

"Lilly an 'me," Sam says slinging her bead-fringed bag over a shoulder. "We'll get busy and pull all them plastic paint tarps down from the living room walls, and I bet we can figure out how to run them brooms. You coming, girl?"

Lilly rolls up a potato chip bag, clips a pink clothespin to hold it closed and then tosses it into her black patent leather purse. She moves her bifocals up into her towering do and snaps her head in the direction of the farmhouse. Sam shoots me an *eye rolling* and follows.

"Let's get the lead out, Sam," she says with purpose, and I smile. They start up the stairs and, halfway across the small verandah, Lilly turns and adds, "I put the finishing touches on our costumes for the belly dance tonight—they kick ass!"

Saundra, dressed as if she's out shopping for a new diamond, saunters over. I wonder when was the last time she ate. Her chocolate pants scream, *I have no ass,* and how can she *not* have flabby upper arms? Doesn't *every* woman over a *certain* age? I try to pull down the sleeves of my Rolling Stones T-shirt over mine.

Removing enormous black sunglasses, Saundra smoothes back her perfectly coiffed blonde ponytail. Helen smiles and then the sun shines a little brighter. I can't help but grin back—she's wearing bib-overalls too. Only hers fit a little different.

"We heard you might need a hand," Saundra says, but her blue eyes say something else. Saundra is doing the best she can to reach out—to help. More than anything, I think she wants to belong.

"I think we can find something for these two broads to tackle—follow me."

Alice Anne took my iPod out of the van for background to our day, seeing as she kind of figured I wasn't into her *sound*, if that's what you'd call it. So now great guitar music by Ottmar Liebert is pulsing through the house, setting a nice rhythm.

Sam and Lilly manage to fill the dumpsters to overflowing with all the extra stuff they find down in the basement. *Bout a hundred years of crap down there!* She mentions on one of their many trips. *The oven is finally on!* Howard proudly announces. Something about a fuse box more screwed up than he's ever seen—I nod my head and hope for the best.

Johnny pretends to be on *The Price is Right* and shows the small group gathered in the kitchen all the amazing things this oven can do to make life *soooooooo much easier.* He gets applause when he's finished, but I'm not sold on the concept of roasting marshmallows over the *nice big blue flame.* Hmmm—too late for more insurance?

"Where in heaven's name should we have our belly dancing performance?"—Ruby asks me as I hand her a light bulb—"It would be the perfect entertainment for the event, don't you think? To be quite honest, however, I'm not sure this area is ready for such an onslaught of culture."

"Ruby—you don't have to shine up a burnt-out light bulb—good grief, give that to me. I think a belly dance jam session will be just the ticket to loosening up folk's checkbooks. That and the beer should round things out about right."

"Perhaps out here then, for the *dance-jam*, darling?" Ruby motions toward the front porch. "We could use this area as a stage. Perhaps Howard could install some temporary lighting, and then there's the need of some sort of curtain. You know—to part *grandly* for the splashy opening number and all—what?"

"I'm not so sure, now that I think about this." I follow her out onto the porch. "I wonder; how carried away do we want to get. It *is* a pizza and beer thing, after all."

The white US mail van comes rumbling up the drive, pulling up to the side of the house. An older gentleman steps out and heads over with a bundle in his hand. I say gentleman, because this guy's got a smart little red bow tie holding his collar in place, and round gold wire-rimmed glasses glint in the morning sun.

"Top of the morning, ladies," he brightly says and gives his cap a friendly tip. "Don't normally bring up the mail in person, though the pleasure's all mine." He gives Ruby a coy wink. "Looks like those hoodlums got to your mail box. It's been smashed flat, sorry to say."

His Midwestern accent is too charming. I notice a bit of egg stuck in his white goatee, and bet there's no wife at home to wipe it away. I swipe at the corner of my mouth and then he does the same—works every time. I reach out and take the hefty collection of letters and magazines.

"Thanks—you coming this Friday for the free pizza and beer?"

"Saw the posters all over town," he chuckles. "I remember hearing about Toad Hollow Tavern from my father, noticed you've named this place Toad Hollow. I've always been partial to toads."

"*Really*—how fascinating," Ruby dramatically exclaims and I shake my head. "I, for one, find them such *divine* little amphibians, don't you agree, Eve?"

"Well—hope to see you there," I say. "I'd be grateful if you'd spread the word!"

"It'd be my pleasure—you ladies have nice day, now."

With another tip of his hat, he quickly disappears into his van; as it trundles away, he taps his horn several times, waving as he goes.

Sam and I are unloading my van up by the barn. The hill is still muddy from the last rain and so steep I am afraid to park down by the boathouse. I've gotten stuck down there before after a spring rain.

"All I know," Sam says, taking an armful of fabric bolts. "Is that you been messin' 'round with things you don't know the first thing 'bout—and girrrl—you best watch your step. Hormones all crazy like yours—look what you already brought back from the other side."

"What are you *talking* about," I ask as we head down the path, carrying armloads of possibilities as I like to think of these fabrics. "Here I am innocently cleaning the duck, and *he* shows up—all sexy looking and..."

Sam stops dead at the foot of the boathouse stairs, I nearly slam into her. She turns and looks me in the eye. "It's time you realize something. Eve Moss. This land—you and Ruby are livin' right on top of a spiritually sacred place that will always belong to the Ojibwa—*always.*"

"But there are only cottages here and...there *is* that Indian graveyard."

"*Child*—I have purposely kept my big 'ol mouth shut on this here subject, but it's time you know. Jus' like you can't own the wind, the earth is pretty much the same. This island will forever be theirs in spirit."

"But—this is now and...God... I feel so guilty. Wait a minute. Leandre was from Niger. He wasn't Ojibwa."

"All I can see is that *here,*" Sam motions around us, "There's this *opportunity* for things to come through—so you be careful, is all."

The boathouse screen door slams closed. "Careful is right!" Ruby quips from above us, then hangs her head over the balcony. "If you two aren't more careful, you're going to miss out on Howard's *Taco Tuesday*—now get up here and let's dine, shall we?"

The door slams and we hear her order everyone to *bloody well put it to rest—grub's on!*

"Did you remember, darling—to ring up the boys?" Ruby asks as we file down the stairs. She flings her fringed shawl over one shoulder; Rocky leaps up into the air to paw at it.

"Yep, Howard found his pipe wrench and will bring it along. Hey—Rocky, watch it there, buster. You get stuck in that fancy-schmancy fringe and you're in big trouble!"

"Trouble's *my* middle name," Ruby says. "Since you simply *insisted* I don a casual-donation look for our Toad Hollow Croak-Off, I *had* to top it off with this silk shawl. Rocky knows fashion sense when he sees it."

"Lilly and Sam sure went overboard with these," I hold up an apron. "Who wouldn't want one covered with grinning, pregnant toads wearing bright red lips?"

"I should think that making it kind of bib-style," Ruby takes it from me. "It has a practical appeal to those who are messier cooks. Me—I never soil my apron."

"No, you don't," I grab it out of her paws and toss it, along with the whole pile, into an IGA sack. "Me, I usually have telling blobs all down my front."

"And every stain, a lovely story!" She grins. "There they are—"

Howard and Johnny peek into the kitchen. I notice that Johnny's shaved all his facial hair off. Now he looks like a slightly older Johnny Depp, since he's grown out his hair a bit more too, it's nearly down to his shoulders. They're wearing tight black T-shirts with the word *Staff* stretched across their chests. A lock of Howard's silver hair flops into his eyes and Johnny pushes it aside, their eyes lock briefly. I've watched Johnny do that for a while and it still makes me look away. As if I've witnessed something terribly personal.

"Let's head over to Bayfield!" I elbow my bag onto my shoulder, load up the boys' and Ruby's arms with sacks, and we parade out the door, toward the duck.

We climb on board, passing things hand-to-hand as everyone goes up the ladder. I rev the duck to life, and down the hill we head. After we splash into the lake and I've switched to outboard, I click on the mike, "It's Friday night—Toad Hollow's hopping, and you're invited!" The pontoon boat passing by toots its horn, and everyone aboard waves. I toot back and hit the gas. With any luck, we may make enough cash tonight to move forward. Sure as hell hope so.

"There, that's the last bloody one," Ruby says with a huff, and climbs down the ladder. "Oh, the porch—or rather—*stage* looks simply divine."

"Howard and Alice Anne rigged the curtains," I point out. "And those white lights wrapped around every pole are compliments of Lilly. She happened to have a case of white lights in a corner of her basement."

"Oh dear—should we be alarmed?" Ruby half-whispers. "Poor darling, she simply can't *resist* a good bargain—then again, who bloody well can?"

"Sam's been popping in on her unannounced," I mention as we head up the porch stairs. "She hasn't seen anything out of the ordinary upstairs—yet."

We're hoping that Lilly the *thrift-sale junkie* can make it through the summer's endless yard sales without re-filling up her lovely home. We'll see.

Since we did use the words *free pizza and beer* and the fact that there are a lot of folks around vacationing in Bayfield as well as on the island, the yard is filling up with cars, vans, SUVs and even a teal pick-up truck with a vintage Airstream in tow. Folks are mingling around, slugging down Nut Brown Ale, donated by the South Shore Brewery in Ashland. Ruby is taking groups around the facility for an *informational tour* as she's billing it. One can only imagine.

Helen and Ryan have friends who play in a jazz band in Duluth, so we have a marimba, French horn, acoustic guitar and a violinist. The three guys have long dreadlocks. I don't get that look on white people, honestly, so weird to me. The gal playing the beautiful melody on the marimba is wearing a peasant blouse that's showing more cleavage than I really think legal. Hope her *girls* stay in there. I'm not in the mood for a riot.

Alice Anne, looking *almost* feminine in her toad apron over a simple summer dress, makes a beeline toward me. The look on her face is not good, or maybe it's the clunky black boots. Why she doesn't tie those laces is beyond me.

"You would not *fucking*—"

—I clamp my hand over her mouth as several heads swing our direction. I toss them a shrug and grin back; they look away.

"You're going to have to *edit!*" I caution tight-lipped with my eyes right smack next to hers. That is some eye-liner she's got on. "Got it? Think *G-rating* and try taking some deep breaths. You're going to blow a gasket—now what's the deal?"

"The God Da—the oven has completely blown out an entire circuit and so—of course—there's been no juice to the chest freezer in the basement, and though the pizzas are still frozen—we can't *bake them!* A gas stove with an electric oven? No wonder the piece of shit was free!"

"Oh shit," I say as a woman I recognize heads over.

"Hello, Eve," Sally Hufferston says and gives me a gentle hug. "I couldn't help overhearing..."—I squint my eyes in Alice Anne's direction—"I've got an idea."

Sally gets on her cell phone and before you can say *We're up blankedy-blank creek without a fricking paddle,* Howard and Johnny come ambling through the now crowded front yard with tray after tray of rectangle-shaped pizzas. The delicious fragrance of oregano, garlic, melted cheese and fresh yeasty dough is working its magic. Sally and her husband John, own Ethel's; a local pizzeria and she sits on the Toad Hollow board and now I have yet another person to add to my list of *those I owe.*

"Testing. Um, hi and welcome to Toad Hollow. As most of you know, I'm Frank Maggio, Mayor of Bayfield." The audience claps and Sam rips off one of her ear-piercing whistles. "We in Bayfield, as well as in the surrounding communities are proud to welcome the establishment of Toad Hollow. A place of safety and—as founder Eve Moss explained to me earlier—a place for second chances."

I hand him one of my old hair-cutting shears. He dramatically snips through the yellow ribbon and then turns back toward the loudly applauding crowd.

"Ladies and gentlemen," the mayor says into the mike. "It gives me great pleasure to introduce Eve Moss, co-founder as well as president of Toad Hollow."

A big round of clapping, and not only Sam, but also Sally, and—you're not going to believe this, Saundra too—are blowing shrill whistles my way. I take the mike and walk up several steps, then several more, and turn to face the audience gathered in a big knot around the base of the porch.

Howard and Johnny stand shoulder-to-shoulder, smiling my way. Sam, Lilly, Alice Anne, Bonnie and of course, Ruby, all send me encouragement. Saundra has an arm draped over Helen's shoulder. I see tenderness in people's eyes, as well as hope.

I clear my throat, and for the briefest moment I'm back in the orphanage—Sister Patty Kay is taking my baby away for what I thought was forever. I was one of the lucky ones. If I can give a few women a shot, it'll be worth it.

"Thank you, Mayor," I nod his direction and he nods back. "I—ah—I can't tell you how important this moment is for me," I wipe away a tear, clear my throat and stand tall. "When I was a young girl...seventeen to be exact...I thought I knew what I was doing. *Thought.* But honestly...what do you know when you're *seventeen!*" The crowd laughs; Alice Anne shakes her head, Helen stares at me with something like awe.

"Anyway, I ended up pregnant and alone and without *any* choices. None. I know that now-a-days we know a lot more about... well, about how to *not* get pregnant—but you know what? Girls are *still* getting pregnant and they need a place where they can feel supported—safe. Toad Hollow is that place. I admit I don't have *all* the answers and there are difficult decisions to be made. But here— here you can weigh your options and choose what *you think* is best for your baby." I look out at all the expectant faces.

"Luckily for me," I give Helen and Saundra a glance; Ruby's eyes are glistening. "I was able to be reunited with my daughter after many, many years of wondering if I'd done the right thing giving my little girl up for adoption. I did." I take a deep breath and realize how grateful I am to be right here—right now.

"Thank you so much for being a part of this, for helping me make *my* dream come true." Big applause. "Seeing this is a fund-raiser—please get those checkbooks and credit cards out! If you have any items you wish to donate, we have a list of things we are still in need of, and all you have to do is contact,"—I motion for Alice Anne to come over—"Alice Anne Kelven, the Director of Toad Hollow." Alice Anne waves to the crowd. "Now—we've got a little number planned for you all—but I'm thinking that the *Fabulous Ladies of the Lake* will look even *more* fabulous if you crack open another beer while we get things set-up!"

With Lilly up front, the four of us (Helen joins in too) do more belly dancing numbers than we'd planned. Since we only know the moves for three numbers—but the crowd demands an encore—we just do the second one over a couple of times. No one is the wiser, and the cheering and clapping keep us swaying to the beat. The jazz band improvises with the music Lilly brought and I'm silently praying to the over-forty-belly-dancing-Goddess that no one is recording our craziness. I sure as hell hope not anyway.

"There's a man on the edge of the roof!" someone yells over the music.

Lilly yanks the cord on her boom box and the jazz band falls quiet. The crowd races over to the side of the house—everyone looking up. We all move down the porch stairs and join in.

"It's that man we saw the other night!" Johnny yells in my ear so loud I smack him on the arm. "Sorry," he says and rubs it.

Alice Anne is suddenly by my side. "It's my mom, it's my mom and she's gone completely off the *fucking deep end!"*

I grab her by the hand and we fly up the porch stairs.

"C'mon!"

CHAPTER THIRTEEN

On the second floor landing I stop suddenly and turn to face Alice Anne. "We have to be calm, we have to focus on her safety. Do you understand?" I look deep into her terrified eyes.

"Christ, shit like this never happened in ER even when I worked *full moons!*"

"Ruby's calling for an ambulance. Which window did she climb out of, do you think?"

"Has to be from my third-floor apartment—the patio windows in my living room."

We move down the hallway and head up her steep stairway. At the top I scan the room and see a short-haired wig tossed onto the black kitchen table seeming oddly out of place.

Alice Anne picks it up. "She's playing like she's—my dad?" She says in a strange voice. "We have to save her—from herself. Christ."

Alice Anne looks at me with tears streaming down her face and through the white punked-out hair and all the makeup, I see the little girl—scared as hell.

"Show me the window—now!" I say in a controlled voice. Alice Anne leads us down a dark hallway that opens up to a long room with windows and a balcony on the right. The doors are wide open; the sheers flanking either side are dancing in the wind.

"Okay," I put my hands on her shoulders and look her in the eye. "I'm going to try and talk her down. I think it best it's me and not you—alright? Besides—for some weird reason, I'm not afraid of heights."

"Hurry!" Alice Anne whispers as I walk onto the balcony. The crowd three stories down is hushed and expectant. I see the outline of Marsha standing on the edge of the roof about five feet from the small deck. Dressed in a white shirt that's glowing in the moonlight, her hair flutters in the wind and she turns toward me.

"I can't get him out any more," Marsha says matter-of-factly. Her tears glint in the moon's glow as they slide down her cheeks.

She's inches toward the edge, her bare feet on this pitched roof, with nothing but air between her and the yard below.

"Who honey? Who can't you get out?" I know you have to keep a person in this kind of danger talking. My heart is slamming against my chest. I have to get this right.

"Don, my husband. He won't get out of my head and I *see* him too—he's in my mirror."

Shit. "Listen Marsha, listen to me," I say softly and move toward her ever-so-slowly. "Don's gone—you said so yourself—that he left you and Alice Anne right after she was born—remember? Sure, you remember. He up and disappeared."

"No!" Marsha yells and scares the crap out of me so that I jump. "He...he never left. Don't you know what *happened*?"

Marsha's voice has become younger somehow—childish—and I have to treat her that way. I have to get through to her and convince her to move closer to the deck, then I can make a grab for her and pull her back off this fucking roof.

I slowly make my way closer to her. "Tell me what happened, Marsha, come here and I'll listen. I want to know what happened. I do."

I figure it's now or never—from the deck I move quickly over to Marsha. She turns to me with a look of fright on her face. I pick her up around the waist and move like the wind back to the balcony and as I do I feel someone's strong arms around me.

In seconds we're standing in the living room. Alice Anne takes her mother into her arms and they cry. I hear the yelps and applause as well as the wail of a siren. I lock the patio door shut. I gently touch the hugging women, then leave them.

The boys suggested we come over to their place. The wine is flowing and our nerves are shot.

"Who in the *world* would have thought," I say for the billionth time. "That she could have *done* such a thing—almost done—or did—whatever."

"Actually," Ryan says as he continues to rifle through his file-box. "It's not *that* unusual for the survivor of a suicide, to invent another personality in order to cope with reality or the reality they're hoping for—remember Sybil?"

"So Marsha's left with Alice Anne by this man with a mustache—left as in he *killed* himself?"

"I found it!" Ryan says as he opens a yellowed file. Clippings and photos fall to the floor. He reads aloud; "A young woman, who recently gave birth, has been temporarily institutionalized due to intense trauma brought on by the apparent suicide of her husband. They had been married only about a year, a next-door neighbor explained, such a happy couple, kept to themselves mostly. But my goodness—when the authorities were removing—Don's body— I've never heard such wailing. I'll never forget it—never. Poor woman."

Ryan scans the article to the end. "I guess the reason it ended up in this file is because Don was reported missing by his probation officer—he had actually been dead over a *week*. Marsha had kept Don's body right in their bed where he died of an overdose. The autopsy revealed his stomach held a combination of cough medicine with codeine in it, and over-the-counter sleeping pills. A *lot* of sleeping pills—she kept him in their bed!"

We sit back in our chairs as though being hit by a blast—
imagining what a horrible tragedy Marsha must have suffered. A
newborn baby bringing all that hope and need into their world,
then Don wanting to get the hell out of it. It's so hard not to pass
judgment on someone committing suicide. How can you not be
pissed? Seems so out of place to even *have* this thought—but had
Don not been able to actually *kill* himself, I'd like to ring his neck.

"Oh, dear heavens," Ruby gasps. "It's mustache man." She
offers the picture she picked up from the floor to me.

"I don't get it," Johnny comments as he fills my trembling
glass. "Why *now,* what happened to set her off on this crazy gig of
dressing up like him—and why'd she try to *jump?*"

"And thank God she *didn't!*" I add and everyone nods, then sips
for strength. I study the eerie photo of Don, looking so much like
Marsha, dressed as Don. "Part of Marsha *wanted* to more or less cut
him out of her. God, talk about a complicated psychosis."

"I bloody well hope,"—Ruby lets the file fall to the floor—
"Perhaps *now* Marsha can accept the fact that it wasn't *her* fault he
killed himself and begin to *finally*—after all this time—somehow
find some peace."

"As they were taking Marsha away in the ambulance," I say,
"she turned and asked me to watch over Alice Anne. At least now,
finally her daughter can know the truth about her dad. He never
abandoned them—then again—I guess—she did."

"Now *there's* a young woman," Ruby says with just the slightest
slur. "Who doesn't seem to need much of anything in the ways of
looking after—why, did you see the way she handled that man who
was about to take some photos, some young man from the local
paper?"

"I only hope," I reply slumping into the boys' cushy chair. "That
he doesn't sue *and* that he's not planning on being a dad one day..."

The boys cross their legs.

CHAPTER FOURTEEN

"**M**y *land,*" Sam comments with emotion, taking the apron parts from me. "Who would'a thought we'd make all that cash for the Hollow—what a night!"

"To think that Helen and Ryan came here last weekend to *relax!*" I say from my work table, zooming my electric shears through an art deco-design stack of fabric.

"It does seem, darling," Ruby regards me over her bifocals, eyebrows skyward. "That perhaps you've found your calling—or rather *it's* found *you.*"

"My calling?"

Ruby sets down the apron she was sewing buttons onto and heads to the kitchen area. Pulling over a stool, she reaches up and turns down the music and then resumes her work. "Second chances—remember? *That's* your calling and I refuse to compete with that bloody platform boom-box whatcha call it—*really.*"

"Sorry. I do remember us chatting about that," I say reaching up and re-tucking my escaping curls under a polka dot headband. "Poor Marsha though, yet if she's lucky, she should be out of that institution pretty quick. They do kind of freak out when you try and—you know—*jump off the third floor.*"

"You nearly give us all a heart attack!" Sam says for the umpteenth time. "Where you get off playin' the hero is—well now, *that's crazy!*" Sam floors her sewing machine pedal for emphasis.

"And to think her husband's been more or less haunting her this whole time," Ruby says with sadness. "People that kill themselves have no *idea* the human wreckage they leave behind."

"I imagine there are many, *many* people in the world who live in some kind of a self-created prison," Lilly adds in a brittle voice." Such a shame most of us have no idea we each create our own reality." Lilly plops her glasses down onto her nose as if that should answer that.

"You go, Lilly!" Johnny chides. "I swear, sometimes you go so deep into things it makes my head spin."

"Deep is what we do!" Sam says with a pride I admire. "We all in this room are *old* souls, old as the hills of this island. I believe we chose this time and this place to be together again and the way I see it—we all been put here for a reason—and I agree with Miss Ruby, that we're here to help folks get that second chance in life. Least ways, find some peace of mind while here."

"I like that," I try it on somewhere deep in my brain. "Now who the hell has seen my..."—Ruby hands me the chalk—"I keep losing that damn thing, thank you."

Running the chalk around the outline of this apron pattern, the feel of the soft fabric under my hands, I feel a peacefulness sweep over me. Odd, but doing this, making these pretty, silly aprons is oddly fulfilling. I felt this way when I worked on my hair clients, but it wasn't such a group effort, of course. I mean, this is a team thing and I think it suits me at this point in life. The rhythm is the best part.

Ryan, meanwhile, has become fascinated with Marsha's case, and how it's morphed into this calamity of split personalities; suicide leading to attempted suicide. But I'm afraid there's going to be some kind of fallout as far as Toad Hollow is concerned. Maybe if we grab the bull by the horns and turn it around.

"Lilly?" I ask when she looks up from her machine. "Would you take over cutting for awhile? I have some phone calls to make."

Ruby follows me back to the office. "What *is* it, darling?" Ruby closes the door behind us, and Howard looks up from the computer. "You've that *look* in your eye."

"Remember that woman from the radio station contacting us a while back?"

Ruby sighs and leans onto my desk. "Oh heavens."

"Hand me that, darling," Ruby points to her favorite copper pan. "Thank you. And exactly how long must I be standing here by the cooker with absolutely *no* wine—it's simply a sin, *really*."

"Sorry—I've been distracted all day long."

I root around in our over-packed fridge and haul out a dark brown wine bottle; and after some fussing I manage to pull its old cork. I carry over the green-painted stool and step up to have a peek at all the different stemware. What I really like is that there are hardly any two of a kind. It's like a cupboard of jewels.

There are four tall goblets that have the same intricate diamond pattern, each a different color. Deep red, dark blue-black, yellow and one that's clear. I decide blue and yellow for tonight.

We clink our freshly-filled goblets and the most wonderful musical *pling* happens, so we do one more.

"I believe Billie is skipping about."

"Oh shoot, I forget those are LP records and old ones at that."

The two-story living room still takes me by surprise. The French doors are open to the evening breeze; a small fire snaps in the grate, its flames softly illuminate the river rock chimney. I move to the hi-fi crouched in an alcove under the stairs.

The wooden cabinet gleams in the firelight, the built-in speakers on either side with their sparkly material are timeless. Nothing sounds like this thing. I lift the middle section up and there's the turntable as well as a radio. I move the needle to the next song and

God Bless the Child begins. I sometimes forget you have to wait for the thing to warm up before you can hear anything. Tubes.

Reminds me of mine—tubes, I mean. Here I am nearly forty-eight and I have these old tubes filled with eggs sorely past their prime. I wonder what past their prime *sperm* is called. Poor swimmers?

As I lower the top down I spy a small, round picture hanging next to an oval mirror. I doubt I'll ever stop discovering something new in this cottage; it's full of stuff going back to when Ed's great-grand parents lived here. Leaning in closer, I see it's of Ruby and her late husband, Ed. They're sitting out on our porch with another couple I don't recognize; not surprising as she'd been coming up here for *years* before we even became friends.

Then I have a closer look and realize it's Charlie with his wife. She died of lung cancer, never smoked a day in her life. I remember when Charlie shared with us that he honestly felt he'd killed her with his secondhand smoke. Imagine.

Rocky leaps on top of the stereo—thankfully the record doesn't skip. He drops a dark clump and leaps away.

"Hey Ruby, will you bring the vegetable tongs? Thanks, buddy!" I mention to Rocky who is happily trotting back into the kitchen, his big gray tail snapping high.

"I can still taste the curry," I say as a smoke ring flips top to bottom over and over up into the sky. I give the flowered pillow a good punching and then settle back to consider the sun preparing for its dramatic descent into the lake.

"Isn't it a *lovely* flavor?" Ruby adds. "Thank *heavens* I was able to secure a case of coconut milk from Lori's grocery store in La Pointe. Why—when I asked the proprietress to order it, she gave me the most revealing grin."

"What do you mean, *revealing*? We're talking coconut milk here."

"She told me how much she loves to cook with it as well, and to be honest, our supper of wild rice and shrimp curry was *her* recipe."

"Before your daring roof-top rescue, earlier at the pizza party part, I couldn't help but notice you chatting with that ego-centric reporter from Duluth—what is that dreadful column he writes? No matter, I only hope you were able to get the Hollow a mention."

"He assured me he'd run an editorial on our efforts," I sigh. "But I could tell when I explained the basic premise—he really wasn't all that interested. Not enough oomph."

"How dreadful. Anyways—Sam and Lilly were filling me in on the latest over at Al's Place, considering Marsha may be detained a time and we're heading into full-tilt tourist season—who will wait tables for Bonnie?"

"I see a man," I say as I hold my hands to my temples. "There's a long, long ponytail involved and birdhouses and a pink trailer and..."

"Actually darling, he's flown the coop." Ruby dramatically sighs. "His daughter, I forget her name, owns a bakery called Grateful Bread—her husband's taken to drinking all the profits."

"Sounds all too familiar."

"Tragic, really. Charlie's gone down to see if he can help put things right—and here's the kicker."

"Gone where?"

"You're ruining my story—honestly, Eve. He's in Vanceburg. That divine little town along the Hay River, you know the one."

"Right. We ate at some place called Artie's or something once."

"*Exactly*," Ruby adjusts her bracelets and admires her latest nail job drawing out the drama until it stretches thin.

"And so?"

"Apparently he's shown an interest in that hussy, Ava Emerson, who owns Artie's."

"Funny," I say looking at her sideways. "I had the feeling that somehow you two would end up together, if not in the same place, well, at least—"

"—Eve Moss, you underestimate me!" Ruby takes a sip of wine and then settles back. "Why—if I'd the mind—I could have any *bloke* I chose. Even that child—Pringles! But all that comes with it is simply not something I'm interested in. Perhaps when I'm older."

I chuckle and she smacks my arm. "Sorry. You guys just seemed, I don't know, *right* for one another."

"Oh, for heaven's sake, darling," Ruby sighs. "You know—I wonder if you don't worry things a bit too much—hmmm?"

I reflect on this. "I would say, on a scale of one to ten, I worry about anything and everything—minor or major—at probably a *ten,* maybe eleven—most of the time."

"You need to learn to be *present.* Try it right now. Look *way* up into this lovely sky and see all the amazing colors and know that *this* moment is what truly counts."

I imagine myself standing in the loft, peering down into the island-model, seeing two miniature ladies out on a dock. I wonder, would I look better as a mini-me if my hair were longer?

Not so red?

CHAPTER FIFTEEN

Several weeks have crept across the calendar. I'm not sure why I feel this way, but it's as though something strange is coming; there's a tightness in my gut I can't seem to quiet. Probably the after affects of all the excitement or my mind pre-worrying something that hasn't even materialized yet, crazy, I know. The crew has left for the day, Ruby's upstairs taking a long, hot bath, and then we're going to make Baked Manicotti with the boys—that's the plan anyway.

Ever since the Toad Hollow grand opening and, of course, Marsha's debut as a roof-jumper, I've been getting more and more email. We did manage to land a really great article in the Duluth News Tribune and then—it went viral! This is according to Howard—Mister Computer Man. Howard created a separate web site for Toad Hollow, which is linked to Ruby's Aprons too. So I suppose that's how this flood of email started.

I'm in the middle of re-thinking our focus for the Hollow, as we're all referring to it now, not only is it a place for pregnant women in crisis, but somehow I want to make it a retreat where women of all ages who have given up their babies can come and talk with others in the same situation. Not everyone, for whatever reason, can find their children later in life. Talking about it might help and I don't want to leave out the children. What about them? This needs to be about both sides. Then there are the men that planted the seed—what have I gotten myself into?

Oh—and Alice Anne has asked us to stop using her full name—too many memories I guess. She's now officially Ali. I like it, suits her better. But I keep forgetting, and then I get the *look.*

Pandora selected William Ackerman so he's softly playing on my computer, the quality's not the greatest, but his guitar strumming is so nice. Rocky is lounging next to me, but his tail keeps flopping onto my keyboard, so I push him over ever-so-carefully.

Now to my inbox. I don't normally get all that much personal email, so I've been ignoring it until I get the web orders printed for the crew. Yesterday, when I opened my mail, there were all these notes from women all over, more or less wanting to tell me that they too had a baby early on in life.

Dear Eve,

My name is Belinda, I'm fifty-five, and have a wonderful family. Great kids and a husband I love. But years and years ago, when I was sixteen, I got pregnant. My family didn't have two pennies to rub together and I wasn't even in the eleventh grade yet! So off to my Aunt's I went, in order not to embarrass my family. I gave my little boy away and to this day, not a moment goes by when I don't wonder about him. But I know that if my family found out, it would just ruin everything. Do you have any advice?

Confidentially yours, Belinda

I roll my cursor around and open another one.

Dear Ms. Moss,

I can't tell you how much I've enjoyed perusing your Toad Hollow web-site as well as visiting Ruby's Aprons. What a busy woman you are! Years ago, when I was a freshman in college, I found myself with child. Since my career path was pre-ordained (both of my parents were highly successful corporate attorneys) I had no other choice than to give the baby away. Presently I am searching to find her, but I continue to hit countless roadblocks. From closed files to missing documents to legal snafus that even in my position (I'm on the legal team for Target Corp.) I can't seem to break through. Could you possibly share your experience of how you were able to locate your child? I'm desperate. I beg you, please feel free to call me anytime, day or night.

Sincerely,
Ms. Kristy Lewison.

Sighing, I think back to the moment I first heard that Helen (who I had originally named Amy, not uncommon for adoptive parents to change the name) was first of all—alive—and then living so damn close. I'm learning that my situation is not what a lot of women are finding, at least not those reaching out to me.

I'm wondering whether I'm over my head. I would love to help *everyone*, but what can I do? It's almost as if people, for one reason or another, aren't able to even *try* to find their kids—seems they have this need to share their pain. But not everyone can physically get to the Hollow.

I honestly know that feeling and the need to share, I do. My computer's email sends out that obnoxious tone-thing again and I read the subject line; *Would love to do a radio interview.* I open up the note and read the lively font:

Hey Eve!
I produce and host a weekly advice program for KAXE Public Radio in Grand Rapids (Minnesota, not Michigan)! I'd love to do a phone interview sometime for our Over the Fence show. We stream live on the Internet and have begun to notice a growing audience of mostly women calling and emailing during the program, from all over the country! A listener alerted me to your Toad Hollow endeavor and great interview in the Duluth Paper and, well, here I am! Contact me and let's set something up soon, Thanks!

Holly Hudson
Outreach Producer
KAXE - Northern Community Radio

While tapping out a response, I nearly fly out of my skin as the closet door snaps open. Ruby appears as if by magic, but actually she had taken the old secret passageway from the cottage—saves time and you needn't go outside.

"You ever hear of knocking? You about gave me a heart attack!"

"Hello there, darling," Ruby bustles into the office and plunks down a green satchel. "It's well past quitting time—you simply must be *famished* after that grueling belly dance class Lilly put us through."

"I think she was expecting to win some awards at the Hollow's opening—I'm not so sure we'll be taking it on the road as Sam suggested. I'm just glad it was pretty dim up there, seeing as the electricity went wacky."

Ruby has set up a small array of cheese and crackers and is busy slicing up a beautiful loaf of bread that Helen and Ryan gave us.

"Iced tea, darling?" Ruby pours from an antique blue quart jar into small juice glasses covered with red roosters. She hands me one and we clink. "I popped the Brie into the oven—here, have a sliver on this divine bread."

"What could be more heavenly?" I ask as the savory Brie and sourdough bread send me. "Howard was right in that we're getting a ton of email from women who gave up their kids, but I just got this offer for a radio interview—"

"—That must be the lovely Holly Hudson." Ruby gives me a sly look. "Actually it was Saundra—divine woman—who heated things up to a proper boil. You'd mentioned it yourself and I simply connected the dots. So to speak."

"I'll have to thank her, because in all honesty, I think going on the air and giving these women a place to chat, or at least to tune in to, could be a really huge help."

"The beauty of it," Ruby offers, obviously warming to the idea. "Is that this way, all those baby boomers who've been in such misery, carrying around the wonder about their secret love child, can finally talk freely about it and *no one's* the wiser."

"I know that Oprah has done tons of shows on this topic," I say. "But I'm sure that all over this area of the Midwest, it's been more difficult. I mean, when everyone knows you, how can you share something that could be really painful, without being judged by your neighbors? Let alone your own family."

"Such a noble cause—going on the radio—but darling, what in *heaven's name* will you wear?"

"Howard and Johnny are on their way over," I mention hanging up the phone. "Howard's excited to help you with the creation of the manicotti filling and has some beautiful greens to share."

"Would you shred a bit more mozzarella, darling?" Ruby bustles over to the stove. "Mine didn't come out right."

"Sure." Grabbing the cheese grater, I come around the side of the stump table. "All these spicy smells of garlic, oregano and basil cooking in olive oil—the marinara is going to be amazing—I'm so glad we still have some of the tomato sauce that you canned in Eau Claire."

"Come this fall, darling, we'll can our own tomatoes,"—Ruby dips into the Dutch oven, blows on a wooden spoonful, then puts it up to of my lips—"And make it just like your mum did, hmmm?"

"God, that's so *rich*—thanks. Could use a dash more salt, and what's the other flavor I'm getting?"

"Could be celery—why—there they are."

There's a knock on the back door before the boys come bursting into the kitchen, bringing all their fresh-shower smells and giving us each a peck on the cheek. Even though it's early summertime, the nights can still be chilly, so we're all in jeans and soft shirts. Since the humidity is back in full force, my red curls are as stubborn as ever, so I pinned the whole works up with several stir-sticks from Al's Place. And besides, with my hair up and away, I can show off the huge hoop earrings Sam thought I should have.

"We were just talking about you, Howard," I say taking the big white plastic bowl from him. "This is enough salad for ten!"

"I simply *love* bibb lettuce," Ruby says with a sparkle in her eye. "We'll have to add it to our list of things to grow next year—since we only *talked* about gardening this year."

"Where does the time go?" Johnny asks as he swivels on a stool. "Hey—an old friend of ours and his partner, along with another couple, are renting a cottage on the island for a week. Our friend owns a salon in Minneapolis and we used to do a lot of photo-shoots together for some of the local press there, and—"

"—When the two of them get together," Howard jumps in as he hands me several goblets. "I might as well be *invisible*. Talk talk talk." He happily grins, then ruffles Johnny's hair.

"Speaking of," Ruby gives a goblet a good tap. "Just *when* are you going to pour the chef more wine? And if you're going to be tonight's assistant, here, tie this on and let's get cooking!" Howard does as he's told and from the look on his face, he's not sure if the dancing-duck apron is his style.

"I think things in here—are under *their* control," I cock my head toward Howard and Ruby who are fussing with several pans on the stove. "Grab your goblet, Johnny, and let's pull up a window seat in the library."

Johnny and I slink away down the hallway. After opening the window in order to let the late afternoon air in, we sit opposite each other and get cozy among all the toad-covered pillows that crowd this marvelous nook.

"You mentioned earlier," I say, "that you'd spoken with our mutual friend—Tony. But before you say a thing, I really want to clear the air once and for all."

"Eve—you don't have to say—"

—I hold my hand up. "I behaved like a little girl, and to be honest, that's how I felt. I mean, I *was* only a kid of seventeen, younger than that when we first started dating. God, that sounds so foreign—*dating*. I'd say it was more like when the hormones started raging, and we were doing everything we could think of to *not* have sex—" Johnny uncomfortably squirms and I realize I'm getting a little too close to home.

After all, we *both* have memories of sleeping with Tony. Either there's a whole lot of truth to what Sam said about group souls coming back together or the universe is playing an amazing trick on me.

"Anyways," I quickly add. "I think this whole experience is actually pretty amazing. I mean what are the odds that of all the people I end up living next to—it's you!" I take a sip and then look into his handsome face.

"Thank you for saying this," Johnny reaches over and we clink our glasses. "Even though I like to think that we're the sum of our past, sometimes our past is not entirely our own."

"I don't think it ever is—unless you live on an island."

We laugh, talk some more, and then head back into the aromatic kitchen and feast on the most incredible baked manicotti you could ever imagine, thanks to Howard's secret cheese recipe. Eventually the boys, after helping clean up, head home.

The sun has begun to set. Ruby and I, with stuffed-full tummies, give several pillows some serious punching, then lie back on the dock and consider the sky.

"Let's invite the crew, Bonnie and those friends of the boys over for a solstice party. We could start in the speakeasy and end up out here."

"Sounds divine, darling. You know—Sam and I chatted a bit the other morning, when you and Howard were going over the accounts, and she mentioned how our cottage is positioned on some sort of energy something or other. Frankly—as much as I love Sam—don't you think that sometimes things simply happen for no good reason at all?"

I warm to the idea. "The older—make that—the *wiser* I become, the more I'm realizing that just when you think you've got things all figured out—"

"—Fresh *shit* hits the fan—doesn't it?" Ruby says and I have to agree.

I pull Leandre's silver-eye amulet out of my pocket and hold it out in the orange light of the setting sun.

"I saw this in the movie, Harold and Maude," I mention as I sit up. Ruby does the same. "They're both sitting out on a dock and Harold gives Maude a ring. Maude admires it and then, instead of putting it on her finger—she tosses it way out into the pond. Then she says something about—this way she'll always know where it is."

"Maude was the *near perfect* character," Ruby takes the necklace from me. "She lived life to the fullest and when she'd had enough—hang on."—Ruby walks to the shore and then quickly returns—"Wind it around this bloody rock. That way we're not copying the film completely—call it an *artistic interpretation.*"

"Remember—Maude *kills* herself in the end!" I mention, taking the necklace and cool stone from her, knotting it this way and that around it. "I *hated* the ending and would always stop it before that obnoxious Cat Stevens song came on. You know—it just dawned on me that Thelma and Louise stole that entire scene of driving off the cliff—the nerve!"

"When are you going to realize—Eve Moss—that everything that's come to pass, will come to pass again and again? There's no new material to be discovered, only new angles and insights and *voices*—such as ours. Now let's get on with it, shall we?"

Bunching up the tightly-wrapped stone, I stand up and toss the necklace as far out as possible. We hear it hit the water with a satisfying *plop.*

Settling back into the comfort of our end-of-the-dock world of throw pillows, wine and thoughts, I watch the moon as it begins to peek out. I wonder if it's true, that all the stories have been told, time and time again.

Not *this* story!

CHAPTER SIXTEEN

Instead of having a solstice party down in the not-so-secret pro-hibition bar underneath the boathouse, we opt for a Wisconsin grill-out, Madeline Island style up by the cottage. This, according to Ruby, means *real charcoal and not bloody propane gas*! I find myself in the opposing what's-grilling-you argument and miss my instant gas Weber grill like crazy. Besides the dude on the charcoal bag looks pretty sinister if you ask me. Wait a second, he looks just like Howard!

Holly at KAXE is tickled that Ruby and I will be coming to the studio to do an interview. Apparently, most of the interviews are done over the phone—*phoners*—she calls them. But she says that this way she'll be able to ensure the very best voice quality, and I figure I need all the *voice quality* I can grab. Ruby is dying to go shopping for a new *interview outfit* although I keep reminding her it's RADIO!

A track of Liz Story is oozing soft piano around the boathouse. It's June already and the vegetable garden idea has been reconsid-ered—*again.* Sam and Howard were able to get Ed's old rototiller going, and so we're diving into this, *but* with a plan. Sam has been boasting of her green thumb long enough, so I figure it's time to see just exactly what that woman can grow. The rest of us are pretty much going to do as we're told. Should be an interesting afternoon.

"Here you go," I say and hand Sam a slew of apron parts. "We really rushed through *that* order!"

"I'm just itchin'," Sam replies, tucking a long braid into her purple headband. "To go on out into that sunshine and get all them handsome plants in the ground."

"I don't know if I've ever seen Howard so focused," Johnny adds. "I forgot how much that man likes to get his hands dirty. He's still out there getting our plot all tilled up and ready to plant."

Johnny is about to use his beautiful white teeth on a thread—I clear my throat and hand him a pair of shears, for about the billionth time.

"'Tis truly a lovely day to fuss with the earth," Ruby comments from the kitchen. "Now that's peculiar—I thought for *sure* I'd just seen Rocky..."

I can barely hear his muffled meowing. I head over and pull open the fridge door; Rocky gives me an irritated *meow*, then hops down and out as if he always sits in there. His tail stands ramrod straight up, twitching ever-so-slightly at the very tip. I have all I can do to not grab it.

"What wonderful creation did Sam put together in her signature carved wooden bowl?" I ask, putting out heavy white restaurant plates with a bold green stripe.

"Girrrl," Sam says between amps of her sewing machine. "That's some of the best damn spinach leaves I *ever* seen. And when I'm done fixin' up that salad, you all gonna beg me for my hot bacon dressing recipe—but don't even ask. Woman's gotta have a few secrets."

"I know precisely why we shouldn't," Lilly says, peering over her bifocals. "That *particular* woman rarely uses anything even remotely related to a recipe. I've had to take notes while she's in motion and I'll tell you—that's no easy thing to achieve!"

Sam finishes up with her sewing and then hands the lot to Johnny. She clicks off her machine, stretches her arms high over her head, and then comes over to help.

"I jus' need to heat this dressing up in the zapper," Sam says and slams the microwave door closed and then taps the screen. "You know—there was a time that I had my *own* chickens." She slices through hardboiled eggs as if they're butter, then sprinkles them over the salad. "I had *a fine* little coop out back, and they was laying me eggs like there was no tomorrow."

"Why have I this sneaking feeling, darling," Ruby comments, handing out napkins and utensils like she was dealing cards. "That perhaps this story would be more enjoyable *after* our lunch, hmmm?"

"It ain't all that awful," Sam says with a dangerous grin. She pours the hot dressing and begins to toss the salad. "Jus' a big ol' raccoon come in there and rip my hens all to—"

"—Okay!" I hold up my plate like a shield in defense. "Let's leave the rest of the story for dessert then, who wants to slice up this loaf of rosemary bread? Thank you, Lilly. Now then, I realize that you lost your hens and we'll hear all about that later, but—what I'd really like to know is—are they hard to take care of?"

"Oh dear," Ruby mutters.

"Lord no." Sam shakes her head, dishing salad onto Johnny's plate. "All they need is a li'l coop, some water and a good grain. The rest is pretty much pickin' eggs and keepin' out them raccoons—fox can be a problem too—you want some ah these red onions, Lilly? I know they give you the gas something fierce."

Howard comes banging into the boathouse. His tanned, handsome face is full of sunshine and smudged with dirt. There's a faded blue baseball cap holding his silver hair at bay.

"The garden is awaiting," he announces with a slight bow. "I'll just clean up and be with you all in a jiffy." He saunters into the bathroom.

"You *white* folks," Sam chuckles as she hips open the screen door. "You go from being ghost-white all winter to turning browner than me in the summer—it's the *craziest* thing."

The crew clusters on the balcony facing out to the lake. It's such a riot eating out here above the lapping water. Enjoying Sam's spinach salad and Lilly's toasted rosemary-infused bread slathered with butter and honey. I wonder if a coop would be better up by the barn or closer to the house for easy access in the winter.

"Hey Sam," Howard says, "where'd you find all those beautiful plants? Wait until you all see the incredible seedlings she's got packed into the back of her pick-up."

"I always get them at Earth Sense Garden Center in Washburn," Sam states with plant-pride. "They always have such *fine* plants and I jus' love to walk around and admire their grounds."

After we finish our sunshine-filled salads, Johnny comes over, stacking everyone's plate onto his. Howard follows him back into the boathouse and the familiar sounds of dish-washing echoes around us. We ladies are busy rummaging around in our purses and handbags; Lilly unfurls a Bar-B-Q potato chip bag and commences to crunch, while the three of us light up our sawed-in-half cigarettes. Sam gets a few more puffs, seeing as she's stuck on her long, thin cigarillos. Wonder if Virginia Slims makes a *longer* model?

In no time at all, I pass around the orange ashtray, marveling at the array of lipstick-colored butts in it. Lilly leads us in a few yoga moves (for proper digestion) and we end the mini-session with my favorite—Mountain Pose.

A quick tidy of the kitchen and then we file up the path toward the barn. The flower boxes underneath the cottage windows on the second floor are bursting with red and white petunias, their long flowered vines swinging in the breeze like long, curly hair.

Ruby and I had hung out laundry earlier, now it's flapping and dancing in the wind. I spy Rocky's shadow leaping behind a teal sheet. Both of the clothesline poles have blue and pink clematis vines slinking up around them, one vine has begun to wrap around a line, heading right for my bra. I swear they grow overnight.

Reminds me of that show, Mutual of Omaha's Wild Kingdom. Mom, Dad and I all clustered around the TV, a freshly made Jeno's pizza hot from the oven. All the stuff we learned about animals and nature and sometimes there were time-lapse shots of plants growing from nothing into, well, whatever they were supposed to end up being. Nature's something beyond amazing.

"Sam, darling," Ruby stops and turns to face her. "These delphiniums," Ruby points to the huge cluster of neon-purples a good several feet taller than her. "They've been here ever since I can recall. But *never* this tall. What in heaven's name was in that mulch you tucked about them last fall? *Do* tell."

"Let's see now," Sam puts both hands on her wide hips. "S'pose there's a summer's worth of my coffee grounds, egg shells by the dozen, any an'all scraps ah things wasn't fit for my plate, and a big load of chicken shit—'bout sums it up."

"I see, well—how nice then," Ruby lets go of the plant stem and it snaps back with the others. She looks at her hand and I know she's dying to wash it with something like bleach.

"I compost as well," Lilly adds lifting her chin high. "I'll get you started. All you need is a plastic ice cream bucket."

"Oh, great," I say as we gather around the back of Sam's truck. "Now I've got to eat ice cream *for the cause*. Ruby gets the empty bucket and my *bucket* of a rear gets bigger!"

Sam un-latches the tailgate and lets it fall open with a clang. "I been meanin' to oil out that creaky door here, but I've come to like the sound."

"My, my," Ruby lifts up a plant and reads the tag. "Brandywine— these make such a lovely sauce. It will be so bloody fun to get canning once again, come fall, that is."

The boys come over, each pushing along a wheelbarrow in various states of disrepair. They park them behind the truck. They've changed into sleeveless T-shirts, long baggy shorts with knee-patches and garden gloves. Sam takes out a basket from the cab and walks around handing us trowels and diggers, and well-washed garden gloves. Mine are covered with pink flowers that match my Keds.

"The plan's pretty simple," Sam offers. "Seein' as Howard got the earth opened up and worked over good alongside the creek over there. We all gonna be plantin' our little friends in nice neat rows that parallel the creek's shoreline."

Sam holds up a map she scotch-taped to the back of an Aussie Grill box. I read that it's a *charcoal only* grill and point this out to Ruby who sticks her tongue out. Maybe I'll have the old brick grill out back re-worked with propane. Do we really need more carcinogens? 'Course, I can't argue with the taste—I bet you can have both.

Sam explains what each team will be responsible for planting, how to read the plastic tabs shoved in next to each plant, and we're pretty much ready to roll. Or dig in, rather.

The now professional gardeners tie on floppy straw hats with colorful ribbon trim (compliments of Lilly), don our festive gloves, load up assigned wheelbarrows—or in the case of Ruby and me, it's a red-paint-peeling, Radio Flyer wagon. And we head over to the rows of overturned earth.

Ruby lays down an old green carpet square to kneel on. "Can you believe the crickets? Hand me that, won't you, darling?"

I remove the plant from its pot, pressing the sides together, and then pass her the plant and read the tab out loud. "Basil, Genovese. Best for Italian pesto, Latin name: *Ocimum basilicum.* Genovese—extremely tender, fragrant, extra-large, dark green leaves. Height 18-24 inches. Start early indoors or outside after all danger of frost. Grows best in full sun. Annual—plant six to eight inches apart."

"Oh, look who's come to help," Ruby lays down her trowel and gives Rocky a pat on his head. "Such a brilliant garden assistant, don't you think? Oh dear—I'm simply not sure if..."

Rocky comes over to my side of the row we're planting, rubs my knee and then proceeds to take a really smelly dump—right smack into the hole I was about to plop an Italian Genovese basil plant into! He carefully covers up his business and then strolls over toward Sam and Lilly.

"I guess I'll put this one," I huff out, *"Away* from his contribution."

"Actually," Lilly says one row over, "Just to be on the safe side—why not dig up his deposit and toss it over there into the woods. Cat-poo can cause taxoplasmosis in pregnant women, and there may come a time when we have someone here in that *very* condition." Lilly and Sam share a smile, then so do Ruby and I.

"He only wants to help, darling—and besides, since we haven't any chicken shit— well, he most likely is assuming it's the next best thing, I should think."

"Maybe we should consider," I offer after letting Lily's comment sink in. "Our own chicken shit-producing plant, right over there, next to the barn. Right about there." I chuck Rocky's items and it lands in a perfect *chicken coop possibility spot.*

"Well," Ruby sits back on her haunches and sends me a look, then a conspiratorial smirk. "Why the hell not?"

"Wow—look at that!" I point my trowel toward the back of the cottage.

A cloud of buttery-yellow moths is swirling and arching above and around the window over the kitchen sink. It's as if they're not a million separate things—but one whole mass of color. I look around—we're all mesmerized—no one's so much as taking a breath. Then, in an instant, they sweep up to form a line of yellow, then in a flash they fly off and away, disappearing into the woods like a silk scarf worn by a ghost.

"That's a sign," Sam announces, waving her trowel around as if it's a wand. "Those young spirits making all that color—they come to bless this garden."

"Moths?" Ruby asks in a pretty incredulous voice so I tap her knee with my trowel. "What could a *moth* possibly know about a garden, for heaven's sake?"

"They come to tell us," Sam replies with that certain glint in her brown eyes. "That we gonna have the biggest damn tomatoes this side of the island—that, and the fact that no moth can resist the smell of fresh dug earth."

"I see the attraction," Ruby says giving the plant she's working on a good bit of attention.

After the plants—as well as all the seed packets—are properly dug into their new homes, the six of us gather in a circle in the very middle of the garden. Sam instructs us to take hands. The late afternoon sun is spinning ribbons of golden light as it slants through the pine trees. With crickets as our rhythmic backdrop, we turn our attention to Sam.

She takes a deep breath and begins. "Oh Great Spirit, whose voice I hear in the wind and whose breath gives life to all—hear me. I ask for wisdom and strength, not to be superior to my brothers and sisters, but to be able to fight my greatest enemy—myself."

She looks at each of us, then continues, "Though we stand on sacred Ojibwa ground—we's *all* your children. Please shine your spirit of love over this garden."

Sam softly sings *Amazing Grace* and we hum along.

Howard and Johnny grill hamburgers and skewers of vegetables coated with Lilly's olive oil and secret herb rub, on the brick and river-rock grill Ed's great-grandfather built. It stands right outside the back porch door and until recently was used as our all-purpose-odds-and-ends holder. That is, until Ruby informed me of its original intent. I love that it was built by hand, even has a little built-in nook to hold the griller-person's beverage.

Bonnie joins us after she and Ali closed the restaurant and so do some friends of Johnny's. One of the couples, Willy and Jax from south of Oshkosh, are fascinating to know. Willy is friendly with a lady who owns Details, a fancy dress shop in Eau Claire that Ruby adores—so those two chat the night away.

We sit on the porch and enjoy the exhausted feeling of a good day's work, mixed with the magical taste that only grilling can give you. I was in charge of toasting the buns, so now, with every turn of my head, my smoky curls remind me that the difference of real charcoal compared to propane is all in the—*charcoal!*

For dessert we have chocolate-swirl ice cream Lilly had hidden down in the boathouse. Now we've got a head-start on our all-important plastic bucket container for composting kitchen scraps. I wonder how long it will take me to finish it off. A day?

Sam and Lilly, as well as the boys and their friends, all head their separate ways. Since the garden is here at the cottage, we'll keep the map taped to a wall in the porch to refer to. I'm impressed at all the plants we put in one afternoon. This is the list that Sam wrote on one side of the map:

Brandy wine tomatoes, cherry tomatoes, broccoli, eggplant, butternut squash, lemon cucumbers, dill, basil, thyme, sage, chives, rosemary, beets, Swiss chard, arugula, red leaf lettuce, leeks, watermelon, snap peas, carrots, red onions, tiny hot chili peppers and a row of sweet corn—for fun!

The spot we finally decided to plant was an old holding pen for either cattle or horses, who knows? But there's a waist-high fence around the entire area. Howard's not sure if it'll keep the deer out and is busy researching the possible problem. We may have to install some kind of electric fence, but I'll be damned if after all this work, those deer think they can just leap right in and have a leisurely snack on us! Is deer hunting in my future?

Ruby and I took long, hot showers, wrapped ourselves in robes, put our hair up in soft white terrycloth turbans and are now sitting in the living room. All feet are up on the green-glitter coffee table and—since it's in the interest of all-things-garden—we're having a skooch more ice cream. Well, it is coated with a *touch* of chocolate syrup and only a *tiny* handful of chopped walnuts, but, oh hell.

"I really like the direction we're heading into." I add, loosening my belt so I have more room for more ice-cream and not giving a damn. "I mean not only the garden but even more than that, our rethinking of what we throw out. Maybe we'll get to the point where we won't even need to make *any* trips to the dump."

The windows, as well as the bank of French doors onto the verandah, are all open to enjoy the night air. From outside we hear the drone of crickets and toads all calling out for someone. I look out the window and can see a crescent-moon sitting high and alone in the sky on a lone cloud.

And it's perfect.

CHAPTER SEVENTEEN

R uby and I are up early; the excitement of our radio-road-trip-adventure has our minds snapping with all the possibilities this may lead to. Or is that the coffee at work?

"Never thought I'd be eating ferns *and* enjoying them so much," I say between surprisingly delicious fork-fulls. "Tastes like broccoli—with attitude. I'm so glad I froze a huge baggie of them, they pop up so early in the spring."

"We've so many Fiddlehead Ferns out back," Ruby adds, carefully dabbing butter from the corner of her mouth. "Such a shame to let them go to waste and you simply never can pick them all, as you can see from the forest of them out there now." Ruby suddenly has that sad look in her eyes that can only belong to one man. "Ed and I used to enjoy this delectable dish every spring. As I recall they're *dreadfully* healthy and with butter, well, you simply can't miss."

Funny how sometimes we over-emphasize the times of triumph, those lost moments when our hearts really thumped with joy and the only thing holding things up was a shared meal of something foraged together. Fiddleheads. Silly name for something that can conjure up such powerful memories, but I know better than to ask Ruby more. The look that crosses her face says it all and soon enough it will be put away until next spring.

"I think a lot of people—like the boys—would be grossed out to see what we're eating for breakfast." I spread strawberry jam onto a half-slice of wheat toast. "But summer's arrived and since we'll be having fresh greens right outside our door—"

"—Why do I feel this is leading somewhere?" With narrowed eyes, Ruby pours us more coffee. "I know you're considering putting in a coop of sorts, but let's give the garden a go first— shall we?"

"I totally agree—I do."

The phone rings, Ruby picks it up as I bend down to give Rocky a few *good morning* scratches on the tippy-top of his furry head.

While clearing away our breakfast dishes, Ruby explains how it's *been so terribly difficult for Eve to decide what frock to wear and I keep reminding her—it's radio, dear child.*

I crank the hot water faucet to full and watch as the gush splashes down on our stack in the sink. Then I lift up the window over the sink a little farther and notice something disturbing.

"*Hey you guys!*" I yell in the direction of the group of deer having a morning munch in the middle of our just-planted garden!

Like a crazed gardener, I push up the sleeves of my terrycloth robe, slam out the back porch door and stomp over to the newly planted rows. Halfway there I realize my mistake. They weren't *in* the garden—they were having a drink of creek water on the other side of it! I somehow imagined them inside the fence, but they weren't. The blush flies up my cheeks, even though I'm alone on this one.

Of *course* I spooked them, so I feel terrible. On the one hand, I love the fact that we have them to enjoy watching, but *on the other side* of the fence, that is. I really do hope to grow some of our own food. This must be why so many give up gardening, it can drive you crazy!

"What in *bloody hell?*" Ruby comes up to stand beside me.

"I thought the deer were snacking on our garden and—"

"—It's a good thing the neighbors already know we're off the boil, now let's finish up with breakfast and be off—my public awaits!"

"Oh boy."

Ruby hops into the passenger seat of my VW van and slams the door good and hard. I've given up reminding her that these thin doors are nothing compared to her traded-in Buick. Dressed in tailored denim skirt and crisp white blouse, her red lips grin back at me with a mixture of dare and excitement.

Morning sunshine reflects off her freshly-colored bob and for the first time I realize how suddenly frail she looks. Funny how me, expert in all things beauty, had missed the sudden passing of time over my dear friend's face. Maybe that's what friends do, they see only what you hope they do and leave the rest up for grabs. Then again, if I were more religious about slathering on the SPF, I guess I wouldn't have all these freckles across my nose and cheeks—and shoulders. Genetics.

I'm decked out in a soft floral-patterned summer dress that used to belong to my mom; I figured it'd give me good luck. We clink our chocolate-laced mugs of coffee and we're off to our first radio interview!

I give the horn a toot; the crew waves from the boathouse balcony and off down the lane we go. The van shudders across the wooden bridge and this time I notice how Howard's fixed up several rotted planks with new ones. I'm not sure when the trees decided to fully leaf out, seems as if it happens when you look away, now you can't see nearly as far into the woods. Our one-lane driveway with the strip of grass in the middle has become a leaf-tunnel once again. The trees along the side lean over and reach across, their branches intertwine above us, competing for sun. I imagine them whispering in one another's leafy ears as we pass underneath.

The traffic on School House Road is pretty crazy. During off-season we wave at every passing vehicle, since we most likely know them, or at least know *of* them. But now that we're on the edge of summer insanity up here, I keep a pleasant smile on and only wave if I'm certain who it is. My black Ray Bans look over at Ruby's rhinestone cat eyes and I'm pretty sure she sends me a wink.

Ruby turns Pearl Bailey down. "My *heavens*—what on *earth* are all these enormous SUVS about? Must cost a small fortune to simply keep their engines motoring and the floating contraptions pulled behind are more like miniature cruise ships."

"We are in the midst of a bigger-is-better craze," I offer as I shift down in order to allow a purple convertible to pass.

I slow us down to a respectable *downtown speed.* As we pass by Al's Place, I toot the horn. Bonnie sets down several plates in front of customers, and sends us a big wave. I can't help but notice she's wearing a frilly blue apron with red trim.

"Bonnie's going to hire a few of the summer-time girls to keep her out of the weeds until Marsha can come back."

"That's lovely of her to hold her place—I know no one else can bake pies like that crazy woman can!"

"Ruby," I say in a voice she knows only too well.

"Oh, dear me—I simply meant. Oh bloody hell, we're all a bit daft one time or another."

We trundle onto the ferry; I pull up to the bumper of a speed-boat, smack beside a shiny-red SUV. Three young-ish children look over. The eerie glow from a suspended TV monitor dances shapes across their bored-looking faces.

"Good *heavens*—I thought *I* was pale."

"You are. Those kids in there are *anemic,* and I bet you the pricey toll over to Bayfield, those aren't carrot sticks being shoved in their faces either. I bet it's a fake-food item like Cheetos."

"After we pay the nice man, shall we go top-side?"

"Yes, please!"

I roll down my window as the ferry pulls away from the pier.

"Top of the morning to you ladies—hey Eve, how are you?" Pringles says.

"Do I know—oh, so sorry, I didn't recognize you without your cucumber—I mean uniform—*smock*!" His pimples have melted away into a deep summer tan, and I have to admit, he looks really handsome in his Madeline Island Ferry Line shirt—for a kid.

"Hello, darling," Ruby peers over her sunglasses for a better look and elbows me. But to our ferryman she says, "You *do* get around then, don't you?"

"Got to make the most of summer—miss. I'm saving up to buy a resort." He says this last part mostly to me.

"So, what do I owe you?" I ask, pulling out my overstuffed, pink, round wallet.

"You wanna go one way," his brilliantly white grin asks, "Or all—I mean both ways?" He chuckles at his oh-so-clever slip of hormones.

"Honey, knock yourself sideways with my credit card." I hand it over sighing. If he stares any harder at my cleavage, well, I should charge *him!*

"There you go—Eve Moss...nice name. Sorry to hear about Marsha and all. Only happy to hear she's going to be just fine. The mind is a complicated thing, especially when the heart gets in the way."

I stare over my sunglasses at him and notice the man that has taken over. I see a wisdom in his blue eyes that I hadn't noticed before.

"Thank you for saying so," I stammer and wonder why.

"Right, okay, well, you ladies have a great day on the mainland." He pushes his thick glasses up his strong nose and moves on to the next car.

We grab our purses and head over to the narrow staircase that leads up to a platform a good story above the lake. Even though it's pretty windy up here, we manage to get our stubby cigarettes lit and enjoy the great view. Madeline Island slowly slides into the horizon, while Bayfield begins to loom ahead of us in the opposite direction. A flock of seagulls swoop up and around the boat; their brilliant white bodies and yellow beaks are stunning against a dazzling blue sky.

As Bayfield comes into view, we head back to the van. I notice that the kids next to us are now slumped against one another, the TV screens a blank gray. I wonder if that's what their minds are—a blank gray.

The ferry makes a soft *tap* onto the pier. Several men toss huge, heavy-looking ropes lasso-style onto thick poles and secure the ship. One of the ropers turns back toward us and gives us a generous wave-off.

The van bumps up Washington and onto Highway 13. Since it's still early morning, the air has that pleasant coolness only a lake can send through the windows. I pull a yellow cotton sweater around my shoulders and settle in. Ruby turns Pearl back up.

Funny, the last time we headed this way it was in the dead of night with dread and fear racing toward Helen. I shake my head and focus on more pressing things, like how we're going to keep the Hollow running until it's more established and is it enough to keep Ali occupied and—is Pringles really too young? I should find out what his name is.

A little over an hour later and *more* than several potty stops, we're tooling into the town of Duluth. Ruby's on her cell, asking for directions, with several maps open on her lap.

"I simply don't *do* north—or south for that matter. Can you provide us with some sort of marker? I'm *terribly* comfortable with high-end retail shopping centers as one's guide."

"Oh, my God—look at that!" I point out the windshield. "Lake Street. How the hell I found it, I'll never know."

"That sounded like such a *lovely* woman from the sandwich shop," Ruby says. "She did her *best* to help us on my phone—Lucie is her name. But you found it all on your own."

"Lot of help you were," I say as I wrestle the van into a parking spot. "Too bad Ryan couldn't get away from classes—but the ladies must lunch!" I crank on the parking brake, flip down my visor, and give my nose a dab of powder, then one more. Check the teeth for lipstick, give the curls a scrunch, and push open the door.

Ruby slams her door so loud a flock of birds take flight in a nearby parking lot. "Sorry. Such a lovely idea of Helen's to meet us here." She turns and reads the hand-painted sign. "Northern Waters Smokehouse."

"She wanted to meet us at a favorite bookstore of hers here on the canal, but it just closed its doors for good not a week ago. Sad how so many independent shops are closing up, especially the interesting bookstores."

"The tide will change, mark my words, darling." Ruby says as we pry open the stubborn door. "Why, look who's here!"

Helen, dressed in faded hip-huggers, a tailored lavender top and all smiles, crosses toward us. Her strawberry hair hangs well past her shoulders in loose plaits that shimmer of health. As she gets closer, I admire *my* freckles dancing across her identical nose. Funny how that seems so important to me.

"Helen—you're *bursting* with beauty," I gush, hugging her good and tight. "I love the extra boost of color in your hair."

"This is so great," Helen replies, then bends down to hug Ruby. "Ruby—you always look like you just walked out of *Vogue*—how *are* you?"

"I'm just *wonderful,* darling. You *do* look ravishing, really you do. If I wore slacks like that they'd simply slip to the floor—I'm hip-less. Listen, dear ones. You two find a lovely table and I'll be back in a jiffy. I've simply got to find that Lucie who led us here," Ruby shoots me a look. "Oh alright, she *tried* to lead us here, Eve somehow figured it out on her own. But that woman's accent reminds me of my England—I'll be back." Ruby saunters off.

"I know you two don't have much time," Helen says, leading me over to a table with mismatched kitchen chairs. "They make several different salads, an interesting cold soup and all their fish is to die—"

"—Helen, slow down, girl!" I say as we thump down at a cozy table with a great view of downtown Duluth. "How are you and Ryan getting on? What in the world have you got around your neck? Bend over here and let me have a good look." I admire the glittering circle of sparkling diamonds. "Did Ryan rob a bank?"

"Actually," Helen blushes, nervously tucking her tresses behind an ear. "My mother gave it to me."

"It's beautiful—now let's talk about me."

"That was just lovely, darling," Ruby says as she snaps her seat belt on. "Such a bloody fun group, and wasn't it grand how Lucie joined us for lunch? Hmmm?"

"She's a riot. Doesn't Helen look great?"

"She does indeed. A bit on the slim side, I should say, but looking like the lovely woman she is. My goodness—I'm simply stuffed."

"Me too. Why in the *world* did we order dessert?"

"A moment of gastronomical weakness, brought on by the sheer unabashed desire for—apple pie," Ruby sighs.

"Well, settle in for the ride," I say while popping on my sunglasses. "According to Lucie, it's going to be about an hour and a half until we hit Grand Rapids. My God, I couldn't get over how high that bridge from Superior to Duluth was—we have to get onto US 2, and then it's smooth sailing."

"Who's to *care* how long a drive, darling? Look at all this lovely landscape we can enjoy. And my heavens—the hills are simply too much."

"Howard sent out a mass email to all the women who've been writing me, so we *might* get a lot of callers on our radio show today—I'm getting a little jumpy about it all."

"Don't be *daft*—you're going to be bloody smashing, darling. Besides—how can you miss with me by your side?"

"That's what I'm worried about."

She smacks my arm. "Smart alec."

We climb the hill in Duluth—actually, Duluth *is* a hill. We're pretty amazed at how the homes are literally perched on tiny little lots, all of them with a panoramic view of Lake Superior. Eventually, the roadway opens up as we leave the city behind.

The open fields we pass show early sprouts of green, just starting their journey toward the sun. We drive by farmhouse after farmhouse, many of which have huge, hulking barns, melting into each other. It must be too pricey to keep them up, and more times than not, there's an ugly metal building nearby.

Cows look up, grass falls from their square jaws. I give the horn a good tapping and since we're in the van, it's more of a bleep than anything resembling a honk. Wonder why quite a few places out here have so many old junk cars parked willy-nilly all over the place. What an eyesore. I suppose it's like anything— sometimes you stop seeing things, yet they're right there in front of you.

We pass the towns of Saginaw, Brookston, Floodwood, and then I pull over at the Swan River One Stop Plaza—a gas station that sells everything. I gas up the van, pee (no seat covers, and who has time to lay TP?), touch up the lips and off we bomb toward the radio station.

"La Prairie," I comment as we pass the sign. "Odd name for a town in Minnesota—hey, we're in Grand Rapids. I had no idea it was the home of Dorothy's ruby slippers."

"Seems to me, darling, that they were stolen. Who in the world would *do* such a thing?"

"Maybe Liza needed some cash. Read me the notes I took from Holly, will you?"

"Oh dear, I must have dropped a bit of coffee on them, but, no bother, I can make out that you need to make a left on Seventh and another quick left—yes, *here*—on First which will soon enough become Canal Street."

"*Get out of town*—look at this place!" I pull into a small parking lot, next to a black station-wagon type car with KAXE bumper stickers plastered all over the bumper.

"Such a lovely spot indeed and *right* on the river," Ruby says as she dabs a tissue on her freshened red lips.

A snap of her purse, and we head over to the impressive-looking station. It resembles a Frank Lloyd Wright building, low-slung portico and whimsical Gotham-City-style microphones flanking the impressive entryway. Well, there's no turning back now.

It's show time!

CHAPTER EIGHTEEN

A woman exactly my height heads our way across the beautifully inlaid wooden floor. The walls are painted cool butternut squash and shades of tea with chocolate accent and wood detailing around the edges, giving the entire interior an artsy feel. Jazz music I don't recognize thumps in the background like a comforting heartbeat.

"You must be Eve," The lovely woman extends her hand. "Welcome to KAXE—how was your drive?" She has the most unusual voice and a really cool asymmetrical haircut too, I like her immediately.

"Simply *divine*," Ruby interrupts and extends her paw, bracelets jangling. "Such a *quaint* town, Ruby Prevost, a pleasure to meet you, darling."

"I'm Holly—Holly Hudson, and *this* is our studio—isn't it something?"

We get a short tour, as it's really not all that huge; several people are working on phones. There's a friendly, casual air. Lots of sandaled feet, soft hairstyles and the smell of popcorn and coffee all mixed together in a soft harmony that's relaxing. She eventually leads us into the main studio area at the end of the hall.

"I'm afraid we don't have much time to chat," Holly says while un-twisting several headsets and handing us each one. "We go live in a few minutes, but to be honest I really prefer to have this type of interview be on the fly. I did glance over the emails you sent me and of course looked over your incredible website and *hilarious* Facebook page. You're doing something really important."

"Well, I—thank you," I stammer and then it dawns on me. "You're adopted, aren't you?"

"Yes, I am."

She sends me a look that says that's all she can share right now. That's enough for me. I glance over to Ruby and she nods.

"You can each have a mike," Holly offers. "I initially only planned on having Eve on the air. But since you explained your— well—shall we say, *unusual* situation of *practically* being mother and daughter, it will bring in another angle."

"Oh, how *desperately* exciting," Ruby warms to the idea. "I *do* so love being an angle."

Everyone puts on their headphones, the hell with the hair! I pull my chair up snug; Holly starts flipping switches as she checks volume gauges and dials on a computer screen. Several round, wall clocks are about to hit the *three-o-clock* mark in perfect synchronicity. The nervousness I felt earlier has slid away and I sit up in my chair with the sudden clarity that I'm here to help others. This is my chance to give back—and I'm ready.

"Can you two hear me okay," Holly's voice comes clearly into the middle of my brain. Weird feeling.

"Just divine, darling," says Ruby.

"Great—I feel like I could land a couple of planes while I'm at it," I chuckle and then so does everyone else.

"Okay ladies, we're about to go live on the air—three—two— one." A small snippet of Pearl Bailey, singing *Easy Street* plays briefly in the background. "Good afternoon and welcome to *Over the Fence live,* on KAXE. This is Holly Hudson and I'm happy to introduce my guests who are here with us in the studio today. Eve Moss and Ruby Prevost, owners of Ruby's Aprons, as well as directors of the newly founded home for pregnant mothers, Toad Hollow, located in Bayfield, Wisconsin—*and* they're related in a rather *curious* way. Welcome to KAXE." Holly glances my direction.

"It's great to be here, thank you," I say into my mike.

"Such a pleasure—I'm sure," Ruby gushes, and I notice she's amped the Brit—of course.

"Let's start off with a little bit of background. You both started an apron-making business on Madeline Island. Why there—Eve?"

"It seemed the natural thing to do. Ruby owned this great cottage...and after we decided to move up there permanently, I knew I couldn't just sit around and watch the leaves turn. So things evolved, and eventually we built up a business that's become really quite successful—knock on wood," I knock on my head, realize it's radio and roll my eyes toward the smiling Holly.

"Eve just gave her head of red curls a good knocking," says Holly. We all laugh into our mikes. "So you have this booming business—I should let our listeners know—Eve and Ruby brought a whole box of their aprons for us to use in our fundraiser. And I have to say—they're really more art than apron. But obviously there's more to your story—what event did you host at your cottage earlier this spring, Eve?"

"Ruby and I, *and* the entire sewing crew," I say and suddenly feel emotional. "We threw the most beautiful lakeside wedding— for my daughter, Helen." I swipe away a tear. Ruby dabs a lipstick-covered tissue on the corners of her eyes as well.

"Can you share with us how you—"

"—When I turned forty-seven, moved to Madeline Island and started looking back over my life—there was this one part that was—well, a big void—an empty place, a lonely place too. You see, when I was still a minor, I got pregnant. My folks were strict Catholics in every sense of the word, so they hauled me away to a convent. I had my baby all alone there—only held her once—then they took her away. I *couldn't* have raised her—what do you know about raising kids when you're still—a kid? Besides how to make babies, that is." I'm getting more comfortable now.

"So Ruby encouraged you to find her?"

"She did—*everyone* did—so I contacted a friend of mine who does this sort of work—helps reunite birth moms with their children and in a matter of days—*bingo!* Not only did she find her, but she ended up living pretty close to us—in Duluth—to be exact."

"Wow—*what* a story—that's enough material for a novel! Have you ever considered writing about your experiences? Maybe it could help others."

Ruby chimes in, "Oh, we've *plenty* of material, darling—trust me on that front. Our little saga has several rather *unusual* twists— wouldn't you say, Eve?"

I slit my eyes at her. "Well—ah—"

Smooth as silk, Holly slides in. "This is KAXE, I'm Holly Hudson and today our guests Eve and Ruby share their experiences leading up to the creation of Toad Hollow. Eve, can you explain the mission of Toad Hollow?"

"It's a place where a pregnant woman in crisis can come and safely not only *have* her child, but have the opportunity to decide what's to become of that child. Whether she wants to give it up for adoption, or needs help finding the resources to keep and raise her baby. But—another situation similar to mine has entered into the picture, and that's that a lot of women—mostly baby boomers—are contacting me to share their long ago, but never, ever forgotten, secrets of having to give up a child."

"Are these women calling you or—"

"Email," I reply struggling to yank the file I brought from my over-stuffed purse. "I brought some of them with me." I hand the bursting file to Ruby who in turn passes it to Holly.

"When Eve and I spoke earlier," Holly says with obvious surprise, "she mentioned that she'd been getting some email, but— there must be over a hundred notes in here!"

"We would have printed off a bit more," Ruby adds. "But we simply ran out of paper. Some of the email notes are *truly* heart-breaking."

"What I'm realizing," I say with a sudden clarity, imagining a light bulb above my head suddenly popping to life—a recyclable one, of course. "Is that there's a need for an outlet or a place, or maybe—maybe *here*, on the anonymous radio waves—for these women to come together. A place where they can finally say it out loud, and not be afraid of being discovered by their family or friends. I can't imagine *not* being able to talk about my daughter now, but I'm realizing that back when I had my child, well—" I start to snivel and wonder where the hell all this emotion was hiding.

Ruby jumps in. "What Eve is so brilliantly describing is that not so long ago, for many, many young women, to be an unmarried single mum oftentimes made you un-marry-able. *Such rubbish*—but that simply was the way things were. I can only hope that now we've realized women have a rather difficult time getting pregnant *alone*—for heaven's sake. *Men...really.*" We chuckle and yet something in my heart—my soul—takes notice. It was my body, mine alone and yet....

"This is Holly Hudson live on KAXE, please join my guests Eve and Ruby after we take a short break." She clicks on a voiceover ad. "How are you two holding up? The show is going really well and look at this." She points to a long console of flashing lights. "Every line in is jammed with people wanting to talk with you, and I haven't even had a chance to peek at *our* email or Facebook or Twitter."

A beautiful Japanese girl, size minus zero, hip-huggers barely hanging on, discreetly enters the studio with an armload of papers. "So sorry to interrupt—" she says in broken English.

"This is Mo," Holly mentions by way of introduction. "She's living with my husband and me for a year, and is helping out at the studio this summer."

Mo sends us each a nod of her beautiful head, hands the stack to Holly and just as quietly, pulls the door closed. I notice a group of people beginning to crowd the hallway outside the studio, peering in at us. Holly quickly scans the sheets, lifting one after the other and shaking her head. She removes her stylish glasses and rubs her eyes.

"These are from all over the nation," Holly says with obvious surprise. "Women at work, listening online, women at hair salons, women who know women, and a few on the other side too—the children. I had no idea." Holly signals us by counting backwards. "—Two, one. This is Holly Hudson on KAXE, Grand Rapids, Minnesota. I'll try and take a few of your calls today. We're on the air live, with Eve and Ruby of Ruby's Aprons and the newly established Toad Hollow. Before I forget to ask—didn't you two learn about being more related than you originally thought—if that makes sense at all?"

"It's such a *sordid* tale," Ruby says and sends me a devilish wink. "I'm not sure if it's suitable for radio—you must have proper ratings and such. But I'll try to clean it up a bit—you see— many, many years ago, unbeknownst to Eve and me, *of course*—Eve's mum and my louse of a now-deceased husband, had a bit of a tryst. Eve was the innocent result. We were friends long before we'd any clue as to our *true* relationship, such as it is. Small world, isn't it?" Ruby sighs dramatically into her mike.

"That's just incredible—I'd say you two have enough material for *many* books. Let's go to our callers who've been waiting patiently on the line. Hello—Please welcome Brenda, calling from the Iron Range."

"Hi. Um, I gave my son up long time ago. I can't be opening no Pandora's box, see. My uncle, he lived with us and when I was fifteen, well, you can figure out the rest. I just hope my boy's doing good, you know?"

"Eve?" Holly looks my way.

"Do you have access to the Internet?" I ask.

She laughs slightly, then it turns into a deep wheeze. "I got you on at work here, so sure."

"We've posted all sorts of resources on our website."

"Thank you. Sure appreciate what you're trying to do."

"Our next caller is Sister Bernadine from Arizona," Holly reports.

"Hello there," a scratchy old-lady-voice crackles into my head. "Eve—you dear child. I don't expect you to recall, but I was the nun who had to pry your newborn baby away. I've looked at your computer site and your pictures and..." Tears are spilling down my cheeks. How can this be? "I'm so very happy you've found your calling, dear. Only, I've always wanted to know—did you knit that yellow sweater for your baby?"

It's a long story, but my mother had knit a yellow sweater for my baby (Helen) while I was pregnant in the convent. Over thirty years later my father told me about it. You see, my parents were so ashamed I was pregnant, they never came to see me—yet my mom took the time to knit this beautiful yellow sweater for her granddaughter. The granddaughter she never met. Somehow, after I gave birth, the sweater was put on Helen before Saundra and her now deceased husband adopted her. It was the link that made it real for my dad.

I fish-lip the mike—nothing wants to come out. I close my eyes for a moment and see the entire scene. My tiny baby disappearing into the arms of that nun—I never realized until this very moment that she had been crying too.

There were many more callers, several not so pleased with the concept of Toad Hollow—one man even suggested *these lost women* turn to God for answers. I asked him what he thought God would say, and after several beats, he suggested I pray and hung up. Nothing against God, or praying for that matter, but sometimes you need more than a belief to help you find your way. You need each other—and I think that maybe God's in there somewhere too, but I'll always put my money on the *each other* part.

After we're off the air, Holly suggests we give Dottie's Hometown Cafe a try as I mentioned that Ruby and I sure could use a good cup of Java and some pie after all that emotional stuff. We hug Holly goodbye and get quite the sendoff as we drive away from the waving staff and many supportive listeners who happened by during our broadcast. We promise to keep in touch, and I think another show is in the works.

Dottie's is the perfect pit stop and there's never an end to the coffee, I have a feeling we'll be stopping a great deal on the way home from Grand Rapids. Ruby and I decide to share a piece of pecan pie. Seeing as it's gotten pretty hot outside, we figure a cold slice of pie would cool us down. We sure earned the sugar. Not to mention all that yummy butter.

After we leave some cash under the now empty plate, we head out the door and clamber aboard my rusted red and yellow VW van. I reach over to put some tunes on, and then think better of it. We've had enough stimulation for the moment I think as I pull onto the highway and begin our journey home.

I wonder if that nun somehow feels that now, now that she knows my mom made the sweater which connected Helen and me—maybe now she can know that everything *does* happen for a reason. It may take thirty years to come to pass, but eventually finding out the truth really can set you free.

As we cruise along the highway I wonder in amazement how so many times in life it seems easier to sweep things under the rug—especially when you have an entire life just waiting to unfold. But as time whips those calendar pages away, maybe you'll find that you want to come clean. Before you're dead and gone, *maybe* you'll realize the truth is always the best road to take.

And secrets are better shared.

CHAPTER NINETEEN

"**D**o you intend to sleep all *bloody* day?" Ruby asks from the threshold of my bedroom doorway. "In less than a week, we've the Ducky Derby and you—being the queen duck and all— well, you'd best get cracking!" She plunks a steaming mug of Java on my nightstand and is out the door in a flash.

Rocky stretches long, does a perfect Downward Dog, then leaps off my bed and heads downstairs without so much as a backward glance. I quickly make my bed as I slide out (in between coffee slugs). I swirl my curls up into a loose do, and nearly poke a hole in my scalp with this stupid hair-comb I'm in a love-hate relationship with. I love how it looks once in place, but I hate how—more times than not—I end up practically drawing blood until it's in right.

While figuring out some sort of *derby-planning outfit*, I keep replaying the conversation I had with Marsha several days ago. I had gone over to visit her in the Behavioral Health Clinic in Ashland. At first I got a small case of the heebie-jeebies. On the way into her room, an elderly woman bent severely over and smelling of peppermint, came rushing over to me and demanded I mail the letter she pressed into my palm—then she disappeared down the hallway, glancing back once to wave. The note was addressed to Tony Bennett in care of Hollywood; I figured *what the heck* and mailed it. Everyone needs to dream.

Marsha seemed pretty much herself, though really tired and a little on the groggy side. But there was something in her eyes I don't know that I'd ever seen before—peace. I had brought my portable beauty-in-a-bag satchel and was finishing up roller-brushing her hair when she reached up and took hold of my wrist. We were sitting in front of a mirror, so I snapped off my dryer and asked her if she intended to *bust my wrist or what?*

In this little girl voice, she asked if Alice—I mean—Ali, hated her. She corrected herself, so I assumed Ali had told her of the recent name change.

I put down my dryer and gave her a good long hug, then asked her why she had thought that. And she explained, (and this is the weird part) she said that she and Don were first cousins. Kind of knocked me sideways. But I bet it's not *that* unusual or at least it's not like marrying your brother or anything, yet it's not something I'd go around sharing with just *anyone.* Apparently Don was really freaked out about Ali and just couldn't handle it. After we chatted some more and I put the finishing touches on her matching mauve fingernails. I asked her to stand next to me and look at herself in the mirror.

Her reflection showed a woman in her early fifties, soft blonde hair, and blue eyes glinting with that peacefulness. I told her to really look—I mean really *see* what a lovely woman she was and all that she had to live for, *especially* Ali. Marsha asked me why I thought Alice Anne needed to be Ali now. I told her that my guess was that she felt more comfortable being Ali—that sometimes you change inside and need to change something on the outside to show the world—and yourself too.

Marsha thought about this for a second, then looked me right in the eyes and said, "I like that." Then she looked back into her reflection. "I think I'd like to be a redhead."

I informed her that it was her lucky day—and now she's chestnut. There can only be one redhead. Sometimes it really *does* boil down to the simple stuff; trying on a new name, or hair color, or—life.

Explains why I'm sticking this *Stop smoking* patch onto my semi-flabby arm. Instead of hiding the damn thing under a shirt-sleeve, I found all these tacky-as-hell stickers and cover the thing in whatever suits my mood. Today's theme is pretty obvious: ducks.

"Well, look what the cat done drug in," Sam says, looking up from her sewing machine. "Girrrl—you gone *off* or what?" She tips her head in the direction of my arm, then lifts her cornrows up and taps a long French-manicured nail onto her nape, indicating the secret location of her own hidden patch.

"You are too much," I say and give Sam a smack on her arm. "Don't you think a picture of the Grim Reaper on your patch is going a little overboard? Besides—you can't even *see* the damn thing."

We're giving the nicotine patch a try; we've *got* to stop smoking.

"Too close to what *might* be," she offers shaking her head. "My little niece come over to visit me and—poor child, she got the gift—she told me he was coming for me if I didn't give up them *cancer-rappers*," I just 'bout bust my bra, laughing like that. We finally come to the conclusion she was thinkin' *reaper*. So that's where she said I should be having him sit. Right on my neck."

"Besides the gift, darling," Ruby says coming out of the bathroom. "Poor dear seems to have your twisted imagination as well. The lucky duck."

Everyone starts quacking; even Howard comes out of his office to join in. Then I notice that *all these quackers* have something brilliantly yellow rushing through their sewing machines in various states of *coming-togetherness*. My duck costume—oh boy.

"Since it's going to be rather warm," Lilly cautions over her bifocals. "We've taken the traditional duck—as in the rubber-ducky type." She lifts up one of the many rubber ducks strewn all over the boathouse. "And well, it's been ramped up a few notches. More of an *adult* version."

"Just you be glad," Sam says with a chuckle. "This ain't no fish derby—whooo— mermaids have *such* a time gettin' 'round."

"I'm sure it's for you, darling," Ruby pulls down the phone and hands it to me.

"Ducky Derby headquarters—this is Eve," I say into the mouth-piece while at the same time turning down Diana Washington.

"Hello, Eve," a man's rather serious voice intones. "This is Mayor Maggio over in Bayfield—and I have been meaning to give you a call."

"Oh, hello Frank," I reply while turning away from the sewing group, suddenly feeling embarrassed about my duck outfit taking shape all around me. "What's up?"

"Just wanted to suggest something for next Saturday."

"Shoot."

"We've managed to rustle together over thirty vendors for the area around Pike's Creek, where it swings by the field back there behind the Hatchery—but we've got a little problem."

My stomach clenches the slightest, and the need for a smoke is smoldering into my consciousness. "Oh?"

"We were planning on using one of Bayfield's very own loading trucks to haul the ducks up to the launch site, but they've all been jobbed out so—"

"—Frank, how am I going to haul thousands of rubber ducks up to,"—Johnny comes running over and whispers in my other ear—"Actually, we've got it covered." I high-five Johnny.

"Oh, that *is* good news—I am so sorry about this. Looking forward to officiating, and from the looks of things, we may get some pretty major press. Could turn into a yearly event up here, maybe even as popular as the Bayfield Apple Festival—and that's saying something!"

"See you Saturday—with heels on," I say and then I let the phone go on up to its crazy deer-mouth home. Would I become the official duck mascot? What have I gotten into—literally.

"Good, very good," Lilly says over the sexy chanting music, as she elegantly slinks by me. "Remember to keep your chin up, Sam, good. Now let's end the Egyptian in a circle with our veil turn—oh Ruby, that *is* a nice touch. Okay, now the waterfall and—good. Take some deep breaths and we'll end today's session with a full run-through of the Great Salutation." We all groan—*we can't help it*—she's a workhorse!

"Damn," Sam says and then slumps into a cushy chair by the window and lifts up her feet onto the steamer-trunk coffee table. "Even with these fans blowing all this hot air around, I'm still about to blow a gasket up here."

"Think of all the water weight we're dropping," I offer, wiping sweat from my brow. "Why—I bet I've lost over a pound already and that was just from coming up the stairs!"

"Oh, rubbish—such poor sods, *really,*" Ruby admonishes. "Why—every one of you is looking so much the better, thanks to Lilly here. Not a *one* of us has dropped dead and that's saying something—imagine."

Sam passes the pack to me and then I offer one to Ruby. Lilly mouths *No thank you.*

"Who would'a thought that with a woman my age," Sam offers while unwrapping a pink chunk. "That after sewin' together a *crazy* duck costume, then doing our yoga-belly dance thing, that my day would end chompin' a Bazooka Bubble Gum. Lord have mercy."

I blow a really huge bubble—Ruby leans over and pops it—leaving me with a face covered with pink goo.

"You are in *such* trouble," I caution, pulling the crap off my face. "Sometimes having oil-slick skin can be an *enormous* convenience." I pop it back into my mouth and shrug. "Now—the booths will be set up by the individual vendors over at the Hatchery, along with help from that handsome Dan from True North Tent."

"Such a *lovely* man," Ruby offers. "He rented us our tent for the Apple Festival—of course he had the wife swing by for payment."

"What all else we got to figure on then?" Sam asks.

"Well…" I confide—leaning in closer to the group, "I got a tip from someone we all know well—Ryan, to be exact—he informed me that a colleague of his that lives here on the island, would be *more* than willing to lend his expertise. *More* than willing.

"Oh, this is *so* bad," Sam smacks her knee. "But you *know*—I could'a misread things over there, wouldn't be the first time—that's for sure. Bein' *human* and all."

"Could you and Eve perhaps speak in a sensible *English?*" Ruby asks with very raised eyebrows.

"Come over here," Sam says and gets up and heads over to the model of Madeline Island. "Good thing we decided to leave that tarp off-a here. Looks like this model has become our *island barometer.*"

Lilly, Ruby, Sam and I gather around it. Howard has taken to keeping it in tiptop shape as far as minor repairs and changing some of the burnt-out lights that needed replacing. Since the local museum hasn't any interest, not to mention room, in displaying Ed's model, we've opted to keep it. Why not—since it's the perfect way to check up on *things,* thanks to Sam.

"Okay ladies, now I'm gonna need some extra energy here, seeing as I gotta try to read something from a time before this place was born."

"Whatever do you mean, darling?" Ruby asks.

"Your Ed made this model with what he knew to be true, and at the time—it was. But see, the earth is like water. It's never the same, one generation to the next, and before all this came to be,"—Sam sweeps her arms over the countless miniature cottages peppered over the landscape—"Why, this was a whole different island for folks. Ojibwa people are the rightful caretakers of this island, always will be far as I can see. Oh, I *do* see now" She steps over to an area south of the cottage.

"It's that development going in," Lilly says and we all follow her gaze. "What do you see—Sam?"

Sam braces herself over the model, closes her eyes and then grins. "Seems like tonight—Eve and Ruby gonna be movin' some of the past into the present."

"You sure that Ed has—"

Ruby, leading the way toward the library, lifts up her hand to silence my questioning. "Ed was a bit of a, shall we say, *collector.* I'm simply *positive* he had a collection of Indian artifacts from the island in *one* of these cupboards." She indicates the green glass-knobbed wooden doors that run underneath all the bookshelves in the library.

"I casually snooped in some of these," I reply, stooping over and opening a set of facing cupboard doors. "Just what are we looking for anyway? Rocks or arrowheads or what?"

"Sam mentioned that the main thing we need to locate," Ruby replies as she begins opening and closing the small doors. "Is this one particular—ah ha!"

"Score!" I say and we grin like the crafty cats we are.

Rocky leaps up onto a shelf, paws a wooden ball out from its base, and we watch as it noisily bangs and bounces, as best wood can, all the way down, finally landing onto the wooden floor with a **bam!** He gives it several expert paw pats and soon it's crashing from doors to baseboards on its journey out of the library and on down the hallway.

"Are you *sure* this is the right spot?" I stage-whisper in the dark. "I mean, the moon is not doing the best job out here and my God, can you believe how loud the toads are?"

"Lovely—isn't it?" Ruby replies with a seriousness in her voice I rarely hear. "Now hand me Ed's solution to this act against nature, and then give me the all important marker."

Shining my flashlight down, through the taped-on toilet paper holder, I point a narrow beam of light onto her efforts. Howard and Johnny are on lookout after having helped us craft our flashlight so it shines this thin beam. Ruby, dressed in black like me, wearing her flowered garden gloves, is finishing up her handiwork. Giving the mound a good pat, she takes the yellow duck and twists it into the earth to secure it.

"That should do it," Ruby says out loud.

Suddenly several bright-as-fricking-hell security lights burst on, shooting daylight-seeming rays of *you're so busted light* all around us!

"Who's there?" A slurred voice calls out from the darkness. "I'm gonna gut jur ass, so hep me!"

Ruby and I are racing down the incline, toward the makeshift dock the duck is lashed to.

"Let's be bloody well off then—shall we?" Ruby pants as Johnny helps her aboard.

"Shit!" I spew, "I left my bag back there! I have to get it!"

"Eve—we've got to dash," Ruby says with panic in her voice.

"Start her up, if I'm not back in a minute—*you leave me and I'll kill you!*" I sprint back up the steep incline to where we were *planting.* The entire area is now awash in bright white work lights. I notice someone limping down the steep driveway that leads to the twenty or so *sites* where one can create their very own *Madeline Island Dream Home.* Whoever it is, he's having quite a time maneuvering downhill in any kind of a straight line, not to mention his obvious challenge as to what foot to put in front of the other—the guy is blasted.

Then I see the dog and hope to get to my bag first.

"Here you are, you little mutt," I say as I toss the mangy creature a fully-wrapped Reese's Peanut Butter Cup. Then I think better of it and throw several more over my shoulder as I race back to the waiting duck.

Ruby and Johnny grab my arms as I leap onto the duck, and we slip away, out onto the mist-covered lake. Howard looks back toward the three of us and shakes his head in obvious relief; then hits the throttle and we're off!

The next morning, as Rocky, Ruby and I are paging through the Rules and Regulations for The Lucky Ducky Derby Festival. My ears perk up when an announcer on WPR says:

"Madeline Island long-time resident, Archaeologist and Ojibwa preservationist, Dr. Kurt Gerhart, has announced an astounding find. While out enjoying his early morning walk, his well-trained eye spied something familiar along a newly excavated area. Apparently, the about-to-be-developed gated community of Gilded Sunsets is actually situated on top of a sacred burial site of the Ojibwa Indians."

"Not only did the world-renowned professor find many rock art recordings. Which, by the way, are stones covered with hand-painted drawings depicting Ojibwa island life—as well as death. He also unearthed some unusually vivid pictographs. These are stone-painted scenes of local wildlife, seasonal celebrations and some exceptionally vivid renderings of Madeline Island's fish. Proving once and for all that Madeline Island is a truly sacred place within the history of the Ojibwa Native Americans. The development is currently suspended, and a Stop Work Order has been issued until further notice."

"Why, isn't that the oddest thing Rocky?" Ruby adjusts her duck-themed apron and flips an omelet high into the air. "Wonder how the good doctor found such a *smashing* treasure trove."

"Some people fish at night—we garden."

CHAPTER TWENTY

I'm standing downstairs in the kitchen; the early morning sunshine is beginning to peek through the shutters, softly reflecting onto the stump table's countless amber-varnished rings. When I first moved up here with Ruby, we tried to count them and stopped at over a hundred. This waist-high chunk of history must weigh in the tons.

With Ruby nowhere in sight, I let Rocky up on the table *only* when there's no food around. He paws at it in hopes of coaxing the rings out to chase God knows where. That's one of the many things I love about cats—they have such a crazy-wonderful imagination.

I'm writing a quick note to the still snoring Ruby, who warned Rocky and me that she was staying up late, finishing a novel she referred to as *a bloody cracking good read.* Sometimes she's unable to put a good tome down until it's all done with. There's been so much focus on being outside, seeing as it's gotten to be so beautiful. I've all but forgotten about the passageway, not to mention the Speakeasy secreted away underneath the boathouse.

Putting the period on my note, I grab my mug of hot coffee, slip my freshly painted toes into flip-flops and head for the basement door. It's so great to only have to toss on an oversized T-shirt and these soft cotton Capri's.

At one time, a bra was optional. But now with too many people coming and going here, I'd hate to scare them away with my so called *hanging jugs of Madeline*. Wonder if one day, thanks to the miracle of gravity, I'll be able to fling them over my shoulder? Man, I sure as hell hope not.

Snapping on lights, I clomp down the creaky stairs of the hidden passageway. Rocky zooms on in front of me, hopefully chasing away all the mice down there. Actually, the slap of these classy flip-flops should scare just about anything. Shuddering as the cool air snakes around me, I nearly spill my coffee.

Ducking down in order to avoid a rather large pipe angling up toward the ceiling, I head over to the wine closet's metal door and give it a good tug. The door creaks open and a damp breeze of an iron smell mixed with something akin to mushrooms comes swirling into the basement.

Finally locating the string with the red-and-white fishing bobber attached, I give it a pull. The naked light bulb pops to life, illuminating rack after rack of dusty wine bottles. Most of this wine is of the homemade variety, compliments of Ed and Ruby's efforts.

Rocky growls back in the corner somewhere—not a good sign. I wrestle with the fussy latch on the false back panel and eventually the stubborn door clicks open. It silently opens outward, clacking against the wall. I snap on more lights, take a sip of coffee, and head down the short flight of metal stairs to begin my journey along the curving passageway.

When Ruby and I first discovered this labyrinth of hidden rooms and secreted booze, we more or less took it all for granted. But re-visiting it now, I can appreciate how extremely desperate anyone wanting a snort must have been. It's pretty lame, if you ask me, but folks up here sure didn't let prohibition stop them from having an occasional slug. I've reached another set of metal stairs, these lead into a spacious storage room, I click several switches and the hooded lights above hum to life.

Even though we've given the passageway a casual cleaning, the metal grid-work that supports the walls and ceiling above are coated in grime and spider-webs that drape downward in creepy shapes and sway in the breeze. Some things are better off left alone and besides, it adds a certain *atmosphere* to the place.

Rocky, who has a memory like a steel trap, is noisily pawing and growling at the rim of a suspicious-looking barrel of Toad Tea. Well, it's really not all that suspicious now that I've been here a few times. There's rack after rack of big wooden barrels lying on their sides; we've decided they all must be empty, but haven't taken the time to check it out. This brings me back to Rocky who is still pawing away, he turns and gives me a half-hearted meow.

"Hey, Rocky—chill a little huh? Let me think a minute, something to do with this plaque. It's been a while."

In the center of the barrel is a patina-coated brass plaque with the words, *Toad Tea Tavern* engraved in the center. On the right is the outline of the very same toad that blazes out of the stained glass window upstairs outside the library. As I rub away the grime, the plague sinks into the wood with a soft clicking sound and—voila! A door reveals itself. I pull it outward, reach around the corner and flip on the lights.

"Wow!"

It still surprises me how vast this basement room is. There's a stage backlit in lavender flanked by ruby red velvet curtains that puddle onto the floor. I flip-flop over toward the lily pad shaped dance floor and recall the night this room was filled with all of Helen and Ryan's wedding well-wishers. Pulling out a chair, I sit down at the very same table as I did that night, and recall Sam and Connie accompanied by the crew, up there singing their hearts out all in celebration of my daughter and Ryan and—love. I smile.

Rocky leaps up onto the table, drops a swath of cloth in front of me, and then dashes off toward the stage area.

"What in the world? Rocky—has Ruby been reading too many cat mysteries to you again?"

I pull the lamp from the middle of the table over for a closer look at the material. It's worn in places, as if it's been held too many times. There are several layers, yet I can feel the outline of a key inside. There's a small black snap sewn into a corner. I unsnap it and the layers open out in reverse like an envelope. A narrow satin ribbon unfurls with a small round tag attached to a long skeleton key.

"This is weird—*Colored dressing room?*"

I close my eyes and try to imagine things as they might have been down here then—and *everywhere,* actually. Sam has told me time and again how we *all* have the sight, it's just that we're so chock-full of fear; we can't tap into it.

As I'm sitting here; trying to imagine what the hell this key is for, I hold it tightly and it almost feels as though it's getting warm—wait a minute—I suddenly feel a familiar pull. My stomach takes a lurch and I nearly toss my cookies.

From some dreamy, underwater state, I hear the barrel-door close with a click; the lights dim, and then come up again. I'm still sitting at the same table, but the room is different, full of people; all the men are dressed in dark suits with bowties, hair slicked back to a light-reflecting sheen. Heavily made-up women in beautiful dresses with odd, low waists sip from stemmed glasses, smoking from long cigarette holders. Off to the side of the stage, a door opens, and garish white light silhouettes a woman.

She steps up onto the stage. I know her. This has to be another dream, but I know there's a reason I'm here. But for the life of me I can't quite get to it. Dressed in a shimmering white gown, hair pulled tight, long, dangling white earrings brush her bare shoulders—Sam, she looks like a skinny Sam. She gives the small jazz group behind her a nod and then starts to sing, *Weeping Willow Blues*.

Something is beating, there's a different sound coming from somewhere, the underwater feeling slides away. I must be waking up. I look around me and then notice the easel over to the far right of the stage with a big playbill of the woman on stage. Then in dancing letters across the top I read, *Bessie Smith live at Toad Tea Tavern.* The pounding is getting more intense. I try to stand and then the room goes black.

"I been poundin' on that damn barrel like a crazy woman!" Sam huffs out, coming toward me. "What kinda mess you whipped up *this* time?"

"I was sitting there, minding my own business," I explain. The sense of being oddly distant, like talking through a tunnel, slowly clears away. "I feel really weird and,"—I look around the speak-easy—"I was back—Bessie Smith—she was singing and Rocky gave me this key and—is it too early for a drink?"

"I called Lilly here," Sam points toward Lilly who has her arms folded over her chest. "Early as can be and told her something strange going to be coming your way. I jus' couldn't get clear on— oh, no *wonder.*"

Lilly picks up the key from the table, takes her bifocals from their perch in her do, and studies the tag.

"I was here," I say, feeling really lame. "Yet I wasn't—and there were all these people and then—Bessie—Bessie Smith was on stage. Oh hell, how in the world can that be. Maybe I'm losing my marbles."

"Don't know why," Sam offers, giving her beaded cornrows a good scratching. "I jus' never can see much of anything pertaining to me. 'Bout drives me *mad*! What else you see?"

"She came from over there." I point and then we file over for a closer look. "There was a door here."

The entire back wall on either side of the stage is covered in a kind of felt material. We had decided to leave well enough alone when getting the tavern ready for Helen's wedding and hadn't given it much attention. We figured it would keep the echoing at bay, after all this is really a big cave.

Heading toward a small set of stairs that lead up to the stage, I turn and re-walk where she did over to where I saw (or dreamed or imagined) her appearing out of the wall.

"There must be a room back here," I say and begin to search around the dark material for a doorknob. "It just feels like stone covered with felt."

"Girrrl," Sam says, hands on hips. "When you gonna learn to look *down* some?" She points to the floor with the tip of her sandal.

"Looks like something's been scraping the floor here," Lilly says and crouches down for a closer look. She runs her well-trained seamstress hands up an edge and then points to a small knob barely visible.

Sam takes the key from Lilly and says, "Something tells me this is *my* door to open. Let's all hope," Sam offers, taking the key from me. "Pandora weren't no *black* woman—Lord, I jus' *hate* surprises."

Lilly and I exchange a look of not knowing what to expect. Sam inserts the key into the center of the knob, turns it this way and that. Suddenly the door pops open and we all jump, then giggle nervously. She tugs the door open all the way as we crowd the threshold.

"Do *you feel* anything?" I ask.

"Sure do," Sam replies in an odd voice. "Like I *know* this place— I've dreamt it. Especially when I was jus' a child and took to the sick bed with a nasty fever; this place gave me hope—a reason. Don't seem possible though—that I coulda' dreamt this place all those years ago—and here it is. Here—it—is." She says with awe in her voice.

I step inside and reach around the wall. "There's something, here." I turn a dial-like switch and suddenly the room is flooded with light.

"Welcome to the colored folks' dressing room," Sam announces and we crowd the long, cramped room.

On the right wall is a big, round mirror surrounded with mostly burned-out bulbs. The countertop underneath is littered with mouse droppings, many lipstick containers, pots of powders, a mug of eye pencils, and tons of brushes and combs strewn around and several black wigs sitting on glass head-stands. I lift one of the tubes of lipstick, pull off the gold top and screw up the deep red lipstick.

"We are talking some dark red here," I say and try some on. "Feels like wax, it's so heavy on my lips."

"Eve Moss," Lilly takes it out of my hand. "Think of the *bacteria!*" She re-caps it and sets it back down like it's about to explode.

Sam chuckles behind us. "Look at all these gowns left in here." She takes one from the narrow armoire on the opposite wall and holds it up to herself.

"That's the one she had on!" I say. "Sam? Are you okay? You look, well—I *imagine* that you look *pale.*" I reach out to her. Lilly and I help her sit down in a red velvet fainting couch off to the side of the armoire.

"You crack me up—'course we go pale. Ashy more like," Sam says after a moment. "Soon as I saw this frock, I had all the answers and it's gonna jus' *mess* with your mind—Miss Eve."

"Oh, great."

"Couldn't you be a bit off the mark on this one?" Ruby asks from the kitchen area. "I mean, you *have* mentioned how it's nearly impossible to see your *own* past."

"It's all here, sister." Sam holds up the small journal. "They was hard times back then for so called *colored folk.* Adeline—your Ed's great-grandma—*was* that woman I felt over at the cabin watching over her child we put to rest. Imagine putting your baby in a hatbox—land. She saw them together and knew it could only lead to grief. No one knew grief like Adeline. She demanded her off and leave all this behind. Not knowing what already was begun."

"So—" Howard's commanding voice makes us all turn his way. "Let me see if I've gotten the gist. Bessie Smith, famous jazz singer and one of Johnny and my personal favorites, I might add—she's here for a singing gig and ends up having an affair with Ruby's husband's father—Thomas."

"I simply can *not* imagine," Ruby interrupts for the umpteenth time. "Ed's father was simply such a *droll* sort of man, tall and narrow and so—transparent, *really.*"

"He *was* a widower and Bessie Smith was a beautiful woman." Lilly chimes in with reason, and we all nod as if this clinches the deal. "Why *shouldn't* they have an affair?"

"A widower with a small child!" Ruby adds and gives the fridge door a slam.

I put down my cutting shears and go over to Sam's station and pick up the small leather-bound book. Turning to the last page with writing on it I read out loud,

"Today Mister Thomas and I had relations, and oh he was so gentle, I about cried. It was glorious and a woman knows when the planets align. But then that woman came in and found us there. I was horrified!"

"That of course," Howard jumps in. "Was Ed's grandmother, Adeline. She had Bessie and her band ordered off the island immediately and then—"

"—She ends up with child," Sam says shaking her head. *"Then* pregnant Bessie gets into a car crash, has her arm took off, then dies the next day. My aunt was the nurse who birthed the child from her dead mama, took her home and raised her up, never telling her who her momma was."

"That—of course," I finish, "Was your mom."

The boys have headed home for the day. We're going to reconvene in the morning and jump into the upcoming Ducky Derby with both feet no matter *who* Sam's grandmother was. The four of us are gathered around a rickety wicker table out on the verandah up at the cottage. The evening sun is still burning in the cooling night air. Crickets are keeping a snappy background noise, while Bessie Smith softly croons from the living room.

"So nice of you all to have Lilly and me up for supper," Sam says around crunches of Ramen noodles. "Damn—this is such *a fine* salad. What all you put in here, Ruby?"

"Believe it or not," Ruby shoots me a look. "This just happens to be an Eve-original. Or perhaps she *stole* it, one can never tell."

"It's really pretty easy," I explain, taking a sip of wine. "I had already made up some coleslaw, to that I added chopped green onions, three packs of Ramen noodles—I break 'em up with a rolling pin. Ruby prefers the vodka bottle. Then toss in some toasted sesame seeds, a dash of sugar, and salt and pepper to taste—simple!"

"But before we continue," Lilly puts her fork down. "I'd like to propose a toast."—We raise our goblets—"Though it would seem that perhaps Sam and Eve may very well share the same gene pool—I'm learning that if you look far enough back—"

"—We're *all* related!" I give Sam a smile that's just ours. We clink like crazy and then end up in a silly hug-fest.

"I must say—I'm just as surprised 'bout this all as you can imagine," Sam says. "But way deep inside of me, the part that's same as you all—my soul—I know that we *do* eventually find home. This place...bein' with you all...*this* is home."

We nod. Her words touch me in a place that's equal parts far away and yet right there in my heart. I look from face to face, thinking back to when we first met. I had that familiar feeling with each of them as if I'd known them all my life. Maybe it's more like I've known them all my lifetimes.

"That's truly lovely, darling," Ruby sits back in her chair. "I've never been one to embrace the mystical. I'm so busy being the *uptight-Brit!*" She dabs at the corners of her twinkling eyes. "But the more I'm around you wonderful women—the thought that we're quite possibly related seems—right."

"A-men."

CHAPTER TWENTY ONE

No matter how organized we've tried to be with this zany Ducky Derby, deep down I know there's gotta be *something* I've missed. One thing's for sure, this costume Lilly and the crew cooked up for me to wear is *not* going to be soon forgotten. Since we're teaming up with Bayfield's Fiftieth Annual Festival of Arts, there's going to be a major crowd to entice over to the Hatchery. Ruby mentioned that she knows *precisely how to work a bloody crowd*; I don't doubt it for a second.

There are all sorts of *artsy types* who stroll through booth after booth of pottery, paintings, and everything in-between along the lake in downtown Bayfield. I hope we have the great problem of running out of rubber ducks for folks to adopt for Toad Hollow's sake, though I believe Lilly has several thousand of the little money-makers on reserve at her place.

As Rocky and I make up the bed, I'm still in a kind of shocked daze that Sam and I have a minor role in the ongoing *melting pot syndrome*. It's also hugely ironic that Adeline was the one to boot her son's lover literally out the door and *her* having had an affair with the likes of Leandre—who I'm *pretty* sure I've met—in one sense or another, anyway. I wish I had time to journal all this, but I'm busier than ever lately.

Seems to me, the more you realize that you're *so* not an island, the more the island becomes you. I mean, there is really no separation in the world; everything is so connected and interwoven. Part of me always found an isolated life intriguing; living somewhere obscure (like here), eking out a peaceful existence while the world zooms by without you. The hell with that noise and honestly, I don't think it's nearly as far as six degrees that we're separated. Not by a long shot.

When I had my salon down in Eau Claire, it never occurred to me that my life at that time wasn't the end-all, even if I thought it was. It's so important to continually explore.

Makes you grow in ways you'll always find refreshingly new and exciting. I had no idea I'd make such an enormous life-change. Yet once things were in motion, I often wondered, what took me so long? Now that I'm here, there's this feeling of the familiar, like this place was waiting for us to shake it back to life.

"C'mon, buster." I scoop up Rocky and head downstairs.

Morning sunshine pours through the open French doors and I can see that the lake is a little rough today, with white caps way out. Ruby must be up and moving, I can hear cupboards being opened and closed in the kitchen. The enticing allure of coffee pulls me along.

Scattered across several end tables, and on all the window sills are blue quart canning jars filled with wildflowers. Mostly white and yellow daisies, but there's a stalk or two of Ruby's Delphiniums in the center of most of them. They're from her amazing patch that has begun to bloom with the coolest colors right outside the front porch door. I'd seen white ones before, but these babies are a vibrant purple.

"There my charges are," Ruby says and waves us in with a spatula. "There's coffee on the fire and—would you get that, darling? My hands are full."

I plunk Rocky down onto a stool and lift up the ringing phone. "Ducky Derby Central, how may I help you?" I sing into the mouthpiece, taking a mug of hot coffee from Ruby.

"It's Ali here—how the hell are you? I'm fine—thanks—listen, we've got a shitload of stuff to haul over to the Hatchery, I've gotta get this grant I wrote late last night emailed and all I have to help me are three *pregnant* women. I swear, if Starr breaks her water today I'm fucked."

I take a deep breath, dream of lighting up a cigarette, and say, "Well—sounds like your day is off to a great start."

"Fuckin'-A," Ali huffs out.

"Look, we're just getting things together over here. Let me give Sam and Lilly a call and see if they can get over there and help out. Sam's got a pickup and Lilly's stronger than any woman I know. So do your breathing and try not to smoke an entire pack of—"

"—Are you *nuts?* I thought I was tough—got my ass chewed out and good by the mother of one of my patients here. Didn't want her grandchild submitted to my damn cancerous cigarette smoke. Jesus, my ears are still ringing—no lie."

"Good. 'Course—you're not going to get a lick of sympathy from the likes of me," I give my patch a rub in hopes that it's sending more nicotine my way.

"Nice bitching with you. Hey—I like what you did to my mom's hair—looks really great."

"She doing okay?" I ask and suddenly get an odd feeling in my stomach.

"Some days are better than others. They want to keep her under observation for a couple more weeks. She isn't sure what she wants to do after she gets out, maybe go back to Al's Place. Or help me out here. I think at bottom, she's really embarrassed—for lack of better words. Christ, the woman went off the deep end, ya know?"

"Could have been any of us," I say and wonder what it must have been like for Alice, I mean Ali, growing up with a mom that wasn't all there. I suppose if that's all you know, maybe you don't miss a thing.

"Listen—gotta go, somebody's at the door. See you there!"

Since I was pacing while chatting with Ali, I've managed to get all tangled up in the cord. I mention to Ruby that they now make phones that don't *have* curly-cords hanging all over the place and she simply raises an already arched brow—that is the end of that. Funny how you can say things without actually *saying* things.

The moment I hang up the phone—it rings.

"Hello there."

"It's your distant—what *am* I anyways?" Sam asks with a deep chuckle.

"You're Sam-the-psychic-seamstress with finely honed automotive skills to boot!"

"Been meanin' to ask if Ruby's managed to burn out that clutch you got in your van. Things not worth the metal it's made outa, but it sure is cute."

"Thanks. I was going to call you," I say and wonder if she—

"—I know that and yes, Lilly and I are only too happy to help out that Alice—Ali. She sure do have a mouth on her."

"Thanks for sticking around. I know you want to get down to Milwaukee and show your sister the diary."

"She's been driving me half crazy, callin' me and wanting me to read from it and all. I think the right thing to do is contact the family and see what they want done with her things but—"

"—You don't want to be *that* famous—right?"

"Bessie Smith is—she's *history*! Then again...I been thinking maybe things should be left alone. I don't need to go stirring up nobody's life and feel the same 'bout mine. Think what them news people would do—*land*."

"I certainly can appreciate your point—but, this is probably my only shot at Oprah."

"Girrrl—don't be too sure 'bout that!"

"Don't tell me a thing. Besides, I have to convert into a duck here shortly."

"C'mon, Ruby," I say, loading one more stack of aprons into my van.

"Sorry, love," Ruby says as she hops in and slams her door closed.

"Love the outfit. I had no idea you had slacks in canary yellow."

"They just arrived this morning," Ruby zips on some pink lipstick, snaps her visor up and clicks on her seatbelt. "Details in Eau Claire had a sale. Let's be off then." She looks over toward me and bursts out laughing.

"You promised not to do that."

"Thank *heavens* it's not terribly hot out this morning," she giggles a bit more.

I shift the van into gear and it chugs up the hill, leaving the boathouse behind. Rocky is out, sitting on the edge of the balcony and I swear he's laughing at me too. Here I am in a *very* tailored duck outfit, complete with duck-covered apron, a huge snap-on tail. Later I'll put on my feather-covered headpiece. Las Vegas move over! It's too warm to wear all the time and besides, it's way too tall for in here.

I'm a little nervous about how low-cut Lilly made the top. When was the last time you ran into a busty duck? Not to mention one with heels with seamed stockings. I thought it'd add some zing to the ensemble. Checking my rather elaborate up-do in the rearview mirror, I shake my head at the insanity of it all. We slowly move by the cottage and I drive us on down the driveway.

"So glad we've all this bloody sunshine," Ruby mentions as we bump over the wooden bridge and up the small incline. "Would be a dreadful *shame* if you had to quack about in the rain. Of course, didn't Lilly say something about your costume being—"

"—A royal pain in the ass when I need to pee!"

"Oh dear."

"Put some music on, would you?" I ask as I pull up to the gate. "I can't get over how early the boys came this morning. Let's leave the gate open, with all the coming and going today I think it'll be easier."

Ruby shrugs. I wait to merge onto School House Road. Summer traffic is in full tilt. Most of the rigs that pass by are *way* too squeaky-clean if you ask me. We head off toward La Pointe to catch the ferry to the music of *Boom Boom Boom* by The Iguanas. Somehow that song seems appropriate.

I slow as we enter La Pointe, as there are crowds of summer folks *everywhere*. Flocks of hungry seagulls dip up and down like flying white potato chips on crack. Not that I've ever been on the stuff, but I can only imagine. I toot the horn as we pass by Al's Place.

"Isn't that a bit *odd*, darling?" Ruby asks as she turns down the tunes. "There doesn't seem to be anyone pottering about in there."

"Oh, that's right," I slow the van to a crawl as a throng of people crosses the street in front of us. "They're over at the Hatchery, setting up a food booth. Bonnie stayed up all night making duck-shaped cookies that kids can decorate—clever woman."

One little girl, with a cotton candy as big as her head, turns and waves at us. We signal her on and I drive us right onto the ferry, easy as you please.

"I think I'll stay put," I mention. "Instead of enjoying the view seeing as I—"

"—Would be *brilliant* advertising," Ruby the businesswoman suggests as she hops out. "I'll follow along with the adoption forms. Now get your head-whatcha-call it and let's get cracking!"

"Oh, what the hell—why not?" I step out of the van just as the ticket person heads over.

"Hey—hello there Miss Duck." The kindly older woman says and then grins my way. "You must be Eve Moss."

"She is indeed," Ruby confirms and comes around the front of the van. "Would you care to adopt a duck, darling?"

This is Earth Momma in the flesh. She's decked out in the standard Madeline Island uniform, short-sleeved white shirt and navy shorts, but along with the cloud of patchouli, her Birkenstocks tell me she's my kinda gal. If I could only get her into my little island salon and take all that gray away. Then again, on her, it works, especially since she has on a powerful deep-mauve lipstick. I count at least eight earrings piercing her left ear.

"You know," Earth Momma leans in toward us. "We're not supposed to allow solicitation of any kind on the ferry." Then she reconsiders the situation. "But I don't remember a *thing* in the employee handbook about donations—how much?"

Besides causing quite the stir simply by being the only human duck aboard, I (with Ruby's help) end up selling a ton of adoptions at five bucks a pop. And most everyone will be stopping by the booths at the Hatchery. I had my picture taken with three couples, four groups of kids, and one guy posed me in his pontoon boat he's taking over to Bayfield for repairs. A dirty old man pinched me so hard on my hind end I nearly creamed him with one of my stilettos. Ruby dashed over and threatened him with an attorney if he didn't adopt ten ducks on the spot. That brings our *ferry take* to an even forty ducks adopted. Cha-quacking-*ching*!

"That was bloody *fun!*" Ruby says as she pulls her door closed.

"Maybe I should wear yellow more often." I comment as I shift into gear and drive up the ramp. "Wonder where Mister Pringles was. I kind of hoped to see him, seeing as I'm ducked out and all."

"You tramp you—why, that boy could be your son!"

"Your point?"

"Good heavens, *look* at all the people here today."

"If Bayfield is *this* busy, imagine the crowd over at the Hatchery."

We chug through town and then south down Highway 13. Lines of cars are passing by us heading to Bayfield. The morning is stunning. More and more sunshine filters through the white pines as we bomb along. Hitting a bend in the road, I keep a look out for the Hatchery driveway's sudden appearance.

"We're here!" I say, as I hang a right onto the paved drive.

The main building is an old, rambling, four-story mansion with pools and water chambers and a myriad of holding tanks out back. Pike's Creek wanders through the woods and then flows along the edge of the Hatchery's property line, allowing a serious crowd of people to gather along the banks in order to witness the journey of the rubber ducks as they float by. Even though it's barely eight-thirty, there's already a small crowd milling around.

There are over thirty booth spaces that I mapped out to form a broad horseshoe once they're all put together. We asked that all the vendors use white canopies, so it looks more, well, clean and not like a flea market. I pull on over to the Al's Place booth. Ruby's Aprons is right next door.

As I hop out of the van, someone yells out that the *duck lady has arrived!* Swinging around, it's none other than Darlene Kravitz, about to take my picture. Ruby, never one to miss a photo-op, runs over and stands beside me. I slip on my headdress and figure I've set the tone for the day—crazy!

Since we've only done one other booth-related event, we're still learning, but Bayfield fills its summers with every kind of festival you can imagine, so there are helpful folks all over only too happy to share festival tips. One I learned early on— bring your own toilet paper. Those little plastic outhouse gizmos can get really rank, but thank god they're around, but they can run short of wipe pretty fast.

"Oh bugger it all," Ruby says while unloading the van. "Thought for sure we packed up more of the—"

I hold up an armful of aprons that match mine—bright yellow and covered with dancing ducks.

"Why—you're becoming more and more like Sam then, aren't you? Smart alec."

"Go figure," I retort back, sticking out my tongue.

The older I get, the more satisfying sticking my tongue out feels. I'll have to think about that more, later. But maybe I do have some psychic talents. Boy, could that come in handy.

"I'm going to walk around," I say to Ruby and head over to the booth next door. "Hello, strangers."

Bonnie comes around and gives me a nice hug. "You have no idea how many people have been talking this event up!"

Bonnie, what a dear she is. She's agreed to donate every penny she makes, after ingredients are covered, to the Hollow. Along with the create-a-duck cookie she's combined efforts with Louie's Meats of Cumberland, Wisconsin. They've come up with a delicious bratwurst made from duck.

Charlie heard we needed his help so he came up from Vanceburg for the day and is manning the grill; even though it's early, he's started the brats going, so there's that unmistakable heavenly smell wafting through the summer air. Charlie as well as Bonnie have on bib-aprons, covered with those very same dancing ducks. Each and every booth is festooned with rubber ducks. It's Lilly's idea and it helps add to the feeling that this is truly a duck-themed festival.

Earlier, there was a 5K-foot race organized by one of the local youth clubs as a fundraiser for themselves. Our event is slated to begin at ten, but I'm sure we'll get a lot of people coming earlier, and that's great. I think Ali told me we ended up with thirty-eight booths—most of them representing different youth organizations or clubs or other non-profit groups in need of a better cash flow. All the money we make from apron sales is going to the Hollow and we're also donating the cost of materials. People who attend buy twenty-five cent tickets to participate in each activity at the booths. The booths then turn them in for money at the end of the event. Smart.

There's also going to be a band here, thanks to a local phenomenon called the Big Top Chautauqua. Very close by is this huge canvas tent complex. It's a unique entertainment spot, a 900-seat, state-of-the-art, all-canvas tent theater. They put on over 70 musical events every year. Since they're *also* a non-profit they heard of our Ducky Event—the Big Top Chautauqua board of directors agreed to lend us this special singer in person. I'm already getting nervous as *I'm* slated to introduce her. A broad in a duck outfit is welcoming a musical prodigy. She and Sam have something special planned as a grand finale. Get ready.

Some of the other booths are selling duck-themed t-shirts and hats and well, rubber-duck-everything. There's a decoy duck decorating contest, pony rides, a small climbing wall, large blowup games, an animal petting area and the booth I'm in front of now. A pet-paw-painting booth.

"I don't believe I've met you folks," I say reaching over the blank, open drawing tablets, to shake hands. "Seems to me you came on the scene after we—"

"—We did. My name's Ana and this is my husband—Mike." We all shake hands.

Ana has hair similar to mine, only a more strawberry red, her eyes shine with mystery. I notice how she holds a rather rambunctious puppy on her lap firmly, but with such love. Mike is tall and lanky with a spiky-messy hairstyle that gives him a definite edge. Women must love him. That and the fact that he's got an addictive laugh—the puppy just peed on Ana and all he did was chuckle, hand her some paper towels, and shrug.

"Now tell me how this works?" I ask more to take the pressure off Ana, but I'm curious too.

She flings her hair out of her eyes and shows me some samples. "We dip the pet's paws in this non-toxic paint and they literally walk across the construction paper, leaving behind their wonderful paw-prints. Then we add more colors and make them as goofy as the mood fits. Or the patience of the dog—cats are pretty much impossible to do this with. The trick is to move really fast and make it as much of a game as possible."

"They're also well rewarded," Mike says, as he gives the puppy a treat. "We're giving all the millions we haul in today to the animal shelter by us in Star Prairie."

"That's great! I can see that treats as well as speed is about your only shot at this," I say with a laugh. "My cat, Rocky, would scratch my eyes out before getting his precious paws covered in paint. I *love* this. Thank you both for coming and don't forget to join in the fun over at Pike's Creek—this is so cool."

Just then, there's a new sound percolating among the mix of the voices instructing so-and-so to turn the tent this way or that, or asking where the table went and who has the wrench and you did *what* last night? If you've ever been involved in a play, even if it was something in high school, this reminds me of that feeling of how everyone becomes a player.

Everyone here today is focusing on a common goal. That alone is wonderful, but there's something else in the air. There's this marvelous seasoning of everyone helping one another. Since this whole event is *about* helping—not about bottom lines and making the grade—everyone is here to help everyone else. I straighten my headgear and head over to the gleaming red tractor rumbling onto the grounds.

"Excuse me," I try to project over the motor's roar. "Have you a permit for that thing?"

The huge front-bucket attached to the tractor, slowly lowers to the ground. Howard and Johnny give me a friendly wave, shut the machine off and head over toward me. They're both dressed in white-and-blue pin-striped bib overalls, the pants cut off below the knees, and tight-fitting brilliant white T-shirts with *Quack Me* stretched across their muscular chests.

Weird, but after all the back-story between Johnny and me—I haven't any ill feelings. Besides, Tony will always be Helen's dad, Johnny's ex-boyfriend, and my—my first love. Will he be my last?

After hugs, they admire my costume, help me adjust the tail, and then we review all the ins and outs of how to get the adopted rubber ducks upstream in order to race them back down. The object is to pay careful attention as to which ducks cross the finish line in what order to award the appropriate prizes *and* to get those all-important press shots. The outpouring of prizes has been a surprise. We even have a shiny (but used) red Jeep filled with all the gear you'd need to camp, kayak, and cook, and finish your novel somewhere along the shores of Lake Superior. Compliments of Apostle Island Kayaks.

"We've finally figured out the program," Howard booms over the band's mike checks. "Since each duck was assigned a barcode, finding the lucky winners shouldn't be hard at all."

"This get-up," Johnny says, "Reminds me of when we first met—remember?"

"Are you nuts?" I reply, self-consciously pulling up my front. "How in the *world* could I forget that *falling out?* God—what an embarrassing moment and trust me—I had Lilly do *major* support work on this baby so my girls are lifted and supported and not bust-out-able."

"Do you need help with setting up anything else before the parade?" Howard asks.

"Actually," I scan the creek, then wave at Ali and the gals. "If you wouldn't mind, see if you can do any last minute running for Ali. She's in charge of registering the duck adoptions. I think we've got things covered and I see that Sam and Lilly are over there too."

"We need to get the tractor to Bayfield," Johnny says.

"Let's fill up the tractor's bucket"—I point to the big boxes on Sam's truck bed—"With those and head on over. Things are pretty darn groovy here."

"Groovy, darling? *Really?*" Ruby says coming up beside me. "That went out with miniskirts and thigh-high boots, anyone knows *that!*"

A clutch of young, giggling girls saunter by, obviously for the boys' benefit. Several wear mini-miniskirts barely covering the essentials. God forbid they have to bend over. Ruby sighs.

"I abso-bloody-lutey stand corrected—don't they look simply *groovy* then, hmmm?"

"Whatever," I add and then, in my *let's get our shit together voice*, "Okay, the day is packed solid and we have to keep things moving. Ruby, go and make sure we have the huge blow-up duck ready for the top of the van. You're going to follow the tractor in the parade with Ali and her gals, tossing out adoption papers to the crowds."

"Right-O," Ruby zips off.

"Let's get the bucket ready," I announce to the boys. "And then we need to all head back to Bayfield. The parade isn't very long, so it shouldn't take too much of our time and then we're back here for the race!"

"Exactly *where* are you going to be sitting for this?" Howard says.

I point to the bucket of the tractor.

"I was afraid of that."

"Am I quacked?"

Chapter Twenty Two

Everyone's lined up to begin the parade that will be routed down Rittenhouse Avenue, the main street of Bayfield. It slopes dramatically down a steep hill, with charming-as-hell bars, restaurants, coffee shops and a bookstore flanking the sides. The street sweeps downward and onto the pier and if you keep going you'll end up in Lake Superior. I like the fact you can see Madeline Island from here. Seems so far off and yet—it's not at all, give or take two miles of really cold water.

The day is heating up and so am I in this get-up. The boys have me up in the sky, inside the front-loader's bucket (imagine a tractor with a big shovel up front, only in the *up* position). I'm pretty comfortable in Lilly's bright yellow beanbag chair and completely surrounded by rubber ducks. My legs are dangling over the edge and thanks to a pair of black fish-net, my varicose veins will remain a secret. These dangerously high black stiletto heels reflect the sun and boy, it's nice to be sitting—my feet are screaming for my comfy flip-flops. Heels were definitely invented by a man.

Right behind us comes the van. Ruby's at the wheel, with Ali next to her and three pregnant gals in the back. One of whom is a *really* pregnant girl named Starr—Watt's estranged sister whom I'm keeping an eye on. It could be that she's just so tiny, not to mention barely sixteen, but her belly is *so* extended—I really feel for her. Ali wasn't about to leave her alone back at the Hollow in her condition. They've folded ducky adoption forms into paper airplanes and plan on zooming them out the windows. Helen and Ryan, as well as Johnny, are back at the festival, holding down the fort until we return.

Since this is an Arts Festival, the parade is made up mostly of floats featuring local artisans with samples of their work. Like the float behind us which has six potters sitting at potting wheels with a piece they've completed secured onto the wheel. There are seven marching bands positioned throughout the parade and many of the local business people wave from convertibles, antique cars, and even an odd cart pulled by a team of sled dogs. A long-bed trailer pulled by a hulking white pickup has a rainbow of kayaks with the paddlers sitting inside doing a routine of synchronized movements with their paddles. Mr. Pringles, without a shirt, is directing the team—he sees me and waves. What the hell are butterflies doing in my stomach?

Janelle, the owner of Greunke's Restaurant, is in front of us and boy, does she look glam in a tailored denim vest and skirt. Saundra, is in her black Mercedes driven by a blonde guy. She's waving out of the sunroof. Helen asked if she could do this, be in the parade, I figured with the amount of cash that lady has donated to the Hollow, hell, she can lead the band! From here all I can see is that her diamonds are going to blind a few folks along the route.

Frank, Bayfield's busy mayor, is saying something official way down the street in front of a marching band and then we'll most likely begin moving our silly selves down and around the marked parade route.

"*Fuck no!*" Ali's voice booms from inside the van.

"What's going on?" I say through my mega-phone as the crowd around us looks on in wonder. Keep in mind I'm over fifteen feet up in the air, dressed like a leggy duck.

Ruby comes rushing over and yells up toward me, "She broke her bloody water!"

"Shit," I say into my megaphone.

There's suddenly tons of confused commotion swirling below me. Howard motions to Ruby, she climbs into the tractor-seat and Howard points at the gears. From what I can make out, he's giving her a quick lesson; she looks up toward me and gives me the *thumbs up*. Am I a dead duck?

He rushes over and tosses up a box of the paper airplanes the three preg-o's had folded. I barely catch it."Ali has to take care of Starr—she's about to deliver—Ruby doesn't know the way, so we're going to rush her to the clinic in Red Cliff. I'm sorry—but I have to drive them! Ruby's going to drive the tractor!"

I watch helplessly as the van backs out of the parade line-up and speeds away. Ruby sends me more thumbs up and then I really know I'm sunk.

"This really looks quite simple, darling," she yells up to me.

As the parade has begun, it's our turn to move. Ruby adjusts several gears; I wish I didn't have such a clear view, the tractor lurches forward with a grinding noise I'm sure Sam can hear at the festival. But we're off!

We begin our slow descent downhill and I start to relax a little hoping Starr will be alright. What a rotten break—literally. But with Ali, she's in good hands.

Clearing my throat, I lift my megaphone up. "After the parade, come over to the Hatchery for the first annual Ducky Derby Race! Come one come all, five bucks could make *you* a winner!" I shoot the fliers toward eager young faces and start feeling better.

We jostle on down the avenue, and I keep up my banter. I can see up the street behind me—there's more to this parade than I thought. Bayfield sure does know how to throw a festival. One of the marching bands is so off-tune it makes me cringe. At least they're giving it their all, and in their white uniforms with red trim, they look cute as hell.

The tractor suddenly shimmies. Glancing over my shoulder, Ruby seems to be having quite a time with one of the gear-shifters. Looks like maybe her bag is caught or something; we start to lurch more and now I'm hanging on for dear life as the bucket begins to swing, rubber ducks are spilling out and bouncing down onto the street! Kids come running over to scoop them up as we shimmy and shake on by the parking lot of Greunke's. The parade is supposed to turn right onto First Street, and end there—but we're not!

"Buggering bloody hell!" Ruby yells from below and I hang on for dear life—at top speed—we're heading right toward the end of the pier!

Just as I'm imagining how this is going to look on the front page of the *Rants & Raves from the Rock*—the tractor lurches to a stop right at the very end of the pier. But I don't—I go sailing high up into the air!

Being a sensible duck, I quickly lift up my megaphone and say, *"Holy quacking shit!"*

Since all of Bayfield was able to clearly witness my incredible flying trick—and then flopping—into Lake Superior, I was quickly rescued and dragged to shore. I won't go into too much detail, but let's just say that the support system Lilly assured me would withstand a walloping sneeze-fit, failed the high-dive miserably. The ever-resourceful Ruby, always looking for that *angle,* had takers for every adoption form she could find. I still may kill her.

Back at the festival, I've exchanged my sopping wet duck costume for a favorite yellow sundress and my flowered flip-flops. Somewhere in Lake Superior there's a big old bullfrog wearing *my* high heels! But I must admit, my feet are much happier now. Since we caused such a ruckus in town, most of the town is over here now. Pays to end a parade with a water act. Now I've become something of a minor celebrity, but Ruby and I don't refer to the finale as being a *Ducky Derby dress malfunction.* And honestly, I could really give a hoot what Janet Jackson would have done.

The boys have taken back control of the tractor and we've sold every last adoption form! The tractor's front bucket is once again loaded up with all the adopted ducks. Their bellies each have a barcode-waterproof-sticker that is assigned to an adoptee for easy identification at the finish line. Howard has it all worked out; we were able to borrow the barcode reader gun from Andy's IGA to scan the little guys. Many local businesses have donated prizes and it seemed that all we had to do was ask. Okay, we did do some begging, but it worked.

"Well, darling," Ruby comes over. "Things seem to have shaped up a bit then. I'm *dreadfully* sorry about your spill—simply can't *tell* you."

"Hey—it sold us out and *look* at all these people!"

"Simply *love* the music."

"It's the backup band for—where did Helen go? And have we heard how Starr is doing?" I ask as we stroll over toward the official Duck Booth.

"Apparently, as soon as Helen heard that there was an issue with Starr—namely that she was about to give birth—she and Ryan headed off to the clinic to offer any help they could."

"Well, speak of the devil," Ruby comments to Helen and Ryan.

"Starr had a perfect little girl," Helen beams. "Ali is going to stay with her a little while longer."

"I was surprised how fast your old van could move." Ryan says. I notice something about him. The furrow in his brow is gone. "Howard is parking it and should be along shortly. So, now that the excitement is over—where's your fancy duck outfit?"

"Ruby will fill you in," I send her a grin. "I've gotta go find the mayor and get this race—racing!"

Mayor Maggio, wearing a huge duckbill mask, is getting last-minute instructions from Johnny as to exactly where they plan on dumping the little money-makers as well as how they're to be kept track of at the finish line.

"Well this certainly is an—well, hello Eve."

"Hey, Frank," I offer back and wave up to Johnny. "Thank you again for officiating and helping us get all these cool prizes together and—"

"—I think it's *you* I should be thanking—you and that crazy driver of yours!"

We share a laugh. It's hard to keep from smiling; he's now wearing his duckbill on top of his head like a bright yellow tiara, in order to talk with us.

"Johnny's got things covered here," I say moving things along. "Here's your walkie-talkie—when you let him know you've announced the start of the race, he'll let those babies go."

Parents and their kids are lined up and down the creek banks. There's a duck trap at the end of the race to capture the little guys—it's actually oil spill containment tubes strung shore to shore—suggested by the guys that run the Hatchery.

Mayor Maggio speaks briefly, thanking the local sponsors as well as the staff of Bayfield Hatchery, the slew of vendors, *and* he reminds everyone of the band that will be playing after the race. Chuckling, he says he's just *sure* Eve and Ruby will be back with more parade surprises next year. At which the crowd gives me a big round of applause. Maybe next year I'll hire a double.

Then he signals to a police officer who in turn, fires a shot into the air while Frank yells into his walkie-talkie—"Dump those ducks, dude!"

"Such a *lovely* man," Ruby says and I have to agree. "The silly bloke's wearing his duck lips upside down."

"I met his wife earlier," I mention as we head over to the finish line to help. "Julie's her name and they own a bed-and-breakfast in Bayfield as well as an outfitter shop of some sort."

"Good heavens—all of us that live up here year 'round seem to wear a dozen different hats."

"I like hats," I comment, adjusting the tie on my straw hat. "Let's go help Sam and Lilly load up the winners so Howard can scan them and see who the prizes go to."

"This is dreadfully exciting—let's go, then, shall we?"

A wonderful spring breeze dances through the trees—trees full of children and quite a few parents too—all pointing and yelling encouragement to the wave of yellow bobbing down the creek. The banks on either side are jammed with cheering people, and I can't get over the number of dogs. Most of them are on leashes, but the added barking is hilarious.

One beautiful golden-colored dog couldn't take it anymore and leaps into the creek, nabs one of innocent ducks in its mouth, and heads back to shore. After plunking the duck down into its master's hand, the dog shakes and shakes, soaking everyone around with water droplets.

The roar of cheers is something I hadn't planned on. Everyone is really getting into the spirit and the best part of this whole thing is that it's going to help families in need here in the community.

Every so often I can make out the distinctive sound of Sam doing her ear-piercing whistle. We timed the duck race from where Johnny dumped them to where the end is and it's about twenty-five minutes worth of racing. Any more than that and I think we'd all go deaf.

"Girrrl," Sam smiles our way, "You two always seem to bring the house down or toss the duck lady or—well, you get my drift."

"Sam's got a little surprise planned," Lilly adds. "But we need to get these over to the back door of the Hatchery where Howard's computer is hooked up ready to read them. Here—"

—Lilly hands us laundry baskets filled with dripping wet ducks that have just been scooped up by Helen and Ryan and off we head across the festival area toward Howard.

Mayor Maggio and his wife take turns up on stage, announcing the winners to a hooting crowd. While the prizes are doled out, Ruby and I are helping over at the apron booth where sales have been brisk. The most popular style is one of Lilly's creations; a bright yellow, sort of French-maid look in that it covers your entire front, but scoops pretty low in the chest area. Young gals are buying them and putting them on right there at the booth, so now the festival looks like a convention of French maids has taken over.

I spy the Pringles guy strolling with a group and have to admire his tanned body, his thin hips swaying seductively in baggy white shorts. He seems to be walking rather close to a beautiful, young

Asian girl. He notices me noticing him and sends me a wink. I think the butterflies have flown the coop.

All of a sudden, out of nowhere, a powerful gust of wind comes hurtling across the entire circle of booths! Hats go flying—all the rubber ducks lashed along the front of the booths rattle and shake—everyone scrambles to hold their tents down. Ruby and I, along with the entire crowd, *gasp*. We watch with wide-open mouths as the *Make Your Own Kite* booth lifts up off the ground and becomes airborne—then sails across the open center where everyone's standing awestruck.

The tent lands perfectly; right smack dab in the middle of the creek. All the colorful kites that were tethered to the booth's four corners float slowly down into the water. The crowd cheers, then the Pringles guy, along with some companions, wade in and help retrieve everything.

Ruby and I sigh with relief. "Now that's what I call a bloody good save," Ruby says while handing a woman a sack and some change.

"What the hell are you talking about?" I ask, folding up four aprons for a dripping-with-sweat older gentleman. "The tent landed in the creek all on its own!"

Ruby juts her chin off toward the woods where the creek begins to come into view. A dark man with long black hair, dressed in a brilliant white shirt, glances my way, bows, and then disappears into the trees. I look back at Ruby and she nods her head as if a light has gone on.

"Leandre," I mutter under my breath.

"Yes darling, I saw him too."

The band has taken to the stage, and right now our local talent; Ric Gillman and Madwood Pro-Motion are getting us in the mood to move, singing a song they call *Nothin' To It*. Ric plays folksy guitar and when he sings, his voice is like a sexy Bruce Springsteen without all the yelling. He's drawing the crowd over to the stage and warming them up.

"Now there's a lovely man," I tilt my curls toward Ric. "Can you imagine living with a musician? Wonder if he sings to his wife like that."

"He is right now," Ruby points to a grinning gal off to the side of the stage. "We chatted up a bit earlier—she knows more about us than I did, *really* I simply can't get over how living on an island—you truly are being *observed* at all times." Ruby nods and her straw hat nearly falls off. "They've a place somewhere on the island, but not anywhere near the water."

"I know *exactly* where they live," a voice answers from in front of our booth.

Ruby and I are both short gals and since the table in front of us is piled high with aprons, we can hardly see over it. We lean over to find out just who's there.

A young woman, long, shiny-black hair wafting in the breeze, is grinning up at us from her wheelchair. One hand, with long, black painted nails, is resting on some kind of control. As she depresses a knob, her entire chair begins to rise up. We stand back and regard her.

She has perfectly applied makeup, a bit on the heavy side, but the thing that is so striking is her brilliant smile. It's as though she's doing her best to put you at ease, to bring you into the fact that though she's in a wheelchair, she's really just sitting down.

I reach over and offer my hand. "Hello—my name's Eve and this is Ruby."

"Oh, I've heard all about the two of you," she chuckles a bit, and then moves her chair even closer to the edge of our booth and reaches over. "I'm Marvilyn. Marvilyn Falling Waters. I just love these aprons you and your company make on Madeline—heard your radio interview too. I just wailed when that nun called in—Jesus, that was touching."

Ruby and I glance at each other, brows ever-so-slightly-raised. "Are you the woman—have you emailed us?"

"I did—you wrote back and told me about Toad Hollow. I got an infection and couldn't make it to your opening."

"Bummer," I offer and she nods. "Hey—don't you have a daughter?"

"I do, good memory. She's about to turn sixteen and man-O-man, can she push my buttons. But she's a good kid. We're renting a cottage on the island."

"How simply lovely," Ruby steps over next to me. "You really must come over for a proper visit."

"Hey, thanks," Marvilyn smiles. "I'd like these two aprons here and do you know who's going to be singing?"

"Yes—we do," Ruby and I answer at the same time.

The prizes have been awarded and the official duck-adoption number, according to our computer man; Howard, comes to an astounding 7,413 and that's counting the bunch that the sewing crew chipped in for as well. We won't have a total for all the vendors' sales for a while as festival attendees purchased tickets and redeem them at each booth.

We're over in an office area of the Hatchery, getting ready for our stage-act. Sam's in the ladies room putting the final touches on her braids.

"I can't believe this thing *shrunk,*" I fuss, while Lilly tries to zip me up.

"I'm afraid it's a no-go—you'll have to wear your summer dress," Lilly says with dismay and then stands back with obvious frustration on her face.

I'm relieved. Being a duck in the parade was enough for one year. I quickly slip back into my dress and step into flip flops. Better.

Lilly and Bonnie wear similar tie-dyed scarf dresses. Lilly's is faded lavender and Bonnie's is yellow. Colorful braided hair pieces with feathers are clipped into their hair.

"Now, Lilly, darling—there," Ruby adjusts a stubborn feather. "Bonnie, pull up the front of your dress a bit like Lilly's—there's a love. Bend down, would you?" She tucks a wisp of Bonnie's hair behind her ear. "Just super." She regards the duo of Bonnie and Lilly before an odd look passes across her face. "Seems rather off balance without Marsha here, she was our third back-up, you know and—"

—Sam begins to chuckle from inside the ladies room (hoot is more like it) and it echoes around the walls of this old building like a super ball.

Seconds later, Ali bursts out of the ladies room. "Johnny told me about this last event and Mom is doing *so* great, we figured—"

"—That you sure as hell needed a third to make a trio!" says Marsha coming out of the restroom in a green scarf dress. Ali hugs her briefly and then dashes out the back door.

Ruby and I quickly transform her hair and makeup, while wiping away tears. The three ladies line up for a final inspection. The trio is a trio once again. Funny, if you look close into each of their faces, you can see the little girls they must have been, right there in their excited eyes.

Then I say to the closed door, "You ready, Sam?"

Sam sashays out of the ladies room and we all whistle. Ruby gives a rendition of her newly-honed, Sam-trained whistle and it's an ear-piercer!

And Sam. She has lifted her corn-rowed hair up and encircled it with a yellow feather-covered band to give the appearance of a crown. Her scarf dress is multi-colored to match the three ladies. Big hoop earrings set off her perfect skin.

Sam walks over to Marsha and takes her hands in hers. "Things gunna be jus' fine now, you'll see."

Ruby lifts her walkie-talkie and after clicking several buttons, she says, "Alright love, cheerio then—or ten-to-four and such, *we're coming out!*" Ruby snaps it off, tosses it into her purple shoulder bag, and motions us toward the exit leading back to the festival.

She turns to regard us. "So—my *lovely* ducklings—Eve will do the introductions, thank you's, and all—then she'll motion you to your places. Sam will lead. Now—not to be a sorry sod, but there's a good lot of press about, so let's keep a stiff upper lip then—shall we?"

"Wait!" I step beside Ruby, and look back at the line-up of beautiful gals. "Look, I know that maybe you're all getting sick and tired of me giving these little pep talks, but what you're doing—what *we 're* doing—can make a difference and—and—thank you. Thank you for—"

"—Girrrl—you the one had courage enough to put your *toe* in the water. And I know how freezein' cold that can be! Yet that ripple you got goin'—well jus' *look* at what's washed ashore!"

I wipe away a tear, "Let's make some waves!"

"Ladies and gentleman," I say, and then lift my eyebrows in surprise—I sound *good!* "Please welcome the one and only Joni Mitchell—accompanied by—Easy Street."

Joni takes center stage, looking perfectly ageless in a loose, pale yellow dress, her blonde hair blowing in the breeze. Sam saunters over and they hug briefly. They join hands and start the lyrics of Joni's famous song, *Big Yellow Taxi.* Before they can even finish singing—*Don't it always seem to go, you don't know what you've got until it's gone*—the entire crowd is clapping and singing along!

Lilly, Bonnie, and Marsha are throwing in soulful *boo-bops* and my god, Joni and Sam look like the beautiful goddesses they are. Howard and Johnny, Helen and Ryan, Charlie, Ruby and I, as well as Mayor Maggio and Julie, are all jamming to this magical music. I look back, out toward the crowd, and see that it's hit everyone.

Waves of hands are raised high—rhythmically moving side to side. I glimpse Marvilyn, her chair elevated above the ground, waving with the rest of us and realize—we need ramps at the cottage.

Ruby and I are out on the dock, surrounded by pillows and wrapped warm in our full-length terrycloth robes. Even though its summer now, the nights really dip down in temperature and then, to top it off, all this fog rolls in off the lake and things get rather chilly. Which is the *only* reason we brought the wine.

"Such a bloody *lovely* tribute," Ruby remarks as she sinks back into a pillow. "I can't recall being so divinely moved, and could you get over the crowd's response when Sam asked if anyone wanted a repeat? Good heavens. Joni and Sam—why, I had no idea Sam knew so many of her songs! They really should consider making a record together."

"That *Big Yellow Taxi* song is so timeless—and yet I have to wonder how many people really *listen* to the warning. You know? I mean, if we don't watch out—there really *could* be a tree museum... and nothing else. Can you imagine not being able to walk off into the woods and smell all this pine?"

"You know, darling—after meeting that lovely Joni—I'm beginning to understand why we need to be *aware* of things. To think that at a moment's notice, a perfectly *lovely* garden-plot could be transformed into a wretched parking lot, why—it's sheer *rubbish!*"

"So many things are rubbish. That's such a great word—rubbish."

"Well, of course it is. Now then," Ruby changes her tone, so I know we're in for a subject change. "What do you think of that Marvilyn—there's a name for the books then, hmmm? Wonder what *her* story is?"

"Oh, I'm pretty certain we'll find out soon enough—I've invited her and her daughter over. Well, you did actually, but I let her know we need a little time."

"Howard and Johnny were over earlier," Ruby says in her *I know something you don't* voice.

"And?"

"They measured things, is all. Howard, the dear, isn't sure *how* we can get her into the boathouse. What, with all those wooden stairs. But I think she'd *so* enjoy a peek into our little factory by the lake."

"We'll figure out something," I reply sleepily.

"Don't you think for one second, you duck-hussy," Ruby sits up and so do I. "That I didn't see you and that Pringles fellow chatting it up earlier. Cradle-robber."

"Pour me some of that," I order. "Can we smoke while wearing these damn patches?"

"Why, Eve Moss—do you need a smoke in order to confess something concerning you and that cucumber-wielding child?"

"Oh, for God's sake no—it's what I'd *like* to do to him that makes me need a smoke."

"Well, in that case, I just happen to have a half—we can share."

Ruby snaps open her gold case. It glimmers in the moonlight, she taps the end, then lights the pre-shortened cigarette with her matching lighter, that just *happens* to be with her as well.

"When you were in the shower, earlier," Ruby hands me the stub. "Helen ran in with some wonderful news—but wants to tell you herself." She holds up a hand. "So don't even ask—my lips are sealed."

"All right," I say, about to take a puff, then I reconsider and put it out. I hand it back, Ruby snaps it into the golden holder and then tosses it far out into the lake. We listen for it to plop. It does.

"There. That's the end of that bloody era!"

"Funny how things keep changing around you, whether or not you care to leap into the fray."

"The old adage is still true, darling."

"That no man is an island?"

"Good heavens, no, not *that* adage."

"Well?"

"No *woman* is an island."

Under the approving glow of a silvered moon, two women lay side-by-side on a long wooden dock connected to an island.

Connected to the world.

ACKNOWLEDGMENTS

Here I am again, right where I'd hope to be, at the end of yet another Madeline Island tale and I didn't get here alone—no sir ree.

First and foremost I can't thank my agent, Alison Bond, enough for *not* throwing away a hard copy (the original, I might add) of *Full Moon Over Madeline Island*. Since I'd lost it, along with everything else, in our 2010 house fire, it was such an awesome surprise when it arrived in the mail one day. Here's to many more years together—what a team!

Throughout my writing journey, I've had the pleasure of hearing from so many of you; your struggles with being adopted, giving up a baby or of never having had the opportunity of finding your child. Thank you for being so candid, so open and honest with your feelings.

I love book clubs! Now that we have Skype—pour the wine, open the chocolate, push around the hair and let's talk about Eve and Ruby! When I'm invited into your kitchens, living rooms—lives—something really wonderful happens. There's an openness, a sharing, that I love. We also manage to laugh a great deal and I never stick to the hour I say I'm going to when we begin. Nice.

On the night of our fire, not one, not two, but *three* neighboring town's volunteer fire fighters answered the call and showed up. They did everything they could to try and save our home. They were our neighbors from Clear Lake, Boyceville and Prairie Farm and they were amazing—thank you all for your grueling work! And afterwards, we were overwhelmed by the generosity of giving that this incredible Prairie Farm community showed us. Shows us still. That kind of caring you never forget.

So many others to thank in the creation of this latest adventure, I hope I don't miss anyone or I'll be in big trouble! Of course, thanks to my Parental Units; Donna Lou & Eric, for their on-going belief in my work. My sister, Amy, for sharing the ins and outs (and hilarity) of hosting a Ducky Derby and brother Kurt for the inspirational work he does with the homeless. Nancy Orth, owner of Starr's Sister Salon in Eau Claire, was the inspiration for Eve's Salon and boy—can she cut hair! Madeline Island resident, Glenn Carlson for showing me around the island during off-season. Author Jess Witkins for helping me realize we all deserve guilty pleasures—why not? And Tim Westergren, the creator of Pandora, for keeping my writing rhythms.

Carrie Maloney and Mark Given for reading my first draft, editing it into a far better tale and tirelessly helping push my writing forward.

And, as mentioned in my first two novels, I'm happy to report there's a pretty darn fancy tractor parked out in the machine shed.

Moving ahead with my dear friend Ken is the joy that puts the smiles into my writing—and life.

Do you honestly think this is the end of Eve & Ruby?

—Jay

To schedule Jay for a Skype chat with your Book Club; jay@jaygilbertson.com.
Become a fan on Facebook.
Learn more of his upcoming novels: www.jaygilbertson.com.

ABOUT THE AUTHOR

© Mark Given swanhouse.smugmug.com

Jay Gilbertson is a native Wisconsin author, beekeeper, hospice volunteer, book review columnist and farmer, as well as producing the nation's first pumpkin seed oil. (**www.hayriver.net**) His first two novels; *Moon Over Madeline Island* and *Back to Madeline Island,* were published by Kensington. His new novel in the Madeline Island Series—*Full Moon Over Madeline Island*—has just been released and is available on Amazon, or you can get signed copies through his website. Jay thrives enjoying the influence of his family and friends. He finds relationships with all their complications and truths to be his most valued teacher and a huge inspiration for his character's voices.

Oh, and he can't sing worth a darn—but boy can he hum!